BERRY HILL

Dedicated to all those who serve our

'Adapt yourself to the things amongst which your lot has been cast and love sincerely the fellow creatures with whom destiny has ordained that you shall live.'

Marcus Aurelius, Roman Emperor 161-180 a.d.

Chapters

1 - Funeral on Berry Hill

2 - Education and Training

3 - Coffee with Kaunda

4 - Thanksgiving

5 - Paddy's Troubles

6 - Midnight in Moscow

7 - The Great Escape

8 - Legging It in Prague

9 – The Falklands

10 - From Russia with Love

11 – Betrayed in Warsaw

12 - The Gulag

13 - Newark Northgate

14 - AGM at Dinan

1

Funeral on Berry Hill

James religiously practised his carefully constructed alibis, founded in truth but lacking in candour, just in case he was ever challenged by adversaries; a prerequisite in his past line of career.

It was difficult to concentrate in the blinding snow blizzard. Advancing years didn't help much either as he peered into the grey gloom. A moving white laced veil spread across his narrow field of vision. Neat sets of ripples forming on the bonnet of his beloved 1959 Rover 90; turning the colour from the original grey blue to a pure matt white. The old windscreen wipers were struggling to cope through the sheer intensity of the snowflake barrage. Two white ice lollipops formed over the wipers swinging in rhythmic unison from side to side.

The weather had been poor as he left Nottingham but now had turned viciously ugly, much like the people he had men encountered in his past life. It would all start gentile enough until frustrations mounted, results were pressing and then Mr. Nasty arrived on the scene, but not quite like the one featured in the children's books.

The gradual elevation increased the challenge of driving in the worsening winter conditions. Passing through the old coal mining village of Annesley Woodhouse, it was no surprise the visibility would steadily deteriorate. In his college days he had taken this route many times before, to see his mate Ken, who lived in Mansfield. This time though he was snug in his beloved old classic car cosseted from the inclement weather. In his youth, totally exposed, he had struggled along on two small wheels of his white Raleigh Roma 80cc motor scooter slip sliding through the hardening snow ruts. There must be an imaginary snow line between the cities of Nottingham and Mansfield.

He rehearsed in his mind, over and over, how he was to explain travelling to Mansfield, this day of all days, and through such foul weather. A chance intervention was always possible, especially during the coal miner's strike. There might be the stray police patrol to intercept him and ask where he was heading and why his journey was so important. Not that they really cared, but it would break the boredom and induce a delusion they were doing something useful in all the civil unrest.

For James such an impromptu interruption would hold no trepidation, he had nerves of cold steel, would remain very calm under extreme stress and importantly could naturally explain away any situation. After all he had come across such random confrontations many times before, whether it be from policemen in their various national uniforms, armed or otherwise, confronted by their thuggish mates in the para-militaries, terrorist militias or worst still the security agents.

Deep-down he was just a normal working-class lad who had tried to be master of his destiny despite the humble beginnings. Living on a post-war council estate can be tough, there is little chance of escape. Social barriers existed in equal measure from within and without to keep you in your 'rightful' place. He could have easily ended up in the RAF after school to have the chance like many others to acquire a skill of some sort to elevate him from the mundane and the mediocrity.

Always at the back of his mind was how was he going to escape, the military seemed the best option compared to the standard jobs handed round to people like him. His father and grandfather had served in the army but the RAF appeared to offer greater skill sets. He had after all he had begun to understand trigonometry and its application for navigation; dead reckoning.

When his school maths teacher, a Mr. Brand, had asked what he was going to do when he left school James gave him another option, the world of chartered accountancy. Little did James know at the time this was to lead him into a life he could have only dreamed of. This was to be the key to cut the 'drag anchors' of his class.

Whether he did finally escape was open to debate, but at least he had made his parents and grandparents proud of him and drew committed friends around him that only others could have dreamed of.

He was heading for the Mansfield Cemetery located on Berry Hill just on the southern edge of town. His true objective was to witness the final and long belated demise of a sworn enemy and traitor. His alibi, whilst correct, suppressed the main objective of his journey. If challenged he would counter with the deflective response, he was paying his final respects to a dear friend of 30 years. Truthful alibis were always superior to a twisted, convoluted explanation. His friend, after all, had been his personal lawyer and most trusted confidant. His planned attendance at the funeral six months ago had been thwarted by a lightning French air traffic controllers strike.

The night before, sat comfortably and warm in his sister's home in Arnold, Nottingham, he had casually scanned the Saturday night's edition of the Nottingham Evening Post newspaper. His sister in her inimitable curiosity enquired,

"If you are looking for the football scores, Clifford can give you those?"

"He told me the sad news already, although by the look on his face I knew the result straightaway. I am looking to see if there is anything about an old college mate. I received a letter the other day from an anonymous sender that a fellow college student had just passed away," James drawing the newspaper ever closer in his failing eyesight, sticking as close to the truth as he dared but without giving anything away.

"Funny they didn't say who they were," remarked his sister.

"I thought that as well, but social etiquette isn't what it used to be, a sign-off would have helped." answered James trying casually to evade his sister's investigatory remarks.

Ah, there it was in a tiny highlighted boxed announcement, hidden amongst all the obituaries, a bland and brief announcement that a Peter Voss was to be buried at the Mansfield Cemetery at 2.30pm the next day, after a short private church service.

The fact that any funeral service was being held at all on a Sunday in such poor winter weather went some way to confirm that it was indeed the Peter Voss he knew. The very Peter Voss, the traitor and author of the death of a dear colleague and perpetrator of his own desperate misery incarcerated in a Russian prison in the Gulag.

James had harboured for a long time an intense personal hatred with a ferocity felt deep to the very pit of his stomach. A final closure of this nagging sore would be a welcome tortured release. Finally, the chance had come to account for this bag of worms and to close the book of an unrelenting sense of unquenched vengeance he had carried since the sad demise of Tony. This was no professional duty to close a long open file; this was profoundly and personally intimate. He had to make sure, absolutely certain, that if it was him, there were no funny games this time. He needed to witness his final extinction from the planet.

Bus services had stopped and many schools were closed and would be for at least another few days. It would never have happened of course in his boyhood days; from the age of five you went to school irrespective of the weather, as long as the snow didn't rise above eye level. Today it seemed kids and even pet dogs took precedence over everything else, including adults, an utter nonsense in James's view.

Continuing stubbornly onwards, travelling in open country road; following the fast disappearing car and lorry tracks blurred in the heavy snow and grey gloom; he went through once again his alibi. The photographic memory pf yester year had long disappeared, one of the reasons he had decided to retire before it was too late. This is how he rehearsed it,

'He was paying his last respects to Malcolm, whom he had first met in Mansfield. Malcolm had a great and whacky sense of humour, an essential attribute when ploughing through the tedious piles of legal due diligence documentation, scattered like confetti in his office. Making sure the legal drafting was faultless and there were no areas of ambiguity; searching for those clumsy constructed clauses, or for that matter unintended legal IED's waiting to be set-off without warning.

He had first met Malcolm, when he had been acting as a company secretary in the same company as James in Mansfield. James was a chartered accountant working as the head of the finance department after a short career in public service. Malcolm eventually left the company to set up his own legal practice, James moved on some eighteen months later for the last decades of his working life and eventually into tranquil retirement. They continued their friendship uninterrupted over some thirty odd years. Malcolm always there to deal with the loose ends left in the wake of James's deal-making. He was his closest friend and he was devastated by his loss.' That should neatly deal with any casual enquiries especially as any follow-up would readily validate the answer.

The information omitted was Malcolm had died suddenly and mysteriously, a lot of James's acquaintances or casual encounters seemed to meet a similar fate, but not in their case purely coincidental or a chance accident. It was true there was a strange phenomenon hanging over James's head; whenever there was 'aggro' directed towards him, someone would get hurt or depart from their mortal spring in bizarre circumstances. Untimely ends in strange course of events; this time James wasn't in the vicinity as far as Malcolm was concerned and after all he was his closest friend and confidant. Surely the fingers of accusation couldn't be pointed in his direction this time. An unexpected death at the age of 50 years old of a close friend though, even if diagnosed with terminal pancreatic cancer, still drew suspicious official curiosity prompting an autopsy, just in case the deceased had been 'elbowed' by unknown malcontents, like the others, on their way.

No doubt Malcolm's involvement in the Russian Gulag affair gave added impetus for further enquiries beyond the norm to confirm that all was above board. James had tried vainly to get to Malcolm's funeral in time but the air traffic controllers in France had gone on a sudden strike and a trip via the fully booked ferries was not capable of getting him there in time. So, six months later he fulfilled his personal pledge to his old and loyal friend who had probably saved his life.

Peter Voss, on the other hand, had just died two days before in the Nottingham City Hospital, apparently it was thought from a second heart attack, but as

James knew full well probably from sheer fright aided by an accidentally induced shortness of breath.

Meticulous as always in his planning, James knew parking would be difficult as the main road outside the cemetery on both sides had parking restrictions; that is if you could have seen the yellow road warning strips in the awful weather. Parking in the largely deserted cemetery would bring unwanted attention, so he decided he would park in the staff car park of the West Notts College; just opposite the cemetery entrance, but less conspicuous. Passers-by would assume an old classic car had been left behind having failed to start in the cold weather, abandoned by one of those odd bearded lecturers with their tank top knitted jerseys and leather covered elbowed tweed jackets.

Hopefully, a little more snow would soon blur his tyre marks and the snow would make it less obvious of his recent arrival. He would not enter the cemetery until 2;45pm to allow for all the mourners to be present at the grave side. He had thought about renting a car but that option bred too many traceable loose ends. The temporary false plates on his own car, despite the car's distinctive marque, would be a better solution. They could always be reset, out of curious eyesight, before returning to his sister's home, at the turn of a tiny chrome handle in the glove compartment. The revolving Toblerone as he called it.

The grey fuzzy outline of the concrete and glass clad building of the West Notts College gradually came into view. Not quite a replica of the Lubyanka in Moscow, headquarters of the KGB and its adjoining guesthouse, a building he had got to know well from the inside. What a depressing building for the young minds of this 'beer and coal mining' dominated town. Built in pebbled concrete it was nowhere as visually pleasant as its' Moscow counterpart. Not quite the conceptual architectural mind-set if you were trying to inspire and raise youthful aspirations. Had no one in the Midlands yet fathomed that architectural design is a vital component of a vision and an instructive pointer to a positive future; a basic unitary concrete and plain sheet glass functionality doesn't cut the mustard.

James could now just make out the entrance to the cemetery and between the partially open iron gates, the fresh tyre tracks and footprints of probably a dozen people giving a clear direction for those wishing to follow. Ahh, I don't have to be a Red Indian Scout to find out where they will be heading, mused James.

James gingerly traversed the main road and swung over into the staff car park of the college giving the handbrake an almighty pull to make sure it was locked into position. It was the one tiny fault James hadn't bothered to rectify on 'Yug', his nickname for the Leeds registered car. One of the teeth on the braking mechanism ratchet had broken and it was necessary to give the handbrake a mighty heave to engage the next tooth and ensure the handbrake was fully engaged.

Despite its age, James had kept the car in pristine showroom condition parking it in an air-conditioned garage every time he was abroad 'on business.' When the car was idling the 2,7 litre 6 cylinders purred away, almost deceiving the driver as to whether the engine was in fact turning over. James believed it was the 'Mercedes of Britain.' Because of short-term sighted shareholders, followed by vacuous marketeers and the bean counters ignoring the pleas of the serious car engineers, a great British icon was lost forever from the British Automotive Industry.

As soon as the small chrome ignition key was turned anticlockwise the red ignition light illuminated and the green light went simultaneously out on the polished wooden dashboard. The long-stroke engine lumbered smoothly to a stop. Almost immediately, with the heater blower turned off, the temperature dropped like a stone, even though still wearing his Abercrombie overcoat. James briskly put on his voluminous woollen scarf wrapping it several times around his neck and chin, sported a dark brown fedora hat pulled well-down over his head to his eyebrows and then pulled out two fur-lined leather brown gloves from his overcoat pocket, both as protection and a precaution from being recognised. Stepping out of the car his light brown brogue shoes made their first crunching contact with the fresh covering of snow. At least the clothing accessories gave him some feeling of warmth and security.

He made his way through the unending blizzard, the snow now collecting on his fedora hat; momentarily he glanced back through his snow speckled eyelashes and tears from the biting wind towards the tyre tracks into the staff car park. They were already disappearing from recognition. Passing through the partially open wrought iron gates, uncharacteristically, his emotions began to be stirred. A deep hatred and vengeful passion unexpectantly engulfed him, almost to the point that he found it difficult to breathe in rhythmic shallow breaths. He focussed on regularisation of his inhalations to maintain his composure. It wasn't so much the freezing cold air that compelled him to carry onwards but the gratifying thought he could lay to rest his personal vendetta and the long running irritation of the last decade.

Months before he had asked for the precise location of Malcolm's grave from his eldest son. So, in his mind recounting the simple map that had been drawn for him, he took the first available turning to the right departing from the tracks of the others taking careful note the direction they were heading. The snow was becoming much deeper so he was forced to walk rather like a strutting flamingo to stop the snow spilling over the top of his shoes and wetting his thick woollen socks.

Malcom's internment was some way away from the entrance down the right-hand-side of the cemetery. As he closed in on Malcolm's grave, he could make out a group of mourners gathered in a circle; as luck would have it just some 80 metres away gathered around a freshly dug plot. The ceremony must have been rather quick for them to be already at the graveside. A minor technical point which should have put James on alert. A small mechanical digger was parked respectfully twenty metres away. Through momentarily glimpses from his tilted head against the prevailing wind, his watery eyes squinting against the cold snowflakes, he could make out ten people, of which two were children. The only sign of grief was from the small children who were turned inwards towards their carer's protection, their small arms clutching tight around the adult's legs, just above their knees, as the coffin was gently lowered into the frozen earth. The widow stood out from the rest, dressed in her full-length black overcoat and hat, her faced masked by a black lace net covering her full face apart from the pale white of her pointed chin. She was too far away and hidden from James to gauge her grief. The others were in a mix of dress ranging from what appeared to be donkey jackets normally found on building sites, whilst others had brown short knee length overcoats. All wore gloves.

James continued towards Malcolm's plot being careful not to break the pattern of his awkward bird like stride; again, a lesson he had learnt through experience to avoid unwanted attention. You can pass people quickly and no one takes notice, but slowed down and heads could turn in your direction.

His wife, Suzanne, had thoughtfully bought a bunch of flowers in advance for James to place in a pot jar bought for the purpose beside the headstone. Malcolm's grave stone was in a grey dappled marble with embossed gold lettering expressing all the standard words, such as devoted husband and father, they were not the words James recalled in his memory at first recognition of his resting place. James remembered one standard joke Malcom used to say to young children,

'What do they call Postman Pat when he is on holiday?'

Off course the answer was, 'Pat,' much to the amusement of the children once they had worked out the simple stupid logic.

Recalling the lame joke in his head James still had to give a wry smile.

"Sorry mate for being so late turning up, but let me make amends by reciting to you a poem I wrote in your honour," said James in a hushed voice.

He then recited in his mind the following:

POEM FOR A MATE

I've travelled down some dusty roads

Both crooked tracks and straight

And I have learnt of life's noblest creed

Summed up in one word, Mate.

I'm thinkin' back across the years

A thing I do of late

And these words still stick between me ears

You gotta have a mate.

Someone who'll take you as you are

Regardless of your state

And stand as firm as Gibraltar Rock

Because he is your mate.

Me mind goes back to '73

To treachery and to hate

When man's one chance to stay alive

Depended on his mate.

With a tin for a billy-can

And slate for a plate

A hell's paradise for bugs

Was bed for me, your mate.

I'd slip and slither through the filth

And cursed my rotten fate

But then I'd hear a quiet word in me ear

Don't give up now I am on my way, your mate.

And though it's all so long ago

This truth I have to state

A man don't know what lonely means

'til he has lost his mate.

If there's a life that follows this

If there's a Golden Gate

The welcome that I wanna hear

Is just, at last you made it here, my mate.

And so to all who ask us why

We recall these special dates

Like that Release from the Gulag in 73, I tell 'em why

I am thinkin' of my mate.

And when I've left the driver's seat

And 'anded' in me Rover plates

I'll tell Ol' Peter at the door

I've come to join me mate.

Those hatred and vengeful thoughts momentarily subsided in James's mind as a few tears flowed down his cheek remembering those years as a relatively young man in the Siberian Gulag with Tony, for a short while his only company, but seemingly forgotten by everyone but Suzanne, his wife and Malcolm his mate. Malcolm by his sheer persistence and guile had managed through sheer tenacity had got James back home where he belonged.

"When you meet up with that 'bastard' before he is sent to an eternal hell and purgatory give him a roughing up from me", said James returning his mind to the main matter in hand.

The cortege by this time were struggling to find small clumps of frozen earth left behind by the mechanical digger so they could throw them on top of the coffin once it had been lowered into its final resting place. Only one person refrained, a smartly dressed gentlemen sporting a strong bow moustache and carrying a leather briefcase embossed with the British crown herald. He was obviously a civil servant from the 'Department', if his pin-striped trousers and shiny black shoes tied with thin black laces were anything to go by. Was he on the same mission as James, but for him on a strictly arms-length bureaucratic basis; to close an old dusty office file? Or, did they still not know who actually Peter Voss really was?

The snow had abated, but in spite of the icy wind, James held back in order to 'clock' the cortege before they moved away and before he went over to pay his own form of respects to the recently departed. He hadn't recognised any of them but did have a tinge of sorrow for the two children who were sobbing quietly. To them Peter Voss was just a lovable grandad, just like him, but what they didn't know was that he was a man capable of acute treachery; placing his nation in grave danger; old men, women and children, there was no compassion, all just for a demented foreign ideology, prestige and a selfish comfortable lifestyle.

Turning to the task in hand, James had brought a small trowel borrowed from his sister, for the purpose of locating the pot jar of flowers into the hard ground. He now used it to wipe away the snow around the grave and to extract the odd surface stone and debris. It not only made him feel better that at last he was doing something positive for the bereaved Malcolm's family but also gave a pretence of activity while he maintained his furtive surveillance. He had thought of visiting Malcolm's widow but in the same instant declined, it was too risky, the 'old foreign state agents' were still active and were on the prowl seeking their own revenge, even decades later, because they had finally realised, they had been well and truly outwitted by an urchin from Nottingham Player Academy, the secondary school for backward boys and forward girls.

As the cortege were about to turn away from the grave and depart, James positioned himself out of their line-of-sight by a conveniently placed oak tree just ten metres away. It wasn't sufficiently quite broad enough to completely disguise his presence but enough to avoid discernible attention. Despite the cold and damp air, James waited another 15 minutes until he was sure they had all left and before any grave diggers appeared to fulfil their remaining duties. He took a quick swig of brandy from a solid silver hip flask presented to him by President Robert Kennedy over an afternoon cup of tea and scones at

'Presidential candidate!

the White House. Then wandered over in the manner of any curious bystander examining a fresh plot in the ground.

Placing the tips of his brown shoes over the lip of the deep rectangular hole he peered into the dark abyss and quietly said,

"How so long have I waited for this moment my friend. You are the vilest person I have ever met. A disgrace to humanity, a traitor to your country and selfish beyond belief. I wished I could have contrived a more painful and extended terminal end for all the grief and suffering you inflicted on me, my family and my friend, Tony. Not only did you betray us, you contrived to increase my suffering through a slow death. You should not be in consecrated ground but buried amongst the filth of a Siberian rubbish dump where you truly belong. Even eternal purgatory is too good for you."

Standing motionless for a few moments as he stared at the brass-plated name on the coffin James then continued,

"I bet when you came out of your coma and saw me stooping over your hospital bed it gave you the fright of your life. Sorry that I stood idly by as that Irish cleaning lady unplugged your machine to do the vacuuming around the ward. I had wondered how many more she would prematurely dispatch on their way before they twigged what was going on. It must have induced your second heart attack from the lack of oxygen. At last, for once your luck seems to have finally run out. I was well away by the time the medical orderlies had rushed in, just another visitor casually walking down the corridor. I am pleased it all worked out so perfectly well."

James looked skywards hoping the good Lord would grant him forgiveness and agree this soul was beyond redemption.

It was as though a great burden had been taken off his shoulders and now, he could return to his wife and family and enjoy the rest of his retirement in contentment. The weather captured the moment too. Suddenly the snow storm had relented, the sun broke through, shedding shafts of bright sunlight between the patches of blue dotted sky. As he gave a precautionary look around, the scene almost resembled one of those chocolate-box pictures, all the greyness had gone and everywhere was covered in three inches of beautiful virgin icing sugar snow. The boughs of the trees were groaning under the weight of the white blanket spread across their branches. He swore he saw a flash of red of a robin in the hedgerow singing his heart out. A new and fresh beginning, summer would soon arrive.

There was still no one around as James returned to his car and wiped off the surplus snow with his gloved hand before using his plastic scraper ice remover with the rubber strip to deal with any ice on the windscreen. Visibility restored and all the covering of snow removed, he tapped the plastic scraper on his heel and placed it into the boot alongside his trusty tool box including a locked compartment for his Glock 26 automatic with a full clip of 10 rounds. He rapidly removed his overcoat, scarf and gloves, placed them on the car's back seat and fumbled in the biting wind for his ignition keys, he turned the key. The red light illuminated, he pushed in the starter button and on came the green light just as the red light went off to signify all was in order. The heating was set to its maximum but he wouldn't use the fan yet until the engine had reached its full normal running temperature. Thrusting the gear selector into reverse he nursed the car rearwards following as best he could the same tracks he had entered by, until at the centre of the road he could make a sharp 90° right turn and make the return trip, via Annesley Woodhouse. The road was completely deserted. Back to the family for dinner at his sister's home.

Tomorrow he planned seeing the old man and at the same time Mr. Brand his teacher when he left school and who opened that gate of destiny for him to follow. Dad had asked him to call round just to see the two of them, just Pa and Mr. Brand, both had kept in touch over the years and were now in their eighties; very intriguing.

"I must pop-in to that sweet shop on Aspley Lane for two big slabs of Cadbury's Dairy Milk Pa loves. He used to have the Fruit and Nut but the old gnashers, whilst still original, are not what they used to be."

James loved driving his 'classic car' so there was a doubling of the pleasure as he made for Redhill and Arnold to meet up with his wife and family again. He hadn't realised just how cold he had become. True, the application of the heater fan at Annesley Woodhouse had made quite a difference but he was still cold to the marrow. His sister seeing him draw up in his car, opened the front door immediately as he approached, he passed in one movement through the open door and stopped at the foot of the staircase throwing his coat, hat, scarf and gloves scooped up from the back of the car over the bottom bannister post.

"You look frozen to death, Bruv," said his sister Sheila with genuine concern.

"Get by the fire and I will get you a cup of tea to warm you through, I prepared an early dinner for us all", she said caringly.

During the time he had been away his youngest daughter, Lapaccia had arrived with her grown-up children, Rosemary and Michael. He had a soft spot for his granddaughter, simply because she happened to arrive at the point of his daughter's first marriage breakdown and he and his wife Suzanne had in effect adopted her as their own until his youngest daughter had moved on. Michael was a completely different character and even when he was a baby was trying to fathom how complex mechanisms worked. Now he was doing a doctorate at Cambridge University in applied mathematics discovering the joys of statistics and behavioural algorithms, much too clever for James educated at the Player Academy for backward boys!

James soon scoffed the two currant scones washed down by a strong mug of sweet Yorkshire tea.

"Dinner's ready," came the shout from the kitchen just as the many hands had laid the table.

Being the fusspot, she was, Sheila had arranged where everyone should sit with James at the head of the table, not her husband. James knew exactly what was coming; the 'third degree.' He might as well have been in 'Langley' being interrogated by the CIA, two strong beams of light shining into his eyes.

A barrage of questions came his way over the roast beef and Yorkshire pudding.

"How was the weather?"

"Did you park OK?"

"Did you find the grave?"

"Were there any other people about?"

"How did the flowers look?"

At this point Clifford intervened and said,

"Give the man a break and let him eat his dinner."

For Clifford a large dinner, in his case eaten twice a day; midday and the evening, was a sacred moment not to be interrupted. James was grateful for the intervention before the line of questioning developed onto more delicate matters. Lapaccia suddenly chirped up with,

"We are off to the Caribbean this summer to deliver a new yacht to Jamaica."

This gave James a chance to divert the conversation and to tell one of his many anecdotes he could summon on queue just from the mere mention of a subject.

"Remember Suzanne In Jamaica when we came back late one night from that evening soiree held by that 90 -year old brewery owner; he who was married to a 32-year-old American model. We swore he must have been head of the local Mafia. Remember looking out into the black sky and bright stars hovering over the night lights of Kingston, the white dinner-suited flunkies who were serving cocktails and canapes by the floodlit swimming pool, it was unreal. It was just like a film set to a James Bond movie. He had grenade nets over his bedroom balconies we originally thought were for the climbing floral climbing plants until corrected. On our late return early in the morning I couldn't open our bedroom door at the motel in Morgan's Creek, the key wouldn't turn so I went next door to see if I could use their back balcony and traverse onto ours, entering our apartment through the sliding doors we had left unlocked. That air hostess had just gone to bed judging from the negligee she was just wearing. She kindly let me in and through her bedroom onto the balcony. That ledge was only 3 inches wide but I managed to shimmy across and make an entry. Our marketing man on the floor below was so astonished he made that wooden trophy on my return to Mansfield inscribed 006½. I am sure he was taking the mickey!"

The rest of the family had heard these stories several times before and they just groaned, smiled, carried on eating and sighed in a condescending way.

James noticed though in the corner of his eye that Michael was staring at him, just as a pet dog would, with tilted cocked head trying to work out what his master was saying. All those behavioural algorithms, formulae, putting the dots together, no matter their apparent lack of individual significance, different ways of observing information and shaping the data were making this young whipper-snapper a bit too bright to be comfortable around. James remembered taking him to the Nottingham Forest football ground and buying him a sausage baguette almost longer than him. Even then, he was questioning the assistant whether his was as big as the rest; the innuendo at his age lost on him but not to the assistant. He would scoff the lot before the second half began. No matter, it helped bring James down to earth from the deadly serious business of his working routine. Magical memories amongst the horrors. Without any introduction or prompting, Michael then abruptly asked,

"Grandad, were you in MI6?"

2

Education and Training

The teachers at Player Academy had done their best to educate the great unwashed class of 40-odd fifteen-year olds. There was no getting around the fact that the 11+ exam scythe of aspiration had cut the bright ears of corn off from the rest of the chaff. James was left with the 'Dumbo's', excluded, along with his mates, from any hope of improving his education and importantly future life prospects. He was trapped. Engulfed like all of his class into a life of servitude and poor career opportunities. Their futures were already set in stone, there was no escape.

Not all though was a lost cause, he had learnt something on the way, particularly how to defend himself. By his second year he was being 'picked on' by the fifth-year pupils simply because of the first signs of a growing academic intellect. Seen as a threat, he was frequently intercepted on the way home and given a thumping, including on one occasion his head being repeatedly knocked against a metal street lamp by a gang of three bullies. The beatings were made worse by James's refusal to back off or go down. Mr. Brand, by pure chance witnessed one such engagement whilst driving home from the school sat in his Austin 10 car, he intervened, and dragging James to one side said to him,

"I can protect you inside school but not outside the school gates, I have a plan for you, young man."

Despite his wiry, less than muscular frame, James was enrolled into the schools boxing club. For the next six months he learned how to anticipate the punches, parry the blows, duck and weave. That would deal with avoiding the bleeding injuries from the severe beatings but that wasn't enough. He was also taught how to attack, punch hard and make it really hurt, especially to the body. Soon he was jabbing with both hands, executing upper-cuts and knock-out 18-inch jabs with either fist timed to perfection. Normally when you hit someone with a swinging left-hand punch their head would move to the right and that sometimes would be enough. If you hit them with a swinging right their head would go to the left with possibly the same result. But if you hit them with a lightning cobra strike straight-on, over just 18 inches they would simply crumple vertically down at your feet if delivered correctly.

Full body punches were to be smashed into your adversary, hopefully cracking his ribs, severely weakening him, for you then to turn to working on his head and finally putting out the lights and for James avoiding the anticipated misery. He was instructed to use his legs, hips and arms as combined, co-ordinated levers, to keep moving on his toes, flattening his front foot to secure the launch pad for another flurry of blows, all the time swerving, bobbing and weaving his whole body and head in perpetual motion.

Those with the unfortunate task of holding the punch bag were often lifted off their feet with the blows that came raining in. After four months to test his readiness, he was put in the school boxing ring over three rounds with the school and Midland Amateur Boxing Champion, Wally Swift. Wally was a bit of a one-hand jabber but he was to show later he could progress to the highest level becoming the British Professional Welterweight Champion. If Wally had made it with both hands who knows what world heights he could have reached.

James was a bit apprehensive at first at such a challenge against a proven opponent, he thought he should feel his way in and get the man's measure. Within thirty seconds, a lightning left-hand jab put him flat on his back from this gifted one-handed fighter. He had been punched before, but not as hard as this, these were sledgehammer punches.

"What did I tell you crackpot lad, anticipate and keep the top half of your body and head moving, don't stand there like a big girl's doll, get into him" said the coach who also doubled as the gym master.

That did the trick, in the future he determined he wouldn't allow his opponents to faze him, he was parrying to perfection and landing a few punches of his own, not enough to claim he had won but at least he had hurt him and was still standing when the final bell went; bloodied but unbowed.

The interview with the visiting careers advice officer from the Nottingham Council said it all as far as future ambitions were concerned. Lined up, just as they did for the 'nit nurse', with no thought of confidentiality or counselling; in turn the pupils were asked the same old questions.

"Name, and what job do you want to do?"

The answers were fairly predictable.

The girls would say,

"On the Co-op's supermarket checkout counters, or the more ambitious a shorthand typist."

For the boys it was,

"Down the pit, bricklayer, the army or for the more ambitious for their gender, a draughtsman."

What a complete farce!

It came to James's turn but this time rather than just a nonchalant grunt and a quickly scribbled pencil note on an A4 paper list, no doubt left in a bin on the way home, the career officer nearly fell-off his chair laughing,

"A chartered accountant, hadn't you better think of something more realistic?"

Before James could respond his maths teacher, Mr. Brand intervened.

"He's deadly serious. He needs to get at least 5 GCE 'O' Levels, with two in Maths and English to enter articles in a professional practice. In order to obtain them he has applied to go to People's College of Further Education for 18 months so he can obtain his school certificates. He is not permitted to take them here.

Mr. Brand and before him a Mr. Briggs had, in their totally opposite teaching styles, drilled into students the joys of algebra and logarithms. Mr. Brand was a thoughtful young teacher who James initially believed was being tested on managing pupils in tough schools before going onto higher status positions in education. He was to find out soon this was probably not true, possibly because he was being 'parked' until the authorities knew how to deal with this firebrand commie, no pun intended. Just a hushed comment from him would bring the unruly scoundrels to order and most of the time they listened intently to his class lectures as though their very lives depended on it. He was seen as one of their kind.

'Briggsy' was a totally different animal. Cruel and vindictive but never without purpose. Knuckles were regularly rapped by the edge of a ruler for leaving a dirty mark on an exercise book. You soon learnt to wash your hands before entering his class. Inattentive chattering pupils would have to have a keen eye out, just in case the wooden block of a blackboard rubber was sent airborne flying directly towards their heads; as fast as a test match cricket ball heading for the stumps. In spite of these frequent outbursts of petty violence, everyone in his class at the age of 10 knew and understood, to an 'A' Level standard, the mysteries of algebra and logarithms.

James never quite worked out which was the preferred teaching methodology, perhaps it was bi-modal.

James resigned himself that whatever he may have been losing out on at the new Bilborough Grammar School with their middle-class chummies, he was getting bucket loads of practical experience on how to handle all varieties of people of whatever age, whether it be on an intellectual level or most of the time the physical. He sometimes wondered though whether at times his own cruel and sarcastic streak was honed from the many rough encounters of a teenager raised on a tough council estate.

"Dream on, but if that is what you want to do, the best of luck with it," said the careers advisor. The response from the career adviser was something he had learnt to anticipate and expect directed towards working class people. What he didn't expect was Mr. Brand turning from the affable mentor to a seething venomous Trotsky revolutionary.

"How dare you talk to my students like that," he said in rebuke?

Before the career advisor could respond, Mr. Brand launched into a tirade on the oppression of the lower social classes and the system they had been preordained to obey. They were not idiots, or imbeciles, but young people trying their best, in the worst possible social circumstances to better themselves only for those who should know better, and were supposedly there to help them, to beat them down at every opportunity. He added he would happily measure his students with any of those from the privileged Bilborough Grammar School 'wallies' and prove beyond any doubt his pupils were academically far superior.

Clearly the career advisor had never been challenged before in so a direct and forthright manner. His face went a bright red with rage and his brow broke into a profuse sweat. Rather than address the opinions of Mr. Brand head on he came out with a tirade of his own, mainly about 'socialist' sympathisers with their liberal revolutionary anti-authority ideas, no doubt drawn verbatim from the Director of Education. In full flow, suddenly his eyes appeared to roll upwards, he clutched his barrel of a chest and fell slowly backwards still sitting in his chair. Pupils were asked to leave as two teachers went to his aid as James looked back at the melee. He saw one teacher gently allow him to drop to the floor still sitting in his chair while the other stepped in and started pumping his chest.

The ambulance arrived within a few minutes and for the rest of the afternoon the school was prematurely closed. It wasn't until the next morning assembly that the school was informed, the career advisor had recovered in the ambulance but would now face permanent retirement. James felt sorry for Mr Brand; he felt some responsibility on account of his defence of his students. James felt no remorse for the career advisor, the guy was a pompous bloated idiot, and in his role shouldn't involve himself in crushing any spark of aspiration a student might possess. Looking back, James pondered whether this was to be the start of the curse he was to bear for rest of his life. Anyone who aggressively crossed his path would suffer a bizarre untimely injury, or worse death, for those stupid enough to engage in this ill-advised tactical approach.

James was idly recounting in his mind the incident as he sat on the half-full upper-deck of the number 32 green Nottingham Corporation bus taking him onto the terminus at Maid Marion Way in Nottingham's city centre. Not exactly an auspicious start for his 18-month tenure at People's College of Further Education having by some miracle passed the entrance examination. Factory workers were already clocked-in to those massive city factories smelling of tobacco or machine oil. Wiping the glass, trying to peer through the steamed-up windows, it was difficult to track where exactly he was. Although he knew the bus would have to stop at the terminus, he nevertheless kept nervously wiping with the back of his gloved hand to check he was on route and today of all days the bus wouldn't take another direction.

Going up Alfreton Road he could relax a little after smelling the John Players cigarette factory he had visited just a few weeks before. They were looking for new recruits and had arranged school visits for prospective school leavers. To James the town seemed to be dominated by the drugs industry. The City was well into 'fags and booze' through the presence of John Players and Shipstones', a brewery in old Basford. For good measure of course, there was the Boots factory, the more acceptable manifestation of the drug sins of Nottingham. Thank goodness there was the Raleigh Cycle Factory to give some measure of a respectability, but even here, it was never translated into a positive image of the City. The film 'Saturday Night and Sunday Morning' put pay to that notion giving an authentic portrayal of everyday bawdy life in the cobbled streets of Radford. Sometimes in life we don't need reminding of how low our social class had sunk, abhorrent behaviour, ground relentless down deep into the gutters. Nottingham was a place you could literally smell the industry, be it the tobacco, the malted barley or even the warm suds of the machine oil. You knew you were at home simply from the smells.

James recognised he needed to buckle down and take life more seriously if he was to make his escape from this squalor and mediocrity. Not fail in the end, like an Arthur Seaton in Alan Sillitoe's book. James's only escape from the depressing greyness was cycling far into the Derbyshire hills leaving behind all this humdrum drabness on his Raleigh three-speed azure blue Palm Beach solid steel bicycle. Take in the pure fresh air and the beauty of the scenery following many mountain streams into tranquil gentle countryside. Later he was to take

34

up long distance running with Notts AC running like a gazelle along the many bridle paths that marked out DH Lawrence's home patch. His speed and fitness over long distances would come in very handy a few years later around the streets of Prague.

He thought to himself,

"Get through the next 18 months successfully and who knows what might open up, certainly better than being a draughtsman or digging for coal at Gedling Colliery. There has to be a way out other than university or the military"

The bus having chugged up to the top of one of the two hills dominating Nottingham in its lowest gear, (the other hill forming the foundation of the infamous Nottingham Castle), the No. 32 green manoeuvred around the large traffic roundabout at Canning Circus, the driver passing the black shiny steering wheel several times through his hands as though he was closing a large valve on an oil pipeline only to reverse the whole process ready for the free-wheeling descent to the bus terminus. The college was 200 metres further on from the terminus. It was the one educational establishment in the city that gave a new ray of hope for pupils, discarded at a tender age, a second chance of recovery. Personified in a brand-new concrete and glass three-story college it was attached to two massive workshops for the building and engineering trades. This could just be the gateway to a life of adventure!

All he had on him was a brief letter asking to present himself for 9.00am at the college reception. The college was not totally unfamiliar has he had been there once before to take the entrance examination, but then he had been with his father. Now he was on his own. After presenting himself at reception he was told to go to the second floor and Room 214 where he would be 'processed'. Processed was not a word he thought should apply to his gateway to fame and fortune. In his darker thoughts he imagined a broiler chicken in a poultry processing factory, electrically stunned in the head, defeathered, eviscerated, passed through boiling water, head and feet cut off and then through the blast freezer for packing and into the cold storage ready to emerge in a carton box of nine or for students like him after being duly reprocessed to a life of drudgery and misery. The only benefit perhaps was the chance of a slightly elevated pay scale, salaried rather than hourly paid, avoiding the piece work exploitation. Surely this is not what was meant. Hopefully the 'processing' and 'outcome' would be somewhat better.

A few of the first-year intake had already arrived, just standing idly around, gathered in small groups nonchalantly chatting away, whilst others were sat in neat rows at their tables pulling out their exercise books. Some, he would get to know better; Brush (because of his haircut), Kenny from Mansfield to be his mate (crash helmet in hand having arrived on his two-stroke Francis Barnett), Raj (a Sikh) and for a nice change coming from a segregated school, some very pretty girls, Ruth, Phyllis and Joanne. A rich mix of girly charms between a redhead, brunette and blonde. Just as he was making his presence known, a 6ft 2ins athletic guy strolled in, he later became to know him as a Peter Voss. Most thought he was the teacher because he looked a good many year's older than he actually was, arrogant and aloof; not as it turned out, just another fellow student.

James was in the second batch of new entrants; the first had arrived three months before defined solely by their birthdays, another farce. As the last of the new arrivals trickled through the door the geography teacher strode in and started the briefing, whilst those first intake students were asked to read an extract from a text book on the subject of surveying; he doubled up on that subject as well. Not all acceded fully to this instruction, preoccupied 'clocking' the new students especially those of the opposite sex. James already felt one of the girls had placed him on her radar screen. Not all the challenges to focus his attention would be his academic studies!

After assigning their small lockers for books stored between classes on the payment of a five-bob returnable deposit; a list was distributed of various stationery materials required to be purchased, pens, pencils, geometry sets etc. Student passes were handed out for the refractory. The remainder of the morning was spent just sitting-in, playing with sand in large boxed tables trying to replicate various contour maps in the geography lesson. The first real opportunity to mix was at lunch as they queued for a generous helping of beef curry and rice and a chat over the eight-cover tables. Despite the rag bag of backgrounds all got on well except for Peter who sloped off to a table all on his own.

"Does anyone know him or should one of us go over to keep him company," asked James?

"Don't bother," said Brush. "He is a drop-out from Nottingham High School. He spent most of his time eulogising his hero Trotsky rather than studying proper stuff until his Dad pulled him out of the High School and told him if he didn't shape up, he would be sent back to his native country, wherever that is, possibly Czechoslovakia."

They say that first impressions count for a lot and so it seemed this time. Peter Voss spelt trouble right from the start. He didn't mix as students normally do but would readily engage in the benefits of the Marxist/Communist system. No amount of counter logic would he entertain, sticking rigidly to his doctrinal mantra. When pressed how he expected his dogma to prevail his immediate answer would be, the same as in 1917, a revolution of the workers. From then on, most students gave him a wide berth but he did knuckle down as his father wished and as James understood later did very well in the final examinations. He went on to obtain his 'A' Levels at Trent Polytechnic and because of his high grades successfully sat the Cambridge University Entrance Exam. That was as far as James's knowledge of Peter Voss's future went, until that fateful day in Warsaw.

The next few years for James went broadly as planned, he managed to obtain entry to his articles, served the full five years and to everyone's astonishment, including himself, qualified as a chartered accountant. Little did he realise that this was only the entrée to a far less predictable and uncertain career path which would attract the attention of 'other's'. His education and training didn't stop on qualifying in his chosen profession, he was to be 'tested' on several missions before it was agreed his line of work would become 'official'.

Mr. Brand had read in the Nottingham Evening Post of James's success at People's College and then his subsequent professional qualification before calling round to see his father. Mr. Brand and his Pa had a chat over a cup of tea and cakes before James came breezing in from the training run home from the accountancy practice in West Bridgford, taking the orbital road but still beating the No. 32 bus taking the direct route through the city. Mr. Brand had enquired what was James's plans for the future, but Pa had replied there were no definite plans yet in place. His son was struggling to find a suitable challenging job after qualifying, anywhere in the UK and was in a bit of a quandary what to do.

Mr. Brand made it known that he felt James had shown great potential and leadership at school and that he knew of someone looking for a bright and resourceful young man, but it would mean a move to South Africa. Pa, whilst realising this meant a family parting and absence for at least a year, he did want his son to have the best chances in life and thought it would be good idea to broach it with James. Pa, looked at his watch saying,

"Ah, it's nearly quarter to six he will be here in the next few minutes."

He didn't need to look at his watch, Sandy the family dog had already jumped onto a dining chair positioned in the bay window knowing a family member was due home. Seeing no sign at the front gate he would dart out of the back door and wait patiently for James's arrival. On the rare occasions James was late he would sulk for hours afterwards.

Pa and Sandy were not the only one's looking out for him.

"Hi James," said Norma, a ginger-haired girl sat on her front gate opposite to his house.

James pretended not to hear, dressed in his Notts AC green tracksuit and with a high stride he put his hand on the gate post and straddle-jumped the gate in one lazy movement only to stop at the side of his house to stretch the leg muscles, Sandy patiently watching at his side, before bounding through the back-kitchen door with him.

"There's someone special here to see you," said James's Pa.

James was somewhat shocked to see Mr. Brand sitting in their cramped living room. He had always pictured him in a large classroom, not at his family home, sat at the dark polished wooden dining table with its lace centred table cloth, in the centre of which was located the ugliest pot sculpture of a bowl of fruit defying the laws of gravity. There was placed on the edge of the table a green file and what appeared some press cuttings inside.

James opened first in a jocular manner,

"Nice to see you Mr Brand, as you can see, I have joined Notts AC so I can run faster than my adversaries this time, before being forced to engage in fisticuffs."

"Very wise young man, two options are always better than one," said Mr Brand smiling at the recollection of a long-lost memory.

"Mr Brand has come to suggest an opportunity for you following your qualification, it sounds very interesting to me," said his father quickly breaking into the formalities and getting straight down to the reason for the surprise visit.

"An ex university chum of mine has a project in Southern Africa and is searching for someone resourceful, can look after himself and understands business," opened Mr Brand.

Mr Brand continued,

"The job is a little unusual in that it is a minimum 12-month fixed contract, based in Johannesburg, but you will be expected to travel around various countries in Southern Africa. The pay is excellent giving you a chance to pay your Mum and Dad back for all their sacrifices. The experience will definitely lead you onto greater opportunities if you are as good as I think you are."

It was nice to hear Mr. Brand had such faith in him after receiving so many rejection letters from job applications. The ability to make some recompense to his parents swung the decision immediately for James, no matter the other details. To sacrifice at least 12 months of his life to help his parents was sufficient motivation on its own.

"Who would I be working for, what's the role and would my travelling costs be covered," asked James trying to maintain the pretence he was still in decision-making mode?

"Officially you will be working for a major African Conglomerate as a business advisor. All your accommodation, travelling costs and out-of-pocket expenses are covered each month. A Peugeot 204 will be at your disposal from the car pool. So, in effect, apart from some pocket money included in your expense allowance, you can leave untouched your monthly salary of £1,000 a month in a UK bank," said Mr Brand spelling out an offer you couldn't refuse unless you were completely insane. He didn't have to throw in the sunshine and fresh juicy oranges to clinch it.

"What do you mean by 'officially', asked James?

"Oh, that's just a contractual nicety, you will be legally employed by the UK Board of Trade but seconded to the Conglomerate," said Mr Brand.

"When do they need me to start," asked James?

"In three weeks, so you will have to first present yourself for a medical and for all the jabs you will need," replied Mr. Brand.

"This university mate of yours, who is he and have you known him a long time," questioned James thinking he needed to ask at least some questions for the pretence of due diligence purposes?

"I can't give you his name for the moment because he doesn't want it to be known how you were selected but I know him well and you can trust him implicitly. He is destined for much higher things, probably a minister of a major department of state. We went to Oxford University together and we became very close friends," said Mr Brand in reassurance.

"I studied Mathematics and Physics, he did his PhD and Masters in Chemistry and Molecular Biology. He's quite a character, you will like him a lot once you meet him."

"What do you think, Dad, should I go for it," asked James paying due respect to his father's opinion?

"It's your decision, son. You are a grown man now. For Me and your Mum we obviously will miss you but your time has come to strike out on your own. Our job was to give you the best platform we could to launch you on your way. What's the downside, just a lost 12 months and sunburn whilst in the meantime finding out what you want to do long-term," said Pa?

"OK, let's go for it."

"Leave me to explain it to your Mum."

Before he knew where he was, James was sat at an oak desk complete with a white phone and a brass green shaded table lamp. The secretary had shown him in and offered a cup of tea and some Palmer and Harvey tea biscuits. Looking through the small paned glass windows over the empty brown leather chair, he could clearly make out Marble Arch. The Arch he recalled had been designed as a grand entrance to Aspley House, the home of the Duke of Wellington sited at the bottom of Park Lane. Unfortunately, the width was made too narrow and it was left as a bit of a white elephant, its use now confined to be an ornate roundabout. Aspley, as he'd known, had been the rough council estate he used to run through on his way to work; now he was within a stone's throw of a somewhat grander house. These side reflections he thought he had to dismiss rapidly from his mind to be sharp and alert for the mysterious visitor, the friend of Mr Bland.

He heard the great wooden door with a huge brass knob open up behind him and a voice bellowed,

"Don't get up young man, enjoy your tea and bikkies before we get down to business. My name is Tony," said the deep voice behind before coming into James's view.

The man before him slumping into the leather chair and kicking both feet onto the desk was not quite what James expected. James first noticed the soles of the leather hiking shoes were studded with steel flat headed nails along the edge of the soles and down the centre. They were hardly worn, the leather unmarked or discoloured. The guy was enormous, over twenty stone with jet black short curly hair and a deep-set pair of black eyes. If he had worn large gold earrings, he could have easily doubled as a gypsy. The large half-smiling moon face then engaged in conversation.

"This is not my normal office. You will soon realise we couldn't meet on King Charles Street in Whitehall. I won't bother you with a recount of your background I already have all I need to know on that front. I am more interested if you are up for a bit of adventure for a lad from the sticks," opened up Tony.

"I thought this was a business project not an adventure," intervened James.

"It is, but with a difference," immediately responded Tony.

"The Department engages in many international development projects and from time to time we second young men like you to supplement our overseas clients when their resources become overstretched. We have a potential problem brewing in Southern Africa and we will possibly have to act to protect our interests and investments," continued Tony.

existing manufacturing facility operating in South Africa. You will work with a designated team from the African Conglomerate, act under their direction and command, but not accountable to them. Once the project is complete you will continue working at their Head Office in Johannesburg on any ad-hoc tasks they may require you to do. Twelve months later, after a great party, you may come home by which time we will throw another opportunity your way."

After a short pause, Tony asked,

"Would you like me to continue?"

"Sounds great so far, just wondering whether I am the man with the skill sets you need, after all I am not an engineer, I am a bean counter", responded James feeling he may be out of his depth.

Tony remarked,

"Don't worry, we have done our homework on your skill sets. We know more about you than even you know. Our personnel vetting boys are quite thorough. Planning and execution will have to be of the topmost order. We are going to have to move plant and machinery from a 60-acre factory site over just one weekend. Together with all the files and systems to a site prepared some 1,000 miles away. The plant and machinery have to be working again by 10:00am the following Monday morning, all done seamlessly as though they have always been there. Still with me, James?"

"Bloody hell, what's the rush," responded James.

"Ah, you have hit the nail on the head and why you need to be there to check it's all done with HMG in mind. We invested £100m's in aiding Zambia, before and after, decolonialisation. Unfortunately, a certain Kenneth Kaunda is getting too big for his boots and threatening to nationalise our assets or put taxes on our operations and our exports to fill their treasury coffers, as they euphemistically call it, with a load of dosh. No doubt diverting some of it into their private Swiss bank accounts. We need to take some preventative actions before he goes too far. We are already leaching stuff out but these assets are too big and visible to be disguised, Tony explained.

"But is this all legit, the President isn't exactly going to put you on his Christmas Card is he, once he finds out what we are up to?"

"It's legit for the moment, but we expect he will issue some Presidential edict we think just before he goes to the African National Congress in six months' time. For the first three months your time will be spent on planning and preparation and then you will travel to the factory for a month, acting as though you are part of an annual planned maintenance team. In fact, you will be preparing the move without the factory personnel realising what you are up to," explained Tony.

"OK, let's go for it."

"Just one final point before I get you to sign your contract of employment. You cannot tell anyone, including your father, about what you are about to do", said Tony altering to a serious tone.

"How can I explain my absence for 12 months," asked James?

"My suggestion in these situations is to follow the truth as far as you can but just be a little economical with the full story. You can tell people you have been struggling to find a worthwhile job, you saw an advert for an intern job in South Africa offering valuable experience of modern advanced computerised systems that was well paid and allowed you to see a foreign country. That's as far as you need go but remember when you cross the South African border at any time you are incognito, no telephone calls and definitely sending no mail with Kaunda's head on the stamp," said Tony smiling in the process.

"How did you know I was struggling to find a job?"

"Do you want me to bore you with the full list of applications you made," asked Tony?

"Don't bother, I suppose you thought I was desperate."

"I wouldn't quite put it that way, let's just say highly motivated and you fit neatly our precise specifications," answered Tony still smiling.

They both then laughed and shook hands as James signed his first employment contract outside the profession.

As he was now on all expenses paid arrangement, James took the taxi back to Saint Pancras Station but refrained from changing his rail ticket to first class. That would not give a good first impression and besides he had to get used to being 'incognito'.

On the train with a cheese sandwich, a packet of Smiths crisps with the blue dolly salt packet and a can of beer he ran through his alibi, as he would have to many times again, before meeting up with Pa and telling him the good news; South Africa beckons. He would get his father as a second signature to his new bank account to take care of his remitted money. He had anticipated already that it wouldn't be long before there was enough dosh to buy a better car to replace the family's Morris 8, they had been managing with for years. Perhaps a nice new Rover 90?

3

Coffee with Kaunda

How life's outlook can change rapidly. James was every morning, preparing the open coal fire for his principal's office in the accountancy practice in West Bridgford, Nottingham; even though he was now a newly qualified chartered accountant. No matter; he wasn't complaining about clearing out the cold ashes of the day before, screwing up balls of newspaper, adding a layering of kindling of wooden sticks before igniting the combustible pile with a match. After a few flickers of flames a few judicious lumps of anthracite placed on the top of the whole pile to complete the task. He ensured the fire got going in earnest with a sheet of the Nottingham Evening Post drawn across the open hearth to draw the air under the combustible mixture until the small flames burst into a roaring fire spreading warmth around his principal's office. Even on the dullest of damp mornings everywhere became bright, warm and cosy. His counterparts on the same pay grade working in the major accountancy firms would face no such perceived indignities. James never minded, his principal had always treated him well and patiently answered all his numerous questions to learn every aspect of his chosen profession.

Times had changed. His career had made a seismic shift. No longer the familiarity of working in a converted kitchen transformed into an extra office, simply by the addition of an office chair and oak table; previously he could peer out of his kitchen window onto the busy Radcliffe Road. On the rare moments working later in the evening to keep onto the ever increasing workload, he would take the luxury of lifting his gaze from the pile of invoices, bank statements and chequebook stubs and view the spectators heading for either the cricket or the football ground located equally distant between the Nottingham Forest and Trent Bridge Sports Stadiums.

His life had been transformed, perhaps with the guidance of his teachers and the support of his parents and grandparents his escape route had revealed itself at last after all the hard toil. He was sat in business class armchair on the BOAC flight from Heathrow to Jan Smuts being waited on by the very smart stewardess. Despite the excitement of a new beginning, he nevertheless was sad to wave goodbye to his old principal and his makeshift office. He was still suffering from the emotional wrench of kissing goodbye in the departure lounge his mother, father and sister.

The white and dark blue jet airliner disappeared into the winter orangey streaked sky over London, the red tail lights shining brightly until disappearing as fading dots into the evening skyline. An evening meal was served after an hour into the two leg 15-hour flight. There would be a stopover in the Cape Verde islands before the final leg bound for Johannesburg. James was able to snatch five hours sleep; at least there wasn't to be the effect of jet lag. Dawn was soon breaking over the African Continent passing over the plains of Botswana, spotting the streaks of sugar cane bush fires clearly visible below. The farmers burning off the weeds and the unwanted bugs of the plantations in order to sanitise and fertilise the soil with natural nutrients.

A light breakfast was served again by a very pretty air hostesses and James braced himself mentally for the momentous challenge he was never to forget. A new continent and a dramatic change in his life. Soon after landing the passengers were disembarking and making for the corrugated covered hangers housing a long factory conveyor belt. At the end were a group of black African porters eagerly pouncing on passenger's luggage to lug to their cars, buses and taxis receiving the tips they relied upon to live. James was to be greeted, strangely by another Mr. Briggs, not this time his school math's teacher, but an employee of the Conglomerate Group instructed to pick him up and take him to the hotel on Bree Street in Johannesburg.

No name signs were required, Mr. Briggs identified his target immediately. Smiling he came over and said,

"James, I presume, welcome let me organise your luggage and get you to my car waiting outside."

Both shook hands. James remembering his manners instilled by his working-class parents said,

"Thanks for meeting me, I think I would have been completely lost without your help."

A porter came scurrying up and grabbed a suitcase in each hand insisting also on carrying James's holdall. Mr. Briggs led the way with the African porter hardly visible under all the cases, all that was visible were two spindly black legs supporting the pile. The porter stuck to them like glue behind them. James was a bit stiff from the long flight and was pleased at last to stretch his legs and to be rid of his suitcases although feeling a little guilty of exploiting the aid of his African friend. Mr. Briggs opened the VW camel coloured combi and asked the porter to put the suitcases and holdall into the back. Mr. Briggs drew out of his pocket a few silver coins, no paper, and without looking to count, placed them into the grateful cupped black African hands. The porter was obviously very pleased with the result and scurried back in case there were still some stragglers he could earn a double bonus from.

Although the city centre of Johannesburg was just 30 minutes away Mr. Briggs was able to brief James on the way to the four-star hotel on Bree Street. He would stay there for the moment until perhaps, if he preferred, a private apartment in somewhere like Sandton. It was possible to walk to the head office on Marshall Street but said he would pick him up at 9:00 am the next morning at the hotel and they would make their way together to meet 'the boss'.

The first thing James did on arriving in his hotel bedroom was to kick off his shoes. Feet always swell a little from a long flight and then went over to look down on the morning traffic below. It was now getting on for midday so he needed to get to a bank and change some traveller's cheques and have a wander around to start to get familiarised to his new surroundings. His first sensation on the street outside was to feel the warmth of the dry sunshine in March. It would be regarded as a beautiful sunny day back home especially given the crystal blue sky. The next sensation was the feeling of shortness of breath. At first, he thought he had taken ill, but then recalled Bryan's warning (as he would now have to call him) that Johannesburg was more than 6,000 feet above sea-level. The effect of the altitude could be quite pronounced for new arrivals especially when gently exercising.

The streets were noisy and bustling with a mixture of whites, blacks and, as they were referred to colloquially, the coloureds. Just like a bag of Basset's Liquorice Allsorts he enjoyed as a kid. A five-lane bank of cars stood at the red traffic lights, later he was to learn these were known as robots. As the lights turned to green the mass of cars revved up and accelerated down the one-way street almost like the start of a Le Mans motor race. Heaven help anyone stupid enough to tempt providence and crossover at the wrong time.

The streets bustled with a mass of humanity going about their daily tasks. Apart from the obvious colour of skin differences, the whites carried briefcases while the blacks balanced enormous loads on their heads. The next thing he noticed were the English and Afrikaans signs stating 'Vir Gebruik Deur Blankes' or 'For Use by Whites Only' on roadside seats. To show some form of égalité but not

James placed the cup in the saucer drinking the last dregs realising he was being subtly drawn straight into something both big and very serious.

"Before I go any further, I need you to sign these two documents; one is a Non-Disclosure Agreement (NDA) and the other the Official Secrets Act," said Tony as though he was handing out the formal expense claims forms.

"I understand the NDA as I may have access to confidential commercial files, but the Official Secrets Act, why that," said James becoming a little nervous as to what he might be getting into?

"Don't be unduly concerned, every civil servant working at our level has to sign it simply because you are dealing with confidential government business and not just private commercial stuff," said Tony, but not altogether convincingly.

"If you can sign the documents straight away, I can give you more details. If you decide it is not for you, no problem, we just file them away to gather dust but you will be restricted from telling anyone that any discussion took place and particularly what was said," said Tony sliding each document across the table in front of James pointing out the places requiring signature and counter-initialling. As there was little downside until a job offer had been accepted, James acquiesced.

"Thanks for that, Betty will let you have your copies before you leave," said Tony.

Tony then launched into a full briefing without notes and references to any files.

"In essence you will be the HMG representative on the project and will ensure that the project I am about to describe is carried out resulting in securing certain assets by removing them from Zambia and relocating them into an fraternity, there were also park bench signs 'Nie-Blankes' or 'Non-Whites' as though they were non-people! Not quite the experience one gets in his home town strolling into 'Market Slab Square.'

At the corner of the next block was the Standard Bank offering currency exchange. He turned into an air-conditioned bank for the next new sensation offering the cash teller his two £50 traveller's cheques with his passport in exchange for some 1,800 Rands. He needed to become familiar with the new currency. He was getting peckish, so he strode across Bree Street at the designated crossing point and popped into an American styled diner 'The Cherokee'. A generous helping of fried chicken pieces and chips washed down with a vanilla milk-shake, made of real ice cream, malt and whipped in ice cubes made to perfection. This was far superior to the insipid version in the Wimpy Bars back home.

He then remembered he must write home to say he was safe and well so spent an hour writing a few pages of a letter and then wandered into the post office close by to mail it to his parents. Mum and Dad didn't possess a telephone. He remembered the words of Tony ringing in his ears only to write the normal stuff as an intern and no disclosure of his real mission. Making his way back to the hotel he thought he would have to pinch himself, somehow, this new world didn't seem real. By seven o'clock he found it difficult to keep awake and decided to have an early meal at the hotel and turn in asking for a morning call at 07:00. The altitude was to dog him for a week before his red blood cells could adjust.

The morning call was not as expected. No insistent buzz from a clock at the side of the bed or a ring from the bedside telephone. There was a knock on the bedroom door and a smartly dressed white uniformed black waiter came in holding a silver tray of a teapot, milk jug and sugar bowl with silver teaspoons and a porcelain cup and saucer.

"Morning Boss, your morning call, its 06:55," he said with the most beautiful white tooth smile no doubt pronounced by the blackness of his skin.

"And what's your name?"

"Jesus."

The total incredulity of the situation was not lost on James. A working-class Nottingham lad had been woken up by Jesus to bring him his morning tea.

This was to be his first real encounter with one of the local natives and the start of an insight into their cultural DNA and a growing affection for his oppressed African brothers, just like his white brothers in Player Academy. They were both from the same cooking pot.

"Breakfast is being served in the restaurant but I have told them not to expect you until 08:00," said Jesus.

The same routine was to be repeated for the next three months until James found somewhere to live not quite in Sandton. James in turn wangled the recruitment of Jesus to work at the head office, as his and other's tea boy, on far better wages.

At 09:00 sharp Bryan strode into the hotel reception drawing deeply on his Marlborough cigarette as though it was to be his last for a lifetime.

"Are you rested for your first day with us," asked Bryan still drawing on his cigarette as though he needed the nicotine effect to reach his toe nails.

"I feel great. I had a little wander around yesterday to get my bearings but the altitude knocked me out by 20:00."

"It gets to all you Pommies," said Bryan amused at the effect.

"We will go in my car as I can park it at the office rather than leave it here on the street."

Both strode through the open dark oak doors of the main office, into a massive open reception, their shoes clacking on the marble floor as they crossed to the reception. There was one armed security man in obvious view. The receptionist asked who was Bryan's friend,

"This is our new man James who will be with us for a while working with Fred and Duncan on the second floor of the accounts department."

"Welkom aan boord," said the receptionist slipping into the other official language, Afrikaans, another new sensation for James was going to have to get used to.

There was no lift, just a wide marble winding staircase covered in a luxurious green and gold carpet. Slightly breathless, they reached the second floor to walk through a wide oak panelled door. The accounts department comprised a very large room made up of a series of twelve desks formed in two rows of six on which each had either an electrically or manually driven Facet rotary calculator and adding machine. Only half the desks were occupied with volumes of paperwork strewn untidily across them and the remainder totally bare. It was later explained it was the year-end and many of the accountants were out on the veldt helping the newly acquired companies to cope with the Group's accounting merger forms. As James entered and was introduce to the few accountants there, Duncan popped his head around the door saying,

"Has the cavalry arrived yet?"

Bryan explained everyone was at full stretch and for the next couple of months James could only expect helping with the laborious consolidation work until the project team could convene and get to work on the mission he was here to help with.

No sooner had Duncan arrived than he was pushed from behind by Fred. James was to learn later Fred knew all there was to know about the computerised accounting systems. He was a portly man with thin horned gold-ringed glasses over which he peered when focussing on distance objects. James later learnt he used to be captain of the BOAC flying boats down East Africa to South Africa, travelling at very low altitude of a few hundred feet over the game reserves to give passengers a better look, scattering the wild animals in all directions. He once had to land on a lake to deal with a cylinder head fault on one of the engines pistons by crawling out onto the wing with a tool box and set of new gaskets. On the roof of the plane was a glass observation dome to carry out the navigational readings by his sextant on night flights.

To add to his talents, he was also an accomplished wood carver producing the most exquisite hand-crafted tables, chairs and grandfather clocks. James did once visit his workshop at the back of his house. It was well stocked with in-progress wood pieces of all varieties and lots of tools; chisels of all shapes and sizes and various saws. When asked if he would like a cold beer, Fred opened one of the two six-foot fridges packed to the gunnels with bottles and cans of Lion lager beer.

With no exchanges of conviviality Fred just said,

"I have got a job for you, young man, I want you to consolidate the monthly group capital expenditure board report."

Without even a glance to Bryan and Duncan, James dutifully followed Fred into his office where stood on his desk were several feet-thick, computer print-outs.

"Here is last month's report setting out the format and here are the returns from our 60 subsidiaries. Make sure the returns cross-check with the account tabs. Duncan will give you the currency exchange rates to use. Let me have the next month's report by close tonight. Nice easy start for you, it's just a simple arithmetic exercise, but if there is anything that looks out of kilter gives us a shout," said Fred brusquely.

James walked back with masses of paper under his arm to see both Bryan and Duncan still chatting away. Bryan said,

"First task eh, any problems I can give you a hand."

James then sat with the rest of the few in the office at first fathoming how the Facet machine worked. Within ten minutes the office was a hum of activity until dead-on 13:00 it was lunchtime. The whole ambiance was so different to his kitchen-based office of before. Lots of like-minded people for company and plenty of accountancy tasks well beyond the challenge of preparing pig breeders and corner shop accounts and their associated tax returns.

He was having a full-frontal exposure to a large-scale international operation spread over several countries and business experiences in manufacturing, engineering, construction, distribution and retailing. New skills were being learnt on fully integrated computerised systems, management and financial account reports and treasury matters. There was also the initiation to familiarising himself with the key executives and main board directors.

After six weeks, the year-end had been completed and the new budgets consolidated and fed into the computerised management information systems.

James was seeing first-hand the practicalities of the workings of a modern, financial systems, instead of just reading about them in American text books. He was also being made accustomed to general management theory as taught at the prestigious business schools of the USA. It seemed by sheer luck he was being mentored into the executive levels of the major international corporate organisations he could have only dreamt of. Pa and Mr. Briggs had been absolutely right to encourage him to have a shot.

Then, as he was getting familiar with the routine cycle, Bryan interrupted the steady workflow and called for six people from the account's office including James to what he euphemistically called the planning room. It was made clear that no note pads were to be used for a 'briefing'. The adjoining planning room gave the experience of an open office but the half- glazed walls and door made it impossible to work out who was inside and to a degree how many. Just dark shadows moving across the long-panelled dimpled glass screens. Bryan stood at a blackboard until Duncan joined them to conduct the next part of the meeting.

"Gentlemen what I am about to tell you is highly confidential and only the Board and you will know of what I am about to say. That is how it must stay until our project is accomplished and even then, you will not be able to discuss this with anyone other than with the people in this room, others who will join you, or the present Board of Directors. Is that fully understood," said Duncan in a serious tone?

"Only one other person needs to know and that is Ian Smith of Rhodesia, our British friends will deal with that when the time comes."

All affirmed in turn excited to know what was coming.

Duncan continued, once it had been established all had responded in the affirmative.

"As many of you are aware, we have a major engineering company in Zambia containing a foundry, 50 numerically controlled milling machines and various finishing processes. We have invested an additional R20m over the last two years successfully servicing the industries in the mining of copper and emeralds; construction and horticulture. We have learnt from our Zambian colleagues that there have been several visits to the factory by Russian delegations meeting with Zambian Ministers asking questions beyond the usual. Their suspicion is that the factory is to be converted into a small arms and artillery factory to arm revolutionary groups in Southern Africa in order to destabilise colonial countries, some of it directed towards us. Kenneth Kaunda, the new President, is being beguiled by the notion, implanted by the Russians, that he will head a new anti-colonial African revolutionary movement.

Of particular importance to us are the plans to nationalise the factory and if we tried to move anything it would be subject to a 100% export duty. There is an African National Congress meeting in three-months' time. We are assuming Kaunda will be wanting to make an official statement to his fellow African President friends at the summit to cement his new leadership role. We have to take pre-emptive action now."

One of the staff James knew as Tim, piped up,

"What does the pre-emptive action actually entail?"

Duncan was now in full flow,

"We are due to start our usual annual maintenance programme in 30 days. In the meantime, a site is going to be cleared in Vereeniging to house all the plant and equipment to be taken from Zambia, including the files and computers. We going to move the whole lot surreptitiously over one weekend, through Rhodesia and into South Africa. We will close the Zambian factory down at

17:00 on a Friday and by 10:00 the following Monday it will be fully operational, 1,000 miles away, in Vereeniging as though it had never been anywhere else."

James couldn't hold back any longer,

"How on earth are we are going to do that?"

"That's what you going to work out over the next four weeks," as though he had been asked a straightforward question how long does it take for that No. 32 bus from the bottom of Helston Drive to arrive at Maid Marion Way on an average day?

For a moment the room stood in stunned silent when Bryan piped up,

"OK gentlemen, we know the mission, let's put our minds to it. All papers will be left in this room under lock and key and only I will have the key."

James couldn't help feeling already the adrenalin rushing through his veins. Not only was this biggest challenge he had ever had but its importance was so profound giving that it clearly necessitated nation states approval.

As they say when you want to eat an elephant take small chunks bit by bit. The team started with a basic structural plan, identified potential alternatives and then started filling in the blanks in detail down to who was going to switch off the last electric light when they departed. Essentially the plan involved certain key phases. During the maintenance programme there was a scheduled limited period for a complete shut down for a few days when factory personnel would be given a few days holiday break. During this period the plant and equipment would be prepared for moving, loosening all the fixing bolts to the foundations, isolation of power circuits, leaving just the low voltage lighting circuits intact.

Around eighty heavy lorries would bring a fleet of fork lift trucks and the machines loaded overnight for the return trip, transported during the day towards Victoria Falls crossing the border with all the paperwork. It needed only one set of documents to be produced and then all the other shipments copied changing only relevant part numbers for the individual packages. The Zambian Border guards would not know the difference as long as the right part numbers, signatures and stamp endorsed the paperwork. The last shipment should mean the last lorry would depart by 22:00 on the Saturday leaving the squad of six from the planning room to do the final checks after the engineers had already left, collect all the files and computers and switch off the last lightbulb.

Following the lorries, the project team would leg it by night and by day in two Land Rovers following the same route stopping for a beer at a bar in Rhodesia to ensure all were safely across the border and then head straight back to Johannesburg. Their remaining task would be to witness the machines working as normal on the Monday morning in their new location; a point of pride that the job had been finally accomplished. The completed plan was gone over meticulously, especially if there were unforeseen hiccups in the process, necessitating other planned alternative options. Each one had to have his alibi rehearsed and ready in case they were questioned at the border or for that matter anywhere else, particularly explaining why they were travelling in Zambia at night and not in broad daylight.

When the time came to depart the Land Rovers with all their baggage were loaded, they were each issued with shoulder holsters, '45 automatics' and two ammunition clips for personal safety. At first James refused saying he would be more of a danger to himself and everyone else. Duncan would have none of it.

"You are in Africa now my son, not the Surrey Downs. Here are two extra clips specially for you, practice hitting a coke-cola can at 50 metres until you can hit it at will. Leave at least one clip though for the trip back. The others will show you how to keep it clean and importantly to take it apart blindfolded and to remember to keep the safety catch always on and never point it at anyone except in anger. If you have to use it, don't hesitate, your life might depend upon it."

If James didn't know it before, he knew it now, this is perhaps the real world, not the one a privilege few enjoy in a civilised Europe.

The countryside of Southern Africa is breath-taking, for quite a bit of the journey there was little traffic except when entering a small town or village. They sped through the countryside day and night until they neared the factory site. It was a great opportunity to talk and get to know his mates other than in an office environment. The others had all been trained in the South African Defence force, so weapons were not an issue for them. For James it made him edgy and nervous.

Housed in sparse barracks near the factory and around five miles from the nearest village, everyone was focussed on the plan. The only occasional distraction was an evening braai (barbeque) and a beer on the dormitory stoop exchanging stories and jokes as mosquitoes buzzed around their heads in the warm night air. Apart from the odd niggly problem such as seized machinery bolts, easily overcome with a welding torch, it was just a matter of ticking off the lists of tasks. The first shipment lorry duly arrived on the Friday evening, the fork lifts already waiting delivered by the advanced party. The work was done in shifts, so no time was lost and James was given the 22:00 to 06:00 to be followed by consecutive eight-hour shifts. Bryan and he were paired up together which James was most grateful for. All was going to plan.

On the Saturday morning, James was shaken from his slumber by Bryan.

"Get up, we have a problem James."

Although James was by now used to the altitude, the incessant work pace had knocked him out and he woke up bleary eyed perhaps suffering a little bit from the extra beers that were much stronger than he was used to back in 'blighty'.

"What's the matter, Bryan?"

"Of all the times to choose, the President has asked us around for afternoon tea as a social gesture," answered Bryan.

"Oh f..k," said James in a rare moment of profanity.

"Precisely. We can't raise any suspicions now; you and I will have to go in our best togs and leave the other here to carry-on. They can have one of the Land Rovers, leave when they are done and you and I will take the second and do the last-minute checks."

But there was another complication. James remembered abruptly something completely overlooked during the planning stage.

They had been so focussed on the physical assets on site, what about the monies deposited in the bank accounts? Once the authorities knew what was happening, they were bound to freeze their money. Then in his mind he thought of another expletive regularly heard around the streets of Radford. He hadn't brought with him the groups head office bank account numbers but did remember the one's used by the valve company in Benoni, a company they had just taken over and James had been involved in transferring everything over from the previous owners. Fortunately, he had retained his authority signature and remembered the bank account sort codes and account numbers. There were three bank accounts in all so he printed out three bank instructions to transfer in tranches all the bank balances to the Benoni subsidiary company at 09.00 on the next Monday morning.

This would mean depositing the letters of instruction at the local Standard Bank before closing at 12.30 lunchtime. He had to weigh the risk that before the bank actually closed for the weekend anyone would twig what they were really up to. His Pa's voice rang in his ears,

"If you are going to do a job, do it well."

So that was it, he talked through his changed plan with Bryan who readily agreed. These South Africans are never fazed, have no fear and are as tough as hell, nothing gets in the way. The others would take one Land Rover transporting four leaving Bryan and him in the one remaining.

Driving to the bank everything was normal, there were a few Africans sat by their huts and a few herding cattle and goats for milking. The traffic in the centre of the town was busy as James strode into the bank to the nearest bank teller to deposit the three sets of bank instructions. Bryan was sat outside on the look-out but also ready for a quick getaway. It took around fifteen minutes before James was sure the bank clerk fully understood the instructions and for him to stand over the telex machine to ensure the transfers were being actioned and a signed confirmation slip handed back.

It took a couple of hours to get to Lusaka and the President's Residence after the errand to the bank.

To James surprise there was very little security at the Official Residence of President Kaunda, they were just waved through and asked to wait in a queue for the President's arrival. Bryan and James spent an hour kicking their heels when finally, an entourage of black Mercedes limousines arrived, the second one sporting the national flag. The President gave a short welcome speech and was most courteous, expressing his thanks that the South African Conglomerate had invested in his country and how well everything was going. James struggled to play along knowing full well that over half the factory, if not all, by now was on its way back to South Africa.

A set of large white wicker tables with glass tops were gathered around and cloth-backed covered chairs again sporting the national flag. Bryan and James sat with another group of white businessmen from Rhodesia. All were offered some champagne except for the President who preferred iced orange juice. All seemed calm and serene until the President gave out a shriek of indignation. Apparently, finishing his glass, he noticed the glass had written on the bottom, 'Made in South Africa.' He went totally apoplectic denouncing the colonial masters and their rape of Africa. It had to stop. He didn't seem to care that the so-called culprits were there in attendance, those evil representatives of the detested colonialists, including the High Commissioner.

Bryan looked across to James saying,

"Ignore it, we get this nonsense all the time, he is just play acting for his cronies. Perhaps that is the only reason we are here is to witness it to demonstrate he is top dog, not us. When we have finished our coffees, we can leave."

James just couldn't wait to get back and carry on.

By the time they got back it was time for James to start his shift over the Saturday evening. The engineers hadn't quite finished but were nearly done, already nearly half of the sheds had been cleared of machines, loaded and on their way. The others had been disconnected from the power cables and the machines unbolted from their concrete foundations onto loading pallets ready to be placed onto the lorries. It wouldn't take long to load and ship the rest.

James felt that factories, devoid of production activity, were such eerie places. At least dozens of engineers beavering away gave some atmosphere to enliven the gloom of the place. The fluorescent lighting gave off a bright light making it easy to see what you were doing. The engineers were going to plan, but James was a little behind boxing and logging all the files and downloading the computers.

Feverishly, everyone stuck to their allotted tasks and James decided to extend his shift by a few hours to ensure there were no loose ends.

By 05:00 Sunday morning everyone had left but for James and Bryan. It was still pitch-black outside and as they went through the bays switching off the lights, they could see through the few skylights a black velvet sky, seemingly studded with bright diamond lights flickering in the eternity beyond. The offices were all that were left. The last remaining light was left on as they packed the computer files tapes into two plastic boxes and loaded them into the Land Rover. It would have been tempting to sit on the veranda of the building, leisurely sipping a whisky while waiting for the sun to rise and then to leave at 08:00am. They knew that the risk level had been significantly raised so it was important to be very alert and wary. They decided to have just another hour's kip, each in turn, and then ensure their automatics were loaded and the safety catches on hidden below their safari suits before leaving.

At first light the full magnitude of their mission became clearly visible. The workshop bays were bare, with the twisted ends of electric cables dangling from the roofs. Bar that is for the foundry furnace. There wasn't the time to empty it and let it cool down. They would leave the vessel full and let it solidify as a going away present for the President! Stamped freshly on the side was 'Manufactured in South Africa.'

At last the pair of them could make their way back virtually doubling back on the same morning route but then continuing on the main road to the border avoiding the five-mile turn-off to the factory. Most of the countryside was rough bushland with the odd brook, lined with green shrubs and trees. They knew they were getting near the border marked by the Zambesi river and Victoria Falls as the vegetation became lush and they began to descend the plateau to the border. As a precaution, Bryan was driving while James took out the binoculars to see if he could begin to see the frontier post. He did, but then suddenly said to Bryan,

"Stop, we have a problem."

"What's up," enquired Bryan rapidly pulling over to the side of the road in a cloud of dust?

"Have a look at the frontier post yourself."

"I can't see anything, just a couple of lorries parked by the gatehouse."

"Look nearer to us just on the brow of that little hill a little to the left," said James.

"Ah, yes there are three more lorries and a few army people around a camp fire. So, what is the problem," asked Bryan?

"The problem is they are all army trucks, see that white circular disc at the back. There were none when we arrived, just two frontier guards, now the army are swarming all over the place. They've eventually twigged us."

Now it was time for Bryan, to express the expletive, "S..t!"

"Let's hope they haven't seen our dust trail. Pull the Land Rover behind those bushes over there and we will cut up the computer tapes, abandon the Land Rover and then leg it to the river."

He took the binoculars and looked behind to the vast flat terrain behind them. He could see some ten miles away into the distance picking out a tiny speck of another dusty convoy travelling at speed in their direction.

"We can't cross by the bridge," said James taking command automatically, obviously learnt in his day as a school captain keeping his rough school friends in order.

Fortunately, they were both wearing boots so the rough stone approach to the river bank was not too bad. They had some cover until they entered the water's edge where they were in open view on the stony bank of the river. There was no time to venture down-stream there could be a patrol by now coming the other way. The water wasn't too deep to begin with but then the river bed fell steeply away and both were forced to swim for it. James leading, immediately launched into a breast stroke. Bryan following said,

"You are not in a lido, there are crocs in this river so get a move on and start swimming the crawl."

By the time they had got two thirds across they were spotted on the bridge judging from the verbal agitation and the pointing of several arms in their direction. In theory they had passed over the border but such diplomatic

Vienna Conventions niceties don't hold in Africa. It was likely they would be chased right into Rhodesia and possibly only stopped if they encountered the Rhodesian Defence Force. James had a quick look back and could see a few soldiers who had been parked away from the frontier making their way down the river bank with their captain pointing a gun at his own men ordering them to enter the river and chase us. James didn't know whether it was because they couldn't swim or the thought of the croc invested waters. He wasn't going to break stroke to find out.

Quickly the pair of them were out of the water onto the stony bank on the other side, although Bryan had to wait for James as he wasn't that good a swimmer. As James managed to get the water level to his thighs, he was running up the bank like a gazelle and soon caught up with Bryan. No doubt motivated by the sounds of zut...zut, as live rounds were fired in their direction. Some were a bit too close for comfort as the bullets pinged off the large stones creating a plum of white smoke. Those training runs had at last come into their own.

One quick glance back to his pursuers gave James a bit of a shock, the two lead swimmers had been grabbed and were pulled under in a red swirling cloud of blood and the sound of bones cracking under the vice like jaws of the crocs. Pistol or not, the others turned tail. A little out of breadth, especially for Bryan and his smoking, they still romped at speed to get well inside the country. Within five-miles the Rhodesian Defence Force Patrol duly arrived wondering what all the commotion was about. A quick interrogation and a wireless call to HQ confirmed they were not a threat and then they were transferred to Harare to freshen up and offered a rental car to get back to Johannesburg.

Chapter 4

Thanksgiving

James reported for work as usual on the first Tuesday and sat at his desk waiting to be briefed by Duncan on what to do next. In the momentarily lull, he and Bryan took the opportunity to make a coffee and reflect on the last few weeks. That morning the steaming black mugs of coffee tasted particularly delicious. They had got to know each other very well working in such close proximity for hours on end. A special bond was in the making that you find amongst the military, especially those found in frontline regiments. Making light-hearted references to their very challenging time in Zambia, Duncan walked in and broke the tranquil mood saying,

"Where's the dosh?"

"I don't understand," said James.

"The R2+m in the bank accounts, didn't you bring the money out as well or did you 'lose' it on the way," said Duncan emphasising the 'losing it' in a sarcastic and accusative tone?

"You will find it all, every last cent, in the Benoni bank account, I thought it would be less obvious transferring it there since they already had intergroup accounts between them," said James using the benefit of a bit of post-rationalisation thought and a little brittleness of his own.

"If we had brought it with us it would have been at the bottom of the Zambesi by now with the crocs."

"We had to improvise for an unplanned delay," added Bryan slightly pissed off with the abruptness after risking their precious necks.

Duncan didn't respond and just did an immediate 180° about-turn to his office and made a call to the Benoni bank.

He returned a few minutes later with Bryan and James looking at each other in incredulity as Duncan was not that type of guy to adopt such an aggressive and insulting tone, especially amongst his mates.

Duncan strode back in and immediately apologised,

"Sorry guys, we have all been a bit tetchy with all that has been going on and we were genuinely concerned for you two when you didn't turn up last night. You guys have had enough excitement for the moment so next week I thought I might give you something in the normal routine. Bryan, if you could go to the contracting division, they are having problems balancing their work-in-progress ledger and you James, as you seemed to have had a yearning for our newly acquired Benoni friends, I want you to act as their temporary company secretary and financial executive until we get somebody permanent. Our American friend, their company secretary, departed the day after you left them. So thoughtful of him!"

Whilst this meant Bryan and James would be working apart, they made the commitment to meet up at the weekend at the Group's Sports and Social Club. Bryan and James then got to work clearing the mass of papers in their in-trays. As the office clock began to show just five minutes before closing for the day, Duncan filed in with Fred and to their surprise the Group Chairman with a crate of cold beers, snacks and packs of crisps.

"I think you all deserve a drink and a slap on the back for a job well done."

The weeks and months went by, James getting his feet truly under the table, socialising at the weekend, playing league football with the local professional club, oblivious he was under a fixed term contract. A month before the secondment termination date, he got the dreaded call from Tony.

"I know you are loving it over there and getting a well-earned suntan, but I have some work for you to do for the Minister and he wants you back in time for a job in the USA," said Tony.

James faced a major dilemma, he knew he had only to give the nod and he could stay on for as long as he liked, but was he being disloyal to his parents? They had sacrificed so much to give him the best opportunities. Perhaps staying and enjoying the good life betrayed their sacrifices and now wasn't the time to judge how far he could go.

For the last few days remaining James stayed with Bryan and his wife Kathy until that feared morning the taxi arrived to take him to the airport. James gave them both a great hug and stepped into the waiting car when Bryan suddenly outstretched his hand and said,

"Last touch!"

James wind down the window, thrust his arm out as far as it would go to touch Bryan's finger tips before the taxi drove away.

It proved not to be the last touch, many years later James brought his wife and son, then twenty years old and toured the Game Reserves on holiday with both Bryan and Kathy. Of course, they took the opportunity to look over once more the Zambesi at Victoria Falls making sure they didn't stray into Zambian territory. They were still on the wanted list decades later!

Now he was on the way back on the BOAC flight to London Heathrow with his parents and sister Sheila anxiously waiting for him. Tony had given him two weeks leave and James had decided the first task was to at last buy that Rover 90 and build a purpose-built garage and driveway at his parent's house to maintain it and keep it mint condition. Only his father would be allowed to drive it other than him.

Driving back to Nottingham in a Morris 8 was a bit of a trial but eventually he was back home. James remembered waking up the following morning just before dusk, there was still a two-hour time gap to adjust for. He rose from his bed and peered into the distance to the city centre. The only star to be made out in the overcast sky was the red one above Shipstones' Brewery, no longer those bright diamond white African stars and the red dawn drawn across the horizon beneath a jet-black sky to greet him. No Jesus either with that beautiful infectious smile; a new reality his Dad shouting upstairs,

"The tea is mashed and the bacon is going on now; shake a leg."

The reality he was born into returned, but today at least they had the excitement of buying a new car. There was also the visit to the bank and drawing £1,000 in two wads for his parents to do with as they liked. His sister Sheila had to go to work so it was decided James would pick her up in the car he had ordered before leaving South Africa, he just had to sign the papers and take the keys.

James had not ordered the car through the normal authorised distributors but from Zipser Motors, a client when he was in practice, run by two emigre Polish Air Force brothers. They had come to the country during the Second World War and had fought bravely alongside our heroes in the RAF defending their adopted country. The car sat in prime position in the showroom with a bold notice just saying in great big red letters, SOLD. Every person visiting apparently admired it and some had decided to buy one for themselves boosting in an indirect way John Zipser's business, much to his pleasure.

James arrived early in the afternoon and once the car business had been regularised, John and James had a chat on South Africa, leaving the mission in Zambia well off the radar screen. By 16:30 it was time to leave and pick up his sister on Talbot Street. He pulled up outside; soon, out she came with all the others from the office. She was in the company of a very attractive brunette, who James was in later years to compare with Ali McGraw, the resemblance was so strong.

"Do you mind if Suzanne comes along as well, she lives on the way home in the Aspley Estate," said Sheila as though a no would have made any difference?

James was a bit miffed because he wanted to show off the attributes of the brand-new car to his sister as well as the sense, he was being set-up. Sheila insisted on sitting in the back and Suzanne at the front, making conversation almost impossible. So, in his shyness most of the journey was to be conducted in absolute silence. Little did he realise that the brunette was to become his future wife. Not exactly love at first sight.

You live in a council house for 20 years and despite its familiarity, once you have spread your wings, it is though you are staying at a regular two-star hotel. It is never quite the same when you have flown the nest and tasted total independence as a young man.

The two weeks went by so quickly and it was time to travel to London to see Tony, same place and same time. Again, James was sat looking out of the window at Marble Arch but this time thinking of all the friends he had made in South Africa, as it turned out, some for life. The tea and digestives duly arrived delivered by Betty before Tony strode in, all smiles and bonhomie still sporting the thick black curly hair.

"I have had some very good reports about you. You surprised many of us as to how good you really are," said Tony.

James always took such exuberant praise with the utmost suspicion. It was always a precursor for a sting in the tail. James didn't respond just gave a wry smile of acknowledgement.

I cannot promise such adventurous missions for the future and the next one falls into our normal pattern. We have had a request by a British Brewery to support them in joint venture with an Austrian Brewery to export their products into the USA. They are looking to open a distribution company in Baltimore, so we need to do some due diligence on both. I would like you to visit both companies in situ, then go with their directors to Baltimore and for you to visit our corporate lawyers in Washington to draft the agreements. At stake are some export grants and export funding support for the USA.

"Are you asking me to do any market research," asked James.

"No, it is simply setting up the accounting systems and producing financial forecasts based on their own market assumptions. We have others to vet the market numbers," said Tony.

This all seemed rather boring work compared what he had been familiar with but obviously better than the mind-numbing grind in a professional practice and the job of making the bosses coal fire. At least there was the chance for the first time to visit the USA and perhaps see some of the sights, particularly as they would be routed through New York.

Two-day visits were organised for trips to the breweries in the Midlands and Vienna. The trip to the Midlands was fairly standard meeting with the various directors, but to James's surprise the one to Vienna was somewhat an eye-opening. Their managing director was an Engelbart, an unsurprising name if you were an Austrian. The timing of the visit was opportune. The brewery was celebrating its 150th anniversary and had been opened for the day to the citizens of Vienna including a visit by the Austrian Chancellor.

Engelbart had booked James in the Hilton and came to collect him that evening for a dinner in the Black Forest. James was sat at the central cocktail bar dressed in his ready to wear Burton herring bone suit trying to order a beer amongst 30 -40 people all in their evening dinner suits and dresses, some of the ladies wearing designer outfits from Paris. He was getting nowhere until Engelbart strode in and said to James,

"You haven't had a drink yet?"

There was a click of his fingers and instantly a barman duly arrived and was told,

"A drink for my very important guest before we go," said Engelbart.

James had seen this attitude before by the Whites in South Africa treating their Black brethren as mere chattels, but this time it was deserved. James was being treated poorly as snobs usually do, especially to foreign hoi polio.

James having been insulted thought he didn't fancy a beer in such an unfriendly environment and responded by saying in a perfect German accent, "Danke mein Freund, aber es ist zu spat," and abruptly got of his high chair to leave.

Engelbart embarrassed, profusely apologised for his countryman's bad manners. They left together in a chauffeured driven car deep into the Black Forest. On the way, Engelbart suggested that his driver was at his disposal for the following afternoon to see the local sites before he went to the airport, James gladly accepted. From a bad start they were beginning to get on well alternating between James's mechanical German learnt from a German exile in Namibia, and Engelbart's perfect fluent English.

James was ushered into a private dining room in the restaurant to an enormous round table set for around fifteen diners. Already sat there were representatives of the brewery's international sales staff with their wives, denominated by small national flags of the countries they represented. Two places were reserved, one for Engelbart and James who both sat opposite. After the introductions they sat down and James gave a puzzled look. Engelbart not wishing there to be a second 'faux pas' immediately noticed something was amiss and said,

"Something the matter James?"

"There is something missing," responded James.

Straightaway and without another word, Engelbart walked out of the room and returned within five minutes, the diners quietly talking to each other wondering what was happening. Engelbart strode back in and behind his back was a Union Flag twice the size of the others.

"There James, does that make you feel more comfortable," enquired Engelbart?

"Not quite big enough but it will do for now," responded James smiling.

There was spontaneous laughter and the 'faux pas' in a silly way broke the ice and it turned out to be a great evening.

James had managed to puncture the image of Teutonic efficiency; he did feel any remaining social barriers were being lowered.

The next morning was taken up with meeting the other directors, managers and brewery personnel. James was learning that Engelbart was a class act. He clearly was widely admired and respected by all his work people being very comfortable walking amongst them at the 'Open Day' at which at its centre was a full- sized oxen being roasted on an open spit. Later that morning he was introduced to the Austrian Chancellor who again spoke perfect English and thanked the British Government for helping them in their joint export efforts.

James did take up the offer of the driver and was shown around the sights including St Steven's Cathedral, the Hapsburg Summer Palace and a special show at the Austrian Riding School. The driver even stopped on the main bridge on the way to the airport to show him the River Danube after James had enquired whether it really was blue. It wasn't, but at least it was cleaner than the River Trent. James thought to himself sometimes in life, despite the occasional mishaps there comes those sublime moments and this was one of them he would never forget.

The local visits done, it was now time to fly to Baltimore and get the trading agreements drafted for both sides and for the lawyers in Washington to produce a draft, in a form the brewery boards could ratify. Given the competence of the two parties and the goodwill between them the documentation and tying of the Board of Trade elements should make the whole process straight forward. James thought that perhaps this was a project Tony wanted to break James's teeth on before being exposed to more complex business matters. Was he being allowed to go through the standard process and learn each element knowing, if there was a problem, it either could be easily remedied or worse, if it failed, it was no big disaster? To a degree James was a little downcast that there was still some lack of faith in him given the great success of the South African mission. He consoled himself by thinking it wasn't really for him to reason why, but just to do, and get on with it.

The first part of the business trip was simply constant travel between airports, a drafting meeting in Baltimore and then the last leg to Washington with all the papers stashed in James's briefcase complete with scrawled notes over the drafts for him to brief the lawyers. Within three days he was at the Washington Hotel just off Pennsylvania avenue. A message had been left at the reception that he would be picked up at 09:30 by the American lawyers.

People think when you go on business trip to 'exotic' places businessmen are living the 'high life'. The reality is somewhat different. You probably travel on hot cramped trains, walk miles through terminals at railway stations and airports, all of them beginning to blur from one to another to the point; you are never quite sure where you are. Having become tired, sweaty and hungry you arrive at an impersonal hotel where you are processed probably in the presence of five or six others going through the same old routine. No one knows you, or cares, the only personal touch being whether you wished to reserve a table in the restaurant for dinner. James always hated eating an evening meal alone and preferred a hot snack in his room after a bath and changing into his dressing gown before settling down to watch the tv for half-an-hour before turning in. He made a call for 06:30 his normal waking up time wherever he was and then turned in to try and sleep as best he could despite the jet lag.

James slept well and decided to go down for an early breakfast in the restaurant and then perhaps take an hour having a walk to stretch his legs having been cramped up over the last few days. As usual the U.S. morning breakfast was outstanding. A menu of fresh iced Florida orange juice, cereals with various toppings, eggs, bacon, hash browns, sausage, beans with hot buttered toast on a variety of breads. If that wasn't enough there was still the flapjacks with maple syrup and boundless mugs of coffee with cream and sugar to suit tastes. James sampled them all but went easy on the quantities knowing that feeling 'bloated' was not the best condition to conduct legal business.

He had brought his overcoat with him to save time and to wander along the streets. The doormen remonstrated he should take a taxi but James refused so he could take in the sights and smells. James contemplated that too many visitors fail to 'clock' the smells as well as the sights. For James though it made the experience much more intense than just a visual reference point. He bought a Washington Post out of one of the street vending machines and strolled back to sit in the lounge and watched the world go by. He read occasionally his newspaper having at first collected his briefcase double checking the contents were all there along with pens, pencils and his pocket calculator.

A smartly dress man came in at precisely 09:30 walked to reception to have James pointed out to him. It was the representative of the lawyers.

"Good morning James, my name is Brad. Me and my associate have been assigned to work with you."

"Please to meet you. I think I have everything you want so hopefully I won't take too much of your valuable time," said James.

"We are available for as long as it takes so please don't feel under any time pressure. We are not looking either to stretch it out as your principals always work on fixing the fee beforehand," said Brad.

"I will take you in my car but we have another lawyer to visit on the way if you don't mind before we sit down with my assistant," Brad continued.

"No problem I am in your hands."

"Splendid, let's go."

The car turned into Pennsylvania Avenue. James knew this because he could see the iconic outline of Congress and the white dome building on his right. Just towards the end, another manoeuvre to the right and they were at the gates of the White House itself. The car came to rapid halt, not far from the entrance gate, and before James had a chance to question where they were going Brad said,

"I will wait for you outside for the next hour and a bit, go to that marine sentry over there by the white post house and he will guide you to your next meeting," said Brad in a very matter of fact instruction.

James did as he was instructed but wondered what the hell was going on. When you are outside the office of the most powerful man on earth you don't have a 'Barny' in the street. Moving towards one of the two sentries he was immediately challenged and asked,

"Where do you think you are going Mac?"

James responded by giving his name and just said he had been summoned to attend having no idea who he was to meet. The sentry asked for his passport that he had been asked to bring with him on the pretence it was needed for the signing of the draft legal documents.

"Follow me, but keep close and don't stray, I wouldn't like to have to shoot you even though you are a Pommy," smiled the sentry taking a more informal approach.

James was shown into a large open hall and was asked to sit on the only chair by one of the many doors until someone came to take him to the meeting room. He could hear the clicks of a secretary's high heels on the marble floors. Closing on him, she said, in one quick military style 90°turn to face him,

"Please follow me sir."

Gazing at each brilliant white door he came to the one with the highly polished brass plate stating simply, Attorney General. When Brad said another lawyer, he didn't say the highest placed lawyer in the USA. James made an involuntary gulp as the secretary knocked on the door and strode in without a reply being heard. James nervously walked in to see Robert Kennedy standing behind his black leather chair reading, in his hand, a document.

"Sit down, make yourself comfortable, I will soon be with you. Help yourself to the tea and scones" said Robert Kennedy.

James sat in the leather clad arms of a stylish highly polished wooden chair staring for the moment at the lush green manicured lawns outside.

After a couple of minutes Robert Kennedy placed the paper on his desk and said,

"James, thank you for coming here at such short notice but Jack and I have wanted to make contact with you for some time."

"I hope you haven't mixed me up with someone else with my name I know you have a trade secretary with my name but he has a better tan than me," said James trying hard to behave normally despite the location.

"Don't be unduly concerned we have the right man; we have done our homework. Mr Briggs talks highly of you as do your neighbours in Nottingham," responded Mr. Kennedy.

James was somewhat shaken with this well-informed casual remark and realised this was no idle conversation. His mind was racing as to what possibly could be of interest.

"I know you are under strict instructions not to talk about your work or pass comment about other personnel, so there is no need for you to respond but just listen carefully now to what I am about to say," said Robert Kennedy.

"Our nations are facing an increasing menace perpetrated by the Russians looking to destabilise our democratic institutions. Even Jack and I are not safe from their ambitions. They are active everywhere to the point they have infiltrated our intelligence network beyond a level we can be comfortable with. Unfortunately, the weakest point at the moment is with you, the Brits, which is frustrating for us given our totally open book policy. Any authorised Brit can wander around the Pentagon or Langley and see anything they wish, no other nation has that ability. Your agents are drawn from your best universities, but some have Marxists' sympathies, willing to go to any length to take-out our democratic institutions".

James began to think this was going down a very serious avenue and feared the worse that his integrity was under question and said,

"Have you any concerns about me?"

"Far from it, you are highly regarded by us, especially after your successful mission preventing for the moment armed insurrection in Southern Africa promoted by our 'Ruskie' adversaries. You and Tony are just the Brits we love, but we have a concern about your higher boss, not just for us but for you two as well," continued Kennedy.

James in his utter naivety had never considered who was the boss above them both; the one Tony was reporting to.

"You know our boss," asked James?

"Do you know well, Peter," asked Robert Kennedy.

"Peter who," replied James making it known that he hadn't a clue, or was he just teasing out the answer.

"Peter Voss," came the reply.

"The Peter Voss I knew at college, he is my ultimate boss," asked James opening up realising the Attorney General knew more than him and it was pointless playing dumb?

"The very one, we think he is a key part of the Ruskies' aims, but that you must never reveal this to anyone else, even Tony for the moment," said Kennedy.

Bloody hell, thought James this was getting into deep state stuff that he was completely ignorant of.

"I certainly knew him well at college and it doesn't surprise me, your concerns," said James.

"Keep your mind open to such a possibility, as much for your own safety, and when you learn of anything to confirm our assertions, I would appreciate you going direct to the Head of MI6, circumventing Tony, making it known I suggested it. Do you agree," asked Kennedy?

James couldn't see an obvious objection for him to behave in this way and thought that probably it was the correct thing to do in the circumstances and confirmed he would. That ended the meeting. The head of the US legal establishment had made his point. Before he was able to leave Kennedy then added,

"We really appreciate James your understanding on a very delicate matter. Before you go Jack and I, speaking of the devil, Hi Jack, just in time."

Jack Kennedy had just strolled in from another door behind Robert Kennedy's desk, smiling in his usual beguiling way.

"We would like you to accept a gift as our token of our appreciation for your contribution in Southern Africa,"

Robert Kennedy with his brother standing next to him opened a desk draw and pulled out a royal blue box embossed with a twin bald-headed eagle on the lid. Holding out his arm he handed it to James and opening it revealed a solid silver whisky flask.

"We have left it for you to fill it with your favourite malt, even though we already know it," giggling at his own comment.

"Obviously there is no inscription but it does have embossed both of our national flags crossing each other in partnership. Whenever you have a sip, think of us," continued Kennedy.

"You have just blown my mind, but thank you for the kind gift. I will treasure it for the rest of my life," said James.

They all shook hands, the Kennedy's smiling in their infectious way and James made his own way out.

James walked down the wide winding tarmac road, past the sentry who saluted and he headed straight back to his waiting car, all the time working out a plausible alibi for the most bizarre meeting of his life.

"What did they want you for and who did you see," asked Brad?

"I have been promoted to Federal Express. They had a gift for our Minister of Trade but it wasn't ready when he was over and they have asked me to deliver it personally for them. I did get a nice cup of tea and scones though," said James thinking how does he think up such nonsense?

On the way back to the UK he began to take in the enormity of his experience. He had been in the company of two of the great political giants of his era, which was to have added poignancy as history later unfurled. From his humble beginnings he had been catapulted into a world he had no recognition of before, all thanks to the belief and support of his parents enabled by exceptional school teachers.

But there was still more. He had been taught another lesson by Mr. Kennedy; James had been very naïve. He was narrowly focussed on developing a career as a financial professional but he was being thrust into another universe. To a degree he was being manipulated and not really the master of his own destiny to the degree he had believed. His only freedom was simply to say no at any stage. He had to recognise no longer could he just accept new assignments and regard them as mere commercial missions and another rung on the ladder of his high ambitions. Something deeper was happening and Robert Kennedy had opened his eyes to it. James thought to himself, be careful my friend, be wary of others and their motives. Some people he would have to trust implicitly, but they would be very, very, limited, the others would have to prove their integrity.

5

Paddy's Troubles

It was a Sunday morning, yearning for a longer lie-in despite it already being 10:00, James could smell the delicious smell of bacon frying. He is doing it again; his father could not stand sitting around alone on a Sunday morning having risen at his habitual time of 06:00am waiting for others to get up. The thought of a full English breakfast with lashings of buttered bread was too great to resist. The morning was so cold the frost was frozen onto the inside of the bedroom windows. Peeping over the warm duvet cover, pulled up to his chin to retain the cosy warmth, there was a clear-patch in one window pane to observe the far hill of the city, three miles into the distance. Dressed in his blue striped pyjamas, James briskly put on his dressing gown and his slippers before his feet were in danger of touching the cold strips of diamond patterned linoleum. Clattering down the staircase he was met with a voice from the kitchen,

"Have a good sleep, son?"

"Great dad. Jet flights are better than a mug of cocoa to knock you out; I could sleep for a week," answered James.

"Here is a cup of tea to get you going for the day and the Sunday paper is over there if you want a read," said his father.

"Couldn't face all that salacious stuff, I am just looking forward to that breakfast," said James.

James was not a one to gossip, particularly about work, nor his father to enquire. Most times things were best left unsaid but both knew what was really going on.

"I have left yesterday's mail on the sideboard, one was by registered post and I had to sign for it," said his father.

For his social class, registered letters were rare and always indicated matters of a serious nature, normally bad news. James thought it best to act nonchalantly hoping his father would think it was a letter he was expecting after his sojourn to the USA. No such luck.

"I think you better open it, it could be important and you might want to go over to 'Jivers' before he goes out, you may want to use his phone. Jiver, as he was nicknamed, was a professional xylophone player, sometimes featured on tv, playing in the variety shows hosted by the celebrities of the day. He was on call all the time, and as a result, a telephone was a necessary tool of his trade allowing his agent to organise bookings. He was the only one on the street who had one, and possibly on the whole council estate. For many, having a phone would only beg the question who could you possibly ring? It was, however, a facility not to abuse and always any user would offer more than the cost for the inconvenience, but most of the time it was refused. Sometimes tv celebrities would visit 'Jiver' on the street in their very posh cars much to the neighbours' delight.

James wasn't a one to disobey an instruction from his father. Even a gentle statement, James would construe as no idle passing comment, but a command. James opened the envelope to see straightaway it was from Tony. There were no preliminaries just a fountain pen written note and some air tickets to inform James that he was to get the East Midlands flight in two days' time to Aldergrove, Belfast. All that was added was he would be met there by a Richard. That was it, except a curious post script saying, '80,000 had flown the coup!'

"No need to disturb 'Jiver,' I just have to go on a business trip on Tuesday for hopefully just a few days," said James pre-empting a question from his Pa.

Having already had his mind deeply disturbed with the conversation in Washington, the less than informative curt message was all adding to the uncertainties. No call from London; solely a brusque note and no explanation of the task.

The flight was like any other, except on walking down the corridor to the plane's door there were two smartly dressed suited gentlemen beyond the departure gate asking again for passports from passengers. This struck James as unusual as he always assumed that once he had gone through the last gate check-in, he could put all his flight papers away. Expecting to be asked for his documentation again, he was just ushered through with a wave of a hand.

James was on his way for who knows what, to meet a Richard. Use to having some semblance of self-control, he felt twitchy, especially as Northern Ireland was suffering from the deepening 'Troubles', He was hoping the luggage had been thoroughly checked for any improvised devices designed to bring planes down into the Irish Sea. Finally, he landed at Aldergrove Airport, collected his luggage and proceeded to the arrivals area. It didn't take a moment for him to see the name Richard scrawled on a large white envelope written in blue crayon. Richard was a very smartly dressed suited young man, probably approaching his thirties, with a dark black beard. He shook James by the hand and said,

"We are putting you up in the company house in Dungannon where you can meet Gerald our managing director, he's expecting you within the hour."

Apart from the heavy army contingent at the airport, several five-man army patrols and many Land Rovers on the perimeter of the airport, the journey to Dungannon was through gentle rolling lush green hills on little used open country roads. Richard didn't say much except to say he worked as the chief accountant at the group's head office just down the road and only had an oversight role over the poultry company. At this reference James was able to at least connect two pieces of scant information, the reference to poultry and the postscript on the registered letter.

James was expecting either a luxury apartment or a terraced house for the company house. He was to get quite a shock, they were ushered through the security- controlled wrought-iron gate, down a long drive way lined by oak trees before opening up to a huge green lawn dominated by a mansion. The entrance was fronted by a gravelled area leading to a jet-black door sporting a highly polished brass door knob. Pulling to a halt, Richard grabbed James's small case from the boot and led the way into the entrance hall. James managed to catch sight of a housemaid scurrying into an adjoining room holding a silver tea tray. James followed Richard.

Dropping the cases in the hallway, Richard led James into the room which the housemaid was leaving. Gerald was a tall dark slim man, black Brylcreamed hair swept back in a parting, thin lipped, dressed in a smart business suit. He stood by a red leather chair. He obviously had warning of the impending visit from the sound of gravel under the car tyres but as James was later to learn the whole estate was surrounded by electronic radar beams and cameras.

"Hello James, welcome, we have been looking forward to your visit. Would you like to join me in a tea and a nice cream and strawberry jam scone," said Gerald?

"Please to see you but I have to confess I am not entirely sure I know why am here but I was told you could fill me in," said James already striking a business tone.

"Let's worry about that later over dinner, just relax and enjoy your refreshment first after your long journey," said Gerald.

Already James was beginning to learn there were certain social graces and a different pace to life in Ulster. Manners were just as important as the business in hand. James began to realise it was quite a few hours since enjoying breakfast with his Pa, having nothing to eat or drink on the way. Tea and scones were just the pick-me-up before dinner at 07:00pm.

James took an instant liking to Gerald, whereas he felt a little wary of Richard. These were just instinctive reactions learnt over his brief life span. James found it interesting whether first impressions were largely confirmed or had to be substantially revised through events and experience. So far, his instincts had served him well. There was only the odd surprise, including the day he met his future wife.

The main topic of the conversation were the problems with republicans and protestant extremists, they seemed intent on killing each other at the slightest provocation. Gerald made a somewhat extreme remark saying he felt the funerals for the victims were in effect competitions as to how many mourners each side could muster. It was a perverse expression of the justice of their cause. In reality they were both sides harbouring murderous criminal thugs chasing causes that could be resolved democratically and peacefully with a little goodwill on both sides.

He did begin to learn later the catholic community had been unfairly locked out of the economic benefits of the country. The British Army had been brought in to prevent a massacre of the Catholics by the Protestants and conversely protection of the Protestants from Catholic reprisals. So intense was the mutual hatred the terrorists were able to feed off their mutual fear and hatred in order to promote their campaigns of domination of their communities through sheer terror.

By the time they had finished tea and scones, there was an hour and a half for James to unpack, freshen up and prepare for dinner and the briefing from Gerald of what needed to be done. He was first down to dinner so took the opportunity to take in the view through the French windows before it became too dark. The view was magnificent. A lush green lawn descending down to a lake dotted by great bare leaved trees. He was reminded of a similar view from Willoughby Hall that he had been accustomed to, right from a baby when his mother would push him there in a great wheeled Victorian pram complete with white tyres and leaf sprung cot. The coachwork would not have been lost on a luxury limousine.

Gerald was just a few minutes later, but no sign of Richard, he had already left while James was changing. A coal fire was burning brightly in the dining room and a series of silver covered platters were already arranged on a giant oak sideboard.

"Let's get started straight away before the food gets cold. We usually don't have a starter just a main course and a choice of desserts. Apologies, entirely my fault, the danger is to overeat cooped up here; little chance to exercise. I fly in Monday and then out on the last flight on Friday to Manchester," continued Gerald.

Despite his slim figure, Gerald it seemed enjoyed his food tucking into the generous fare of delicious dishes. James paced himself thinking Gerald could do all the talking while James finished his helpings.

Eventually James piped up,

"So how can I possibly help you?"

Gerald then gave quite a long dissertation of his issues. In summary they had a subsidiary in the Group operating as a poultry business. There had been a control failure indicating 80,000 chickens couldn't be accounted for. Bingo, that's where the 80,000 came from thought James. As it was 1st April James thought this had been an elaborate wind-up by Tony but it soon became apparent there were much deeper and more serious problems in store. HMG had invested millions of pounds expanding the poultry processing factories to five times the current production levels over the next eighteen months. A production control problem was not only unwelcome, at this stage, but could jeopardise the whole project, the government possibly pulling the funding rug from under them.

Probing by James revealed another massive problem down the track when questioning the capacity of refrigerated lorries to take this massive increase in product to their main market in GB. The company had relied exclusively on Protestant hauliers. James suggested he started immediately on the production control issue first but in the meantime could Gerald list all the Catholic hauliers in the Province? Gerald response was positive, except he did add,

"The Protestants won't like it."

"They can go and f..k themselves, we are not going to allow them to be a political barrier to a practical solution," answered James tersely perhaps a little of it had rubbed-off, the South African bluntness emerging.

Within a week the production control weaknesses had been identified and importantly a range of system changes introduced that were not only robust but could be the firm foundation for a much greater enterprise. Tony called late that Friday afternoon enquiring how James was getting on.

"Are the chickens back in their coup," he quipped?

"All tucked up in bed with a nice cup of cocoa," replied James.

"Are you coming back today then," said Tony?

"I am afraid not, I need to deal with a logistic issue first before I can leave, it may take a couple of weeks to resolve that one," said James.

"What's the problem", asked Tony?

"Don't quite know yet but it could be complicated and delicate, give me a couple of weeks and I will let you have a progress report," requested James.

"Fair enough, but take care my friend I am learning it is getting a bit tasty over there," said Tony.

Over dinner Gerald produced a list of 25 potential hauliers and usefully adding the number of refrigerated lorries each had. Most had at least two, whilst a few others had up to ten. A quick calculation and James concluded he needed to convert at least ten of them and for them to commit 100% for at least one lorry.

"I will be onto it, this week," said James.

"I will arrange a car for you and change from time to time your registration plates and sometimes perhaps the car, just as a precaution," added Gerald.

"Is that really necessary," asked James?

"It's getting a 'tidge' tricky at the moment. Not only is it necessary, but for some visits to the haulier it is better they pick you up than you go alone into bandit country," answered Gerald.

James thought Gerald might be over doing the security stuff but then came the visit to Donahue's in County Armagh. James was making good progress in his meetings although there was still some scepticism amongst Catholic hauliers. That could only be overcome by exchange of haulage service contracts and a significant rise in business. Donahue's were located on an isolated farm in the county of Armagh. This was considered bandit country and cars driven by suited gentlemen with short haircuts were bound to attract suspicion and possibly worse. There would be no army protection. James took Gerald's recommendation and organised for Barry Donahue to pick him up by the courthouse in Armagh town centre.

Barry was a barrel-chested hard lump. Not fat, but you knew he was physically tough. He picked up James dressed in a grey cardigan that didn't quite meet the top of his trousers. It was apparent his trousers were kept up by green striped braces. Despite his slightly unshaven appearance he was quite an affable character. He suggested they first went to the haulage sheds to show James the space for five lorries with one parked in situ. A conversation could take place over a tea and biscuits to outline what a deal could look like. On arrival he could see acres of potatoes fields and grazing cows far into the distance. There were five-hangar like sheds built adjoining one another with one set of sliding doors slightly ajar sufficient to gain entry.

James followed Barry into the vast open space containing the five inspection pits and at the far-end sets of tools neatly stored against the wall. You couldn't help but be impressed especially as there was standing in one bay a brand new 40-foot refrigerated Volvo lorry.

"Bloody hell, why haven't we been using your lorries before," said James?

"I suppose that is why you are here," answered Barry.

They then walked across the huge concrete yard and entered the farmhouse. As he sat down James said,

"And what makes you think you are good enough to work for me?"

That wasn't a very clever opening statement by James in such a sensitive political climate. Barry rose in his chair clearly offended and took a swing. James ducked as he did so and before he could try with the other arm said,

"Whoa, I meant no offence, I am genuinely trying to help you. You well know our Protestant friends would love for my initiative to fail and I need to ensure I don't give them the pleasure."

Calm was restored and as the discussions continued both agreed to a service contract for two years committing three refrigerated full-time. For Barry, this meant purchasing another two lorries but with a guarantee of their income for at least two years. Effectively Barry's business had been given the boost it needed to establish his business long-term. Just as they concluded and shook hands a buzzer went and Barry shot up out of his chair and peered out of the window through a pulled curtain, now in gathering darkness to see two sets of car headlights approaching. He turned to James and said,

"We have unwelcome visitors you must hide immediately they must not know you are here," said Barry exuding for the first-time petrified fear.

James could already hear footsteps of nail studded boots on the hard-concrete yard. There was no time for the best options. He looked at the fireplace, looked up the vast chimney and noted there were some protruding half bricks for the first ten feet before smoothing out further up. He climbed up and near the narrowing of the chimney firmly wedged-in his feet, tucking his bottom on a stone piece fortunately well-positioned. Within a couple of minutes, the door swung open and he could hear several people entering the room. There were several voices all speaking Gaelic as far as he could make out. He worked out there were about six people in all with various names. One seemed to ask Barry something followed by an instruction leading to Barry leaving the room.

Were these drug dealers or worse still terrorists. James thought they better not decide to light a fire or I am in real trouble. Not exactly the time of the year for Santa Claus to come down the chimney!

James thought he must try and pay attention, try and work out names and hopefully confirm how many people were gathered. For an hour and a half, he half sat there his legs beginning to become progressively numb. He had worked out there were six and applied their names to the voices but there were two additional names came up he could not place. One was the name of Duggan, a frequent reference but no voice to attribute it to. The other was what he believed was not a person but the 'Scilly Isles'. Nothing made much sense.

Just as quickly as the visitors had arrived, they left with a few words exchanged with Barry.

As he heard the cars drive-off Barry put his head into the chimney and looking up said,

"You can come down now they have gone," beckoning James down with an outstretched arm.

James looked a comical sight, his suit and shirt covered in black sooty patches. "Hold on I will get the vacuum cleaner," continued Barry.

As Barry energetically set about removing all the loose soot James exclaimed, "Steady on with the suction I could get all excited," said James laughing.

The comical remark diffused a very tense moment.

"Who were they," asked James?

"Pleased don't say a word about tonight otherwise I am a dead man. They were the Derry Brigade of the IRA," said Barry.

"They commandeer isolated places around here like mine to avoid recognition and will assassinate anyone who betrays their whereabouts."

"What did they say to you", enquired James.

"Well one of them said he could smell soot. I told him a bird had fallen down the chimney a few days ago with a load of soot. That is why they daren't light a fire in case it caused a fire in the chimney until it had been properly swept. They did give me the standard warning except they said knee-capping would seem an act of mercy if I talked," reported Barry.

James just played the scared business man and swore he would tell no one as he was just as at risk as Barry was. In a peculiar way this brought the relationship between Barry and James that much closer as soldiers experience during combat.

"Look Barry let's get on with the business. I will grow your business gradually, a little behind the others to begin with, in order not to draw too much attention so close to the events of today," said James.

It was quite late before James returned with a worried Gerald waiting in the lounge delaying retiring to bed until he was sure James was OK.

"Did it go OK," asked Gerald?

"The business side brilliantly, but we had some unwelcome visitors," replied James.

Having recounted the whole event Gerald thought pensively for a moment and then said,

"We ought to tell Special Branch and leave them to deal with it."

"I wouldn't want to put Barry Donahue at risk," countered James.

"Don't worry I have a contact who will keep the information highly confidential and knows how to protect informants," answered Gerald.

James felt a little uneasy that he had opened so much to Gerald but also realised it was important the security forces had all the information they could lay their hands on; lives were at stake.

As with all strategic business problems they go deeper than you at first imagine. It took several weeks to bed-in the new haulage logistics. James began to realise the need for a more robust distribution system in GB to cope with the sheer scale of the production volume about to be switched on. James had kept Tony fully informed of his work and just as his work was drawing to a close Tony on one of the routine Friday afternoon calls said to James,

"You need to get out of Ireland soon, stuff is 'hotting up' and we are picking up malevolent background noise."

James couldn't quite grasp what this might mean for him until the next Monday when he was breakfasting with Gerald. Gerald unusually was first down for breakfast and was tucking into a bowl of cereal. Normally, Gerald had hot steaming porridge with a slug of honey in the middle, but this time the cereal was different.

"No porridge this morning, what's that stuff you are enjoying," asked James?

"It's a new cereal I bought over from GB, it's a muesli called Alpen. It's great, try some, I left the packet for you on the sideboard," said Gerald chirpily.

As Gerald spooned the last of the cereal into his mouth and James sat down to enjoy a bowlful of cereal swimming with full cream Irish milk, Gerald casually said,

"I had a call from Special Branch last night."

James immediately switched his mind back to the situation at Donahue's farmhouse, wondering whether there had been some developments. Gerald continued,

"They told me I have been put as number 81 on the IRA's Death List."

James thought if anyone was serious about knocking you off, they wouldn't advertise the fact beforehand to avoid risk of capture. He responded by saying,

"Did they tell you who number 80 was," asked James?

Gerald didn't give a direct answer except to say,

"They told me not to be concerned and they would take care of matters."

Taking a serious tone James then said,

"Is there anything they suggested we need to do to make sure you are OK?"

"I am use to this nonsense; they are just thugs trying to terrify everyone to bend to their will. Don't worry, I will be OK but you need to know your next on the list, number 82," answered Gerald.

James nearly choked on his cereal but outwardly showed no reaction as much to reassure Gerald as to any thoughts for his own safety. He reflected on Tony's comment and realised there might be something to worry about and perhaps he shouldn't stay any longer than he needed to. Changing the subject, James went through the progress he had made and believed he could finish his work by Friday once all the service contracts had been signed off.

"You have done a great job for us but more than that I shall miss your company. Please feel free to come and see us again anytime, you don't need to have a reason," said Gerald.

"That's very kind of you. I have learnt an awful lot particularly how to approach people. You sometimes need to realise what pressures they may be under and not necessarily the ones under your nose," said James.

"That's an important lesson especially around here. As it is your last week, I will be your waiter over breakfast. I know what you like," Gerald said with a cheeky grin.

Friday soon came around and James made for the late afternoon flight from Aldergrove to East Midlands. Tony had been right; you could feel the tension in the air and James was pleased that at last he was on his way home but sad to leave Gerald behind. Travelling cross-country he decided to take a short-cut down a country lane just fifteen miles from the airport. Suddenly a figure stepped out from behind a tree wearing a balaclava waving 45-automatic in his hand. James came to a hard stop and the gunmen, probably a teenager, gestured for James to wind down his window. James pretended to put on his handbrake in case he got the opportunity to make a rapid getaway.

"Where are you going," asked the gunman?

"None of your f.....g business came the swift reply," James resorting naturally to his roots from a rough council estate.

The gunman was so shocked he went silent and dropped in his momentarily disorientation the pistol to his side, just as James in that split second drove off running over his feet in the process. Luckily for James, the gunman was forced to release the pistol, letting it drop to the ground for it to go off with a stray bullet, while as James saw from his rear-view mirror, hopping around in total agony. Luckily for James there were no back-up snipers covering the position. Probably for the first time in his life James went into deep breaths and a degree of shock realising the gravity of the situation he had just escaped from. He needed to be more prudent and patient next time the red mist came down over his eyes.

Finally, he arrived home for his Pa to immediately say as he came through the door,

"Cup of tea, son?"

"You don't realise how much I need it," said James.

"Jiver came over last night to say someone called Tony wants an urgent word," said his father.

"The tea first and then I will go and see if I can use Jiver's phone," said James.

James learnt Tony was wanting James to come to London the next day for a meeting in another office. They were to meet at a café on the Albert Embankment at 09.30. No rest for the wicked.

Exiting from Vauxhall Bridge Underground, James checked his bearings knowing he had to walk eastwards on the pavement nearest the river. Sure enough, he found the café not too far away and Tony waiting inside tucking into a thick bacon sandwich laced with HP sauce. Tony ordered the same for James without asking, together with two mugs of tea. Tony duly shovelled in four teaspoons of sugar and washed down the chunky mouthfuls of his hot sandwich. In between gulps of tea and as James tucked into his delicious hot snack, Tony in a cryptic conversation told James they were due for a meeting at 10,30 and James could expect some detailed questioning over some recent experiences. James immediately sensed the subject was to be the Donahue episode, but who were the other people he was about to meet?

Shortly after they left, Tony picked up the tab and returned along the same route James had just taken. Suddenly, Tony made a sharp right turn into clearly a well-secured building but unusually for London no name plates outside. Passing through three security gates manned by armed guards they were ushered into a meeting room. Three gentlemen strode in dressed both casually and suited. Under the last persons arm was a very thick file containing papers of non-uniform sizes and colours. After a brief exchange of introductions, the first person turned to James and asked him to recount again what he had heard at the meeting in Donahue's farmhouse. As James brought up Duggan and Scilly Isles the head man turned to the others as though to confirm some information.

Once the intense interrogation had finished, James asked across the table,

"Is there a problem?"

"No problem, just a very grateful thank you for what you managed to do in difficult circumstances," said the interrogator.

"Sorry I don't understand what you mean," said James looking across to Tony with an expression of what the hell was going on.

Before there was a response Tony intervened by saying,

"What I am about to tell you stays in this room. The information I had gained proved the final link they needed in current investigations to one place, one time and one perpetrator.

The Scilly Isles happens to be the holiday home of our PM. Duggan is a well-known assassin operator for the IRA. Last week Duggan decided to visit Saint Mary's, booking in a hotel for three days. He has involved himself in some tourist guided tours, one of which was to the island of Annet. His purpose was to make radio contact in Penzance for the clearance to execute the plan. It required him to launch a helium balloon as an aerial on the uninhabited island, except for a colony of puffins, an ideal location. What he didn't know was that the guy in the boat dropping people off at the other islands, mainly Trescoe, was from the SAS. He had been dropped off first and the others later to the other islands. A mist came down, the others were picked-up, he was left on the island alone the fellow tourists not noticing one was missing on their return."

"Bloody hell," exclaimed James realising for the first time the magnitude of what he had uncovered purely by accident.

"What happened to him."

"There was another visit after four days and his remains were found on the beach. We got a RAF helicopter to come and pick his body up in a plastic bag and dumped him out in the Irish Sea. We thought he might like that," he answered with a satisfying grin.

Before leaving, Tony said,

"We have recommended an MBE for you, but you can't tell anyone, even your Dad. I will present it to you"

6

Midnight in Moscow

Tony and James left the MI6 building together. They walked the short distance to the tube station at Vauxhall Bridge before Tony turned to James saying,

"You are one of us now."

"What do you mean," asked James?

"I will explain later, let's get back to the Marble Arch Office and we can talk further. I have ordered some sandwiches, including cheese and Branston pickle your favourite," explained Tony. James loved Branston pickle, a delight made known to him by his future mother-in-law, Hanorah.

Sure enough, a coffee table in front of Tony's desk had been laden with not just the sandwiches, but various crispy snacks, fruit juices, Jacob chocolate biscuits and a Mocha coffee pot complete with a sugar bowl and cream jug. Lunchtime had well past and so James knew immediately this was going to be no 10-minute wrap up chat before catching the train back from St. Pancras.

They both walked in to sit on a pair of red leather sofas adjoining a coffee table. "When I said one of us, I meant you are now a full member of the operational team," said Tony.

"I thought I already was given my contract. You are not suggesting I was just an intern did you," asked James?

"No, your contract was with the Department of Trade but you have now earnt a place as an official MI6 operative. I am aware you have had a few exciting experiences, all that was unplanned, but in a strange way gave us growing conviction of your potential for the security services," Tony adding some explanation.

"I am no secret agent," said James.

"I know your name is James but forget the James Bond stories and all those seductive ladies, we don't work like that, never have. Most of the work is boring, repetitive and mind numbing and worst of all, the ladies you are likely to encounter are as ugly as sin. Stick to your girlfriend if I were you. Your contract remains with the Department of Trade but from now on you need to expect to be pulled-in at short notice for the odd mission," continued Tony.

"Are there personal risks attached," asked James?

"No more than is usually the case. Where there may be some risk, you will operate under full diplomatic immunity," answered Tony.

"The opportunity for you is that it will open up an invaluable network of highly influential figures in government and international companies; perhaps for an outside career later on."

"That's a relief, I was beginning to become concerned," responded James excited by the level of work and opportunities for advancement but concerned at the scope of the hidden potential dangers.

"As you know I came from a discipline in chemistry and biology. I have a fellowship at two of Oxfords' Colleges and had a successful career as an entrepreneur exploiting their research. So great has been my success in turning research into successful commercial ventures that I am considered the greatest private benefactor to the university's research programmes since Henry VIII.

My work has led me involuntary into an area of vital national interest, the defence of the realm. Even Prime Ministers have to understand our national defence is his or her prime responsibility.

I need to share with you a grave concern held by many at senior level. We have been made aware that the Russians have been working on a weapon that is so lethal it dwarfs the effect of any nuclear bomb. Unlike any other weapon of mass destruction, the benefit for any aggressor is, that after its use, it has the capability of subjugating a whole nation without destroying its physical assets. The ultimate weapon if you like. We have been following the same development path as them, but have run into the same brick wall as they have. We can produce the nerve gas agent but it is highly unstable. It lasts a few minutes and then a series of chain chemical reactions sets in that neutralises its full potency.

In parallel it so transpires I had been working on a cancer vaccine, I too encountered the same kind of issue until I found a molecular safety trigger that acted as an off switch. That's where you and I get intimately involved. We have a cunning plan, more of a cunning a plan than the professor of cunning at Cambridge University could devise.

What I am about to tell you is of such vital strategic importance that it involves the defence of the West. Our work will be reported direct to the Prime Minister and the President of the USA," said Tony seemingly for the first time more engaged in an area in which he had an expertise and an intense personal interest.

"Now you are really beginning to scare me," responded James.

Tony, continued unabated,

"Don't be, let me go on. My research discovered a molecular mutation I had not expected. I hadn't, I fully admit, recognised its value until someone from Porton Down suddenly came into my research laboratory on an unannounced visit. Porton had beaten the Ruskie's in producing a nerve gas agent of such power that if delivered in an appropriate way would be more powerful than their attempted version. Their unresolvable problem was that their substance too was also highly volatile and acutely unstable, the substance once fully formed, disintegrated within minutes of creation. A chemical fix was needed to stabilise it, and apparently, I had been the one by accident to discover the solution.

Bizarrely, the man from Porton Down didn't arrive on his own. Accompanying him were twenty fully-armed 3rd Parachute Regiment Troopers. All my stock was removed and I was escorted to Porton Down for an interrogation in spite of my high security status, such was its importance."

"I understand the importance, but why are sharing this with me," asked James?

"Because young man in the initial stage of our mission you are going to part of the cunning plan and I need you to play along. I had thought about holding it from you but the risk was you would become suspicious and the mission failed. You are going to accompany me to Moscow, you will be under diplomatic cover, ostensibly to check out the Ruskies' chemical arsenals they have assured us they have disposed of under an international agreement," said Tony.

"I wouldn't know one end of a test tube from another," said James.

"The Ruskies know I am a respected international chemical expert and they either know or could easily find out you work for me. They would expect I would come with a colleague. We don't want to arouse any undue suspicions so you will be going as my bag carrier," said Tony.

"I see, I always wanted to visit Russia having had two years of earache at my further education college of its virtues," said James.

"Yes, we know all about your friend Peter," said Tony.

"Is there anything else you don't know about my background," asked James?

"Not much," replied, Tony.

"Do you remember when your cricketing pal Phillip invited you over to see his sister's G.I. boyfriend and to have a look at his brand-new Chevrolet Impala? Well, while you were busy admiring the car, the G.I. was over to your mother chatting to her about you and the neighbourhood, including Norma your secret admirer."

"Blimey you are thorough," said James somewhat surprised by the intimacy of the intelligence gathering.

It slowly dawned on James that he had been really naïve. The sequence of events from the time he left school was no haphazard chain of events. There were others masterminding his future with him acting as a puppet on a string. He didn't feel resentful since he was being allowed to escape from the fate of Arthur Seaton in order to grab all those many new opportunities or challenges coming his way. Guys from his social background could only dream of what he was doing.

"When do we go?"

"Next week, so take a few days deserved rest while I sort out your passport, visa and diplomatic clearances."

James was expecting to take the flight from Heathrow on a BOAC flight but awaiting them after passing through the departures gate was an Ilyushin airliner carrying some red Russian writing but clearly marked were the bold initials CCCP. Their suitcases safely stored in the hold; both clutched their locked briefcases carrying the really important papers bearing the crown crest. On the flight they placed them in the overhead locker. James was about to remove his overcoat when Tony said,

"Don't bother with that, you will need it, the heating is pathetic."

Sure enough, it was freezing and the only refreshment was a thick black tiny cup of coffee not even some milk to calm it down or a few nibbles to snack on.

The arrival on touchdown after freezing in a metal tube for a couple of hours was unlike any experience, even for James's limited familiarity of air travel. As soon as their feet touched the ground at Moscow Airport, they were met on the tarmac beckoned away by two gentlemen in long black leather coats to a VIP segregated arrival area. No documentation checks, they were quickly ushered into an enormous black car carrying an official flag on its bonnet and driven out of the airport to a five-star hotel right in the centre of Moscow. The hotel couldn't have been any closer to the Kremlin located on the Rue Tverskaia. It was no normal hotel; guests were duly selected and vetted for short stays and no doubt the premises were peppered with various hidden cameras and microphones tuned into every action and word. Even the privacy of a toilet could not be guaranteed. On each floor there was a security guard, most of them were fat ugly women in drab overcoats; the heating didn't extend to the corridors.

Tony suggested they first had dinner in the hotel. There was no abundance of readily available alternatives amongst all the grey stone buildings and sparse commercial signs. The traffic lights seemed to be the only source of colour other than the profusion of red flags and posters of the Russian President. Afterwards, perhaps they would take an evening stroll around the fortress walls of the Kremlin and take a short diversion to the Lenin Mausoleum before turning in. At least they could be out of earshot or possibly even prying eyes. They couldn't be too late turning in. The time of the first meeting was set at

8,30am so they needed to be ready by 8.00am to be escorted into the Kremlin for the meeting with a certain Andrei Gromyko, the Minister of Foreign Affairs.

The next morning and still clutching their brief cases, handcuffed to their hands all night whilst asleep, Tony and James were summoned into the hotel reception and a driver whisked them the very short distance to the Kremlin. For James, used to the trolleybuses running to Trent Bridge via Market Square passing the Romanesque Nottingham Council House, this was a completely different and strange looking world. Surrounding the Kremlin were constructed very high red brick walls guarded outside its perimeter by ornate buildings more akin to an Asian skyline rather than a European one.

He mused that this was the very place Napoleon so triumphantly entered, the heart of the Russian Empire, seated himself on the very chair that had been absented abruptly by the Tsar Nicolas, only for the departing Russian general to set the whole city ablaze. Literally a pyrrhic victory leading to an horrendous and deathly return to Paris leaving in the return trek over 70,000 of his troops either starving or dying in the freezing cold winter. A hard lesson for a doomed strategy carried out with courageous tactics. The Nazis had tried the same but decided to head south, to their cost, for the Ukrainian oilfields instead and the waiting death trap of Stalingrad.

It was as their black car passed through a wide-open gate, close to one of the many towers dividing sections of the high fortress red walls, did James sense a feeling of real fear and trepidation. Is this how the Christians felt, sent into the Roman Coliseum to be used as the spectator sport for the senators and baying citizens of Rome? This was the epi-centre of a feared military power, noted for its ruthlessness, suspicion of foreigners and no respecter of the individual, nor democracy. These were no gentle intellectuals, they were pitiless in their pursuit of their grip on power, no doubt instilled into their DNA by the communist revolutionaries of Lenin, Trotsky and Stalin. The first two were intellectuals in their own right but Stalin wasn't, he was just a peasant thug, driven by an iron will for power at whatever cost. The human sacrifice on an industrial scale went to justify the hardship to achieve the 'ideal'.

It was plainly evident this was no idle exchange meeting between state officials, they were seeing probably the most second most powerful man of the Russian Council next to Leonid Brezhnev. James turned his glance to Tony who sat on the wide black divan leather seat totally relaxed, still clutching his briefcase on his lap, the mass of his body bouncing to the rhythm of the car's soft suspension. His eyes were transfixed on the road ahead. So tranquil was his demeanour it wouldn't have seemed at all odd if he had produced a bucket of popcorn, plunge his mighty fists into it, like a crane grabbing handfuls of the toffee covered popcorn whilst watching a film at the cinema. In a peculiar way James was able to draw strength by his calm and bulky presence.

The car made a rumbled arrival over the cobblestones, somewhat different to those rough irregular lumpy versions in the housing estate of Radford. These were smooth and geometric and neatly laid out in fan-like patterns. As soon as they arrived a hidden hand opened the rear barn door of a bullet and bomb car for a sentry to utter the words,

"Пожалуйста, следуй за мной джентльмен."

James hadn't a clue what was said, but Tony turned to James and just said, "Follow me, young man."

Through the main entrance steel doors, they walked along a deep piled red carpet running along a light grey marble floor adorned on either side by a great expanse of cream painted walls with elaborate gold ornate carvings. The vast expanse of the floor and walls was broken by enormous oil paintings depicting various heroic scenes from the 1917 Revolution. At the end of the corridor he saw two sentries dressed in what appeared to be toy soldier uniforms, exaggerated tall hats, guarding enormous double cream doors liberally covered again in gold leaf. They must have been fifteen-foot high; the doors that is. Their leading escort, as they approached the door, suddenly did an 180° about turn and placed his arm outstretched beckoning them to stop exactly where they stood. Their escort knocked on the door and James could just hear a muffled voice coming from inside. The doors were opened in unison by the two sentries and all three marched in to what James felt was a huge ballroom with several crystal chandeliers hanging from the high ceiling. A sort of very upmarket Sherwood Rooms Dance Hall he had gone to on his first date with his future wife. At the distant end was an enormous mahogany office desk in front of a statue of another double headed golden eagle. Placed to one side a bare red leather covered boardroom table with seating for at least ten people.

It occurred to James that interpreters might be required but there were no other people in the room once their 'commissionaire' had left. He needn't have worried, the man lifted his gaze and rose from his desk and said in perfect English,

"Welcome comrades to my humble abode, please take a seat at the table. Would you like a coffee or perhaps some Russian tea? Sorry we seemed to have run out of the Yorkshire variety."

He smiled as he said it, obviously believing the intended self-deprecating humour would not be lost on his English guests. This was not what James had expected, here was a man, very charming, highly intelligent and well at ease with the enormous power he wielded. James had seen him on newsreels, he and the other sombre characters like a clan of godfathers in the mafia, standing in line on parade in the Red Square watching the military parade and the missiles on their carriers. This was a world away from that.

The tea duly arrived with some digestive biscuits embossed with of all things, 'McVities.' James remained tight-lipped, leaving the meeting entirely in Tony's hands, after all his was just a bag carrier. It was then that Andrei got down to business and asked the first question,

"Where is your list? Let me review it."

Tony had already unlocked the security lock on his briefcase in the car and immediately flicked the switch for the clasp to spring open and he pulled out from the open case just one A4 piece of paper. He slid it over having checked the list for himself and Andrei perused what appeared to be a list of five addresses and then said.

"I see your MI6 guys are still on top of their job. That's the very list we have already organised for you and your colleague to visit. We will drive you to the first site today and the remainder tomorrow and the following day. You will be transported by an official car and some of the others by train. I will furnish you with the necessary high-level security passes. The passes will give you the same entry rights as any one of our politburo ministers and you will be able to ask any questions of our scientists as long as it is in the presence of one of our representatives."

"How will I know the representatives who need to be present," asked Tony?

"That's easy, they will be dressed in long black leather coats and will be carrying a Kalashnikov," he replied giggling as he said it.

"Take as long as you like, and perhaps, we can meet again before you leave in case you wish to ask any further questions while you are here. Possibly, we can have five minutes with comrade Leonid in between him retargeting our nuclear warheads," continued Andrei breaking out into more vigorous fit of giggles.

Tony responded by saying with a wry smile, "As long the coordinates don't correspond to my home address."

At this Andrei handed back the paper as though it was a shopping list for Tesco's and the commissionaire duly arrived on queue to escort them back to the waiting car.

Nothing was said as they visited the first site on the list close by and then returned to the hotel knowing full well, they could be overheard or their conversation recorded. They decided to have another walk around the Kremlin that evening, but this time by the river Moskova. They had dinner at the hotel and slipped out into the cool evening air. It was colder than they thought as their breath formed vapour trails around their faces.

"What do you think to our meeting and first visit," asked James?

"They are lying, there is another site they built 18-months ago and didn't volunteer to correct our list. They have cleaned the sites out and most of their most senior scientists have been moved out with the sensitive measuring equipment," said Tony.

"How do you know that," asked James.

"Because I dropped in a couple of nonsense chemical assumptions with the so-called scientists at our first venue and they never corrected me. It wasn't because they were scared to give away state secrets, they were basic errors that anyone reading public journals should have alerted them to my deliberate error," answered Tony.

The next four visits, some of them sat in a railway carriage with two armed guards stood in the corridor throughout the journey, went as the others before. Except on the last visit there were KGB agents dressed as Andrei had described. Perhaps a little final joke on his part. The evening of the last visit, just as they had finished their dinner, was interrupted by the sound of a major bustle in the hotel reception as though a coachload of tourists had just arrived. As they left the dining room, they could see Andrei striding across the massive reception area heading directly their way saying loudly,

"How about a nightcap my friends at the cocktail bar, I have organised a meeting for 10.30am tomorrow before you go back to London on the afternoon flight?"

"Don't mind if we do," replied Tony.

Sat together at the cocktail bar Andrei opened up first by saying,

"We can talk business tomorrow, but I hope you enjoyed your visit and you are now able to report your findings to your lords and masters."

Delivered again with a quick fit of the giggles. James couldn't help but feel this was utterly surreal. Not only were they meeting one of the most powerful men in the world but in a setting totally alien to anything James had experienced before. It was though they were guys having a friendly chat at a Nottingham pub instead of a mission to verify capabilities of annihilation of each other's country using their massive chemical arsenals. This was truly Alice in Wonderland. Any minute the 'Mad Hatter' would arrive.

James could hardly sleep that night so exhilarated was he by the magnitude of the events unfolding around him. He did manage to get some spurts of unconsciousness so didn't feel too rough the next morning. The same routine was followed on their last day as on their first meeting with Andrei. Again, over tea, but this time with a selection of ginger nuts and custard cream biscuits. Andrei asked for a report on their visit and whether there were any questions. To James's surprise Tony did ask whether the list he had prepared was complete and that the personnel was a full complement at the various establishments. Andrei replied in the affirmative except to say there were a few senior people who had gone down with the Asian flu and a couple had gone on a skiing holiday in Bulgaria, but other than that, what they saw was the normal contingent.

Just as James bit into his first ginger biscuit the door opened and in walked Leonid Brezhnev unsmiling and looking extremely stern emphasised by his bushy eyebrows almost meeting over his nose. Andrei introduced them, and in Russian, James assumed he gave him a quick summary of the visit. Leonid then half-smiled at each of them in turn, turned to Andrei and said a few words in Russian and walked away giving Tony a hard stare. James was metaphorically pinching himself at the encounter, sad that he wouldn't be able to relay the experience to his father.

On their return to London, again an official car was waiting at Heathrow and they were driven straightaway to Whitehall and the Ministry of Defence. The same routine, but on this occasion in very rudimentary furnishings, they were shown into the Minister's office where he was waiting with a senior civil servant standing at his side holding a brown file. Tony gave a full account of the visit and his conclusions. Basically, the message was there was nothing to worry about concerning their chemical research and production establishments, the equipment was basic and their scientific knowledge likewise. He did add, however, that the absence of some personnel, despite the explanation, and the poor apparatus down to cracked test-tubes indicated they were working on a new nerve agent elsewhere evidenced by the absence of modern laboratory testing equipment.

At the end Tony also said that Leonid had told Andrei to keep an eye on him and that there was more to me than Andrei thought. He knew more than he was letting on. Blimey James thought, Tony understood Russian perfectly and possibly Leonid was making sure Tony knew he was onto him! Tony and James returned to Marble Arch allowing Tony to give James a greater insight into the whole mission.

This time Betty brought a huge selection of Jacob chocolate biscuits which James duly devoured as Tony, feet on the desk went through the gaps in information to give James a better understanding of the huge issues at stake.

"The Russians were as active on the nerve gas as the UK was. Our policy would be to formulate a defence strategy but the Ruskie's have no such moral constraints. If the circumstances arose, they would have no hesitation of deploying such a weapon and neutralising countries of the West. Their facilities maybe rudimentary but their new establishment could be a state-of-the-art. They certainly know we are doing the same and now it was a race to get to a final product before the other side perfects their technology."

Then came the astonishing announcement,

"We have got to let them have samples of our nerve gas formula but tamper with the formula by a fixing agent."

"And what would that achieve," asked James?

"Stop looking at the current, think beyond, we are playing chess here but for high stakes. They are determined to produce a stable version of what we have but we have to divert them from their objective. We must be able to tamper with their efforts and effectively neutralise them without them knowing it," continued Tony.

"Sorry to be slow but I don't get this," said James.

"Look," said Tony showing slight irritation at James's slowness of thought. "They know we are close to perfecting our own version but they don't know yet whether we have been able to fully stabilise the random reactions. Let's give them a stabiliser but one which has a delayed time trigger that degrades the chemical agent's acute capabilities within a couple of months. The Ruskie's of course will test their first batch of production but because this is really nasty stuff will be impatient to store it as soon as they can until such time, they feel forced to use it. It will appear everything is alright but our hidden trigger will be secretly working away disarming all their stocks without them knowing it."

"Nice idea but how on earth do we get to them acquire our samples and formula for the stabilising agent and how can we convince them they have the real McCoy," asked James?

"You see you are not as dumb as you think you are. That's your next mission," said Tony casually.

7

The Great Escape

Returning to some sense of normality James was able lead a normal life. His less than first romantic encounter with his sister's work colleague was rectified by their first date when they met again at the Sherwood Rooms Dance Hall in Nottingham.

Another growing passion was about to commence. James needed another transport option; he decided to buy a motorbike. His mother had always forbidden him to buy one, probably wisely in his teenage years, but now he was a grown man. He was able to make his own decisions and self- risk assessment analysis. His pockets bulging with spare cash he could indulge in his juvenile fancies.

Studying at college, he and his pals would spend part of their lunchtime wandering around 'Bunny's', a large motorcycle dealer in Nottingham selling mainly second-hand motorbikes and scooters. There they were in all their glory, the great British marques; AJS, BSA, Matchless, Norton, Vincent and Triumph. For a few special weeks in pride of place they were able to drool over a 1000cc Brough Superior, made in Nottingham. The very same motorbike that the Arabian adventurer T E Lawrence met his bizarre end, strangled by his own scarf in the wheel of his motorbike, rather than by the blade of an Arab scimitar or through the crosshairs of a lucky sniper firing from a captured Royal Enfield rifle! This may well have been the omen for many of his enemies who would meet their own version of weird terminations from their mortal spring.

Whilst all these marques conjured such romantic thoughts of great bikes and adventures, his dreams were always punctured by the reality. The sight of dirty oil spill trays underneath many bikes told their own story. British engineering wasn't quite up to scratch, crankcase gaskets failed, allowing the bottom of the bikes to be smeared in weeping oil. He didn't much fancy either the idea of cleaning and lubricating the massive drive chain to maintain full efficiency and to prevent the chain 'popping' of its ratchet locking the rear wheel. Not a good idea when you are winding along the roads at 60 to 70 mph. There had to be a better option to indulge his passion. Perhaps he must seriously consider the new-fangled electric start Japanese or German motorbikes and not allow his national emotions to get the better of him.

Widening his scan of the motorcycle magazines his attention was captured by the sight of a new BMW model. Trust the Germans to resolve his engineering doubts with a bike that not only did not leak oil but also had the luxury of an electric start. No danger then of breaking a leg on an ill-executed kick-start. If that wasn't enough there was another beautiful engineering solution, a shaft driven rear wheel. No messy rear chain wheel to deal with every 3,000 miles. No front drum brakes either, instead huge hydraulically operated disc brakes. Unusually for the Germans, it was also exquisitely designed and finished with two enormous opposing twin cylinder barrels protecting both legs should you happen to pull the bike over. For James, this was the perfect epitome of a modern motorbike. A bike with an enviable reputation for reliability and furthermore one that could last a lifetime, if well maintained. The hardest decision would be the colour out of a choice of just three; black, red or blue.

As luck would have it, there was a local approved dealer in Basford; Wheelcraft. So, one Thursday morning, he legged it to the showroom to meet what would turn out to be his mechanic for decades to come, Roger. The colour decision was not too difficult. In the middle of the showroom, in pride of place, was a beautiful new blue BMW R75. He fell in love with it immediately, but then came the dull administrative stuff, cheque book out, registering the bike in his initials, insurance and importantly the protective gear; a full-face helmet, boots and gloves, plus tailored leathers and rain-proof overalls. Then came the big day just a week later. How to get the beast home?

Riding an 80cc Raleigh Roma scooter was one challenge; this machine was much heavier and the engine nearly ten times the engine capacity. The drive home had to be executed with great care. So powerful was the bike he never changed out of first gear all the way. Gradually through continuous practice he became more and more comfortable riding it to the point he was able to use all the gears and eventually travel as far as the Motorcycle Grand Prix at Assen.

He still drove his beloved Rover, especially in his courting years, but for pure self-indulgent pleasure and an ability to escape the day to day humdrum, a motorbike ride along the winding country lanes or even sweeping at speed along the autoroutes was just the antidote to life's cares and stresses. At the motorway cafés it always drew attention. On the continent he found it difficult to escape the interest of grandparents, parents and children alike, curious about a Brit riding on a German bike so far from home.

Two years had passed by since his return to the UK, during which James had been engaged in mainly conventional business assignments. These were helping out with acquisitions, disposal and start-ups. It was his latest assignment that would lead him to his next unconventional project working with a chemical company. 'Jiver' had come over the road to his parent's house to knock on the door to say he had received an urgent phone call from someone who would not give his name but wanted to speak to James immediately.

James returned the call and thanked 'Jiver' again for his patience and forbearance.

"What was all the urgency," asked James's Pa?

"A storm in a teacup," answered James. "It was the office making sure I would be around by the end of the week as they want me to go on a European business trip and wanted to confirm flights for me. I managed to persuade them it would be cheaper and more convenient if I could use my new motorbike. I could then have the flexibility to add on a few days and do a bit of touring around the alps."

"You are really enjoying yourself, aren't you? Make the best of it son before the responsibilities of family life consume you," said his father pleased James had finally broken out of his humble dull beginnings.

"Dad, I do have to pinch myself at times that I have been so lucky to lead the life I do. If it wasn't for you and mum's support, and my teachers of course, I would have never got out of the starting blocks," said James finding a natural timing to show his deep appreciation of his parents sacrifices and unstinting support.

"One day Dad, I will show my appreciation in a more tangible way," said James.

"You have done enough. You have helped out every month with the housekeeping money and bought us a nice Morris Mini that we adore. Your happiness is thanks enough," countered his father.

James had been quite economical with the whole truth. Tony had called him saying this was the time to enact the latent plan aired since their last visit to MI6. James had an inkling of what he was referring to. Tony must have worked out the deception and now he was prepared to deliver it. Odd though he readily agreed to the motorbike.

It seemed just like yesterday after a two-year break when James strode back into Tony's office as Betty scurried as usual on his arrival to the back-office kitchen for the tea and now obligatory Jacob chocolate orange biscuits.

"Hello James, take a seat while I explain perhaps one of the greatest missions of your life," said Tony.

What an intriguing opening for a meeting thought James, this had to be deadly serious. Tony preceded to give not only a brief on the mission but to admit some suspicions held against James but now dispelled. The reason James had been 'rested' and employed over the last two years on conventional work was to eliminate the remote possibility that he was a suspected 'mole' in the organisation. This came as a bit of a shock, but James on hearing the rest understood why. Apparently, a security leak had occurred of information only known to Tony, James and Peter Voss. Through a process of elimination, it became certain Peter Voss was the problem. So thought James, Robert Kennedy was right in his suspicions. Rather than expose him, Tony had suggested to the Head of MI6 they would use Peter Voss as a conduit for disinformation, given he was now known to be a trusted informant of the Russians.

James sat on the edge of his seat eager to know more about the cunning plan. In essence, it was to deceive the Ruskie's into believing that a 'doctored' version of the nerve agent developed by Tony was the real McCoy. Somehow the manipulated version had to be delivered into the Ruskie's hands in a convincing manner, allow them to test it, and then copy it on an industrial scale. Hopefully it would be added to their chemical warfare arsenal and then surreptitiously, through an implanted catalytic chemical agent, the stock of nerve gas in the arsenals would degrade unperceptively within weeks whilst in cold storage. Easier said than done thought James.

Tony came out with a very surprising suggestion,

"How do you fancy a trip to Dubrovnik," asked Tony?

"Where's that," asked James?

"I thought you had a GCE 'O' Level in geography. It's in Yugoslavia," said Tony.

"But what am I supposed to do there; go sightseeing," responded James?

"Precisely, that is exactly what I want you to do. That brand-new motorbike of yours would be a perfect cover," said Tony.

"Cover for what," went on James?

"Ah, that's the exquisite bit. Under your seat there is a lockable small box for documents and cash, a perfect place for a strip of secured phials, if Peter is the leak, we can let him know you are courier unaware of your doctored cargo and then give the Ruskie's a simple opportunity to steal your packages from you. We will make out you are meeting up with some Swiss pharmaceutical people to arrange the tests for our forthcoming version of nerve gas in a neutral country. We expect he will tip off our Andrei friends, find your parked bike, unlock the hidden box under the seat and take the phials. To disguise their efforts, they may make a swop to cover their tracks. The Ruskies can happily organise the manufacture on an industrial scale from the benchmark samples," said Tony winking.

"So, you want me to sit on a bandolier of lethal nerve gas cartridges that could wipe out a nation as I rattle along across half of Europe!"

"Well not quite. It is the nerve gas with the implanted chemical neutraliser. Whilst in the aluminium files they are quite harmless.

Let's say we manage to leave carelessly parked your motorbike in a convenient spot for a thief to extract what they are after. If they take your bike as well, we will buy you another new one with perhaps a few nice luxury extras," said Tony almost licking his lips at the prospect of deceiving the enemy and capturing a traitor.

"I'd better go and fill the tank," said James knowing the nation came before his adoration of his bike.

It would have been futile attempting to rationalise the personal risk he was being ask to take, not so much from any possible leaks from his hidden cargo but from an arrest as a spy. The enormous prize was worth it. Personal risk wasn't a significant factor. In effect it would enable the disarming of the Russian's entire chemical warfare capability for decades without them knowing it. What a better way to have a verifiable disarmament without all the summits, treaties and site testing. Afterall, ordinary British infantrymen had taken much greater risks for Queen and Country. James motorbike was delivered to Wheelcraft for some 'guest engineers' to doctor his bike ready for departure.

Rather than take the direct route to his destination James decided to do what he would have planned if this was purely a leisure trip, he made for Hull to the North for the ferry to Zeebrugge. After securing the bike with leather straps in the bowels of the ferry, and changing for dinner, he went to the boat's onboard shop to buy a small camera so he could play the full tourist part snapping away at anything of touristic interest.

His trip coincided with the tenth anniversary of the new ferry route, and as he had bought an expensive camera, he was offered a free gift of a small travelling/shopping bag. For a car driver that would have been fine but for a motorbike rider with limited luggage space it was totally inappropriate. He courteously declined the kind offer to the sales assistant, to be then offered a large stuffed dog. This presented the same problem except he fathomed he could strap it to top of the petrol tank with his leather straps and what better way of avoiding suspicion than by appearing to be a total looney biker!

In the excitement of the first long trip on the continent on his dream steel stead, James almost forgot the objective of the mission. Having breakfasted onboard ship, he was soon purring along the main roads of Europe. He hadn't though overlooked the travelling routine to keep safe and alert. There were self-imposed rules for long distance rides on two wheels. Never ride for more than two hours uninterrupted. Stop for a coffee break, or meal, or spend 20 minutes filling up and chewing something sweet to keep the sugar levels adequate.

He had quickly navigated through Rotterdam and was on an open road, flat and straight, observing the Dutch road signs flash by feeling the wind on his face. The first leg would be the longest to Klagenfurt on the Austrian Border, around 750miles if there were no hold-ups. This is where a powerful motorbike comes into its own. At traffic jams he could niftily squeeze through between the lines of cars and lorries. He could easily travel at over 80mph, the only irritation being the regular frontier stops and toll booths fumbling around for passports and loose change whilst still holding the bike upright between his legs.

Most of the trip was on flat terrain until the land begins to gently crimple and then you see in the far distance the blue tinge of the alps. James hadn't booked any hotels since there should be plentiful choice of accommodation especially in the more expensive hotels. It was also a way of avoiding the risk of discovery of getting to arrive at a fixed pre-determined point. He also made it a rule that as soon as it was nearing five in the afternoon, it was time to plan and lookout for the hotel for the night. He had, however set his sights on reaching Klagenfurt and on this occasion would break this rule. He had, however, booked a hotel on his final day for his ultimate destination in Dubrovnik in order to localise the discovery risk and to meet his Swiss friends. This third leg of the journey he had estimated was less than 400 miles from Rijeka. Tomorrow was to be a gentle ride for the second-leg of just 150 miles to Rijeka only to be extended if the first day didn't go broadly to plan. He looked forward to the best part of the journey, from Klagenfurt and a blissful meandering romp through the Alps, with no time pressures, taking in the scenery and stopping on the way for sightseeing and extended meals.

Tired, hungry and with his legs and arms aching from being so long in the saddle, it was nearly 8pm when James turned into the main square of Klagenfurt. There, plum in the centre was a typical Austrian style old-fashioned hotel. The town was deserted and so was the hotel; he was the only guest. It was a public holiday and the restaurant was closed. The only employee around was the manager who apologised profusely that the restaurant was closed but would be prepared to make him a few sandwiches. James was then shown into what appeared to be the Hapsburg's private bedroom complete with four poster bed, his two panniers in hand and the stuffed limp dog under his arm.

His 'other luggage' was locked securely under his seat, theft alarms activated, should the bike be touched or moved by unwanted thieves; including the engine immobiliser. Luckily, it was parked in full view of his bedroom window. Even with these precautions he thought it was a hell of risk given the high stakes, but Tony remained relaxed. After all it for credibility he had to give some pretence of precautions, the aim was for them to be overcome with some difficulty by experts before his Swiss friends made contact, the precautions would be gauged at the expected level of an ordinary motor biker trying to take the normal precautions against theft of his bike. Not too easily but severe enough in order not to arise suspicions that all was not as it seemed.

Seeing the high polished wooden floors and the beautiful carved dark wood furniture James hesitated before entering the hotel bedroom saying he should remove his dusty leather boots first. The manager would have none of it, beckoning him to go straight-in while he made the sandwiches and a pot of coffee. By the time James had changed, the manger gave a polite tap on his door and walked in with a large platter of several different sandwiches that could feed four not just one. Despite this, James hadn't realised how hungry he was and scoffed the lot with a couple of cups of black coffee. Before he turned-in he went for a short walk around the square, seated himself outside a bar for a cold beer keeping all the time a furtive eye on the bike.

The next morning, he didn't leave until well past 10am after a good breakfast. He would soon be over the border into Croatia and then perhaps lunch amongst the mountains before heading for Rijeka and his next overnight stay. As it turned out this day was going to take longer than he thought. The border near Klagenfurt is at the top of a mountain pass. Despite being out of season the traffic had built up and just at the foot of the climb traffic was already moving at walking pace. There must have been an accident. He contemplated he should be patient for a while, travelling at walking pace until whatever the obstruction was, he could clear it soon. The road anyway was narrow with many blind bends, so to travel on the outside risked meeting head-on the occasional heavy lorry thundering down the road the other way. Not a happy prospect.

Two hours later he was only halfway up the mountain road and the traffic had come to a virtual standstill in both directions. Waiting for 20 minutes to check for the possibility for any vehicles in the opposing direction, he decided to go for it and steadily manoeuvred up the mountain hugging very tight the stationary vehicles, especially on the bends, listening out for anything that maybe coming the other way.

An hour later he was at the top and was stopped by a Croatian soldier complete with rifle slung over his shoulder. In German he was told to stop and asked for his passport. This is it, he thought, they have already twigged my mission and will search his bike as though it was a normal custom's check for drug smugglers. Other soldiers were milling around doing nothing despite the building traffic jam. The frontier was marked by two sets of half-barrier red and white painted horizontal poles. Clearly, the military had closed the border for some reason. Noticing the address on the passport as Nottingham the soldier looked at him and said in perfect English and bearing a broad smile,

"Are you Robin Hood?"

"Close," came the reply.

With that, and to James's complete surprise, he beckoned him to cross the frontier immediately, gestured to the others to let him pass, passing the queue on the other side of the road. Whether he was a fan of Errol Flynn, a motorbike devotee, or just to avoid a motorbike and its rider having to wait in the baking sun, James couldn't surmise which. Obviously, the Croats were not in on the ruse. As it turned out James wasn't going to make Rijeka not much before 5pm anyway so he decided instead to stay in a B&B outside of the town.

The day after was to be the ride of his life. His piece of string on the map to judge the distances hadn't taken account of the pronounced ria coast of

Croatia. You could see the next headland across the inlet just a few short miles away but it was a good fifteen to twenty minutes to get there, so deep were the inlets. Realising the leg would be at least another 100 miles, James was force to adopt a different riding technique. The traffic wasn't heavy so early in the summer season and as there were no trees, you could see well in advance for any oncoming traffic. Rather than just keep to his side of the road he would use all of the road tarmac including rounding the bends. This meant the average of 35 to 40mph could be increased to 50 to 55mph, one hell of a difference when travelling such a long distance.

From being an initial irritation, the ride turned into one of sheer exhilaration. This was motorcycling at its best. Constant change of speeds, gears and direction, leaning into the bends defying the centrifugal forces trying to pull you into a straight line. He still kept to his disciplined routine of stops but had an unexpected surprise at the first fuel stop. The pumps had no gauges; just a man with a stop watch. The fuel was so cheap it wouldn't have been worth the hassle to argue about the odd half-litre difference. Precious time was eating into the day making it necessary to avoid the food breaks and keep riding relentlessly onwards to make the hotel before nightfall.

Despite James best intentions, dusk had fallen and he had not yet arrived in Dubrovnik. The headlight was always switched on; even during daylight hours. The pencil beam of his headlight was picking up the rocky side of steep cliffs, and then as he turned in the other direction, it would point out in a solid stick of light into the inky blackness; out to sea towards the rapidly fading feint outline of the horizon beyond. One careless mistake could either lead to crashing into a very hard wall of rock, or worse still, disappearing off the edge of the road down a three-hundred-foot drop into the sea.

The ride was turning from a blissful carefree adventure into a creeping nightmare. The constant need for keen concentration was taking its toll. Nearing finally his destination, but no idea where the hotel was, James was relieved to see the flicker of a twinkling light, resembling a space station suspended in the heavens. It turned out to be a petrol station on the verge of closing before midnight. The manager kindly offered to fill James's bike and gave him directions for his hotel along the same main road lit by the odd streetlight. Fortunately, the hotel was easily located on the same road very near the end, making navigation straightforward. Giving the manager a generous tip for the inconvenience, off James toddled relieved he was nearing journey's end, feeling absolutely shattered but contented he had finally made it.

Arriving at the hotel the night porter was expecting him, directed him to the underground car park. James relieved himself of his side panniers and tank top bag complete with a by now even limper looking stuffed dog for the night porter to take to his room. As luck would have it there was a late cabaret show on so James was offered some steak and chips at a table at the back next to the kitchen door before the chef left after the show. Sometimes in life there can be a silver lining when all seems so dark and forbidding. After some food and a hot coffee, he went upstairs one floor to his room, noted his luggage had been delivered intact, had a hot shower and slumped onto the bed passing-out through the sheer exhaustion.

Old habits die hard. After just six hours deep sleep, he was wide-awake again as the strong dawn light penetrated the thin linen bedroom curtains. Drawing the light drapes back he couldn't believe the vista that awaited him. Not the grimy skyline of the city of his birth, or the red star over the local brewery but a deep blue sea stretching to the horizon. His room was not just one storey up but the next to last floor at the top of a twenty-floor storey hotel built onto the side of a cliff. Below him an Olympic sized swimming pool enclosed by a series of concrete steps to the water's edge, and to its left, a rocky terrace garden complete with sun lounges and umbrella dressed tables. Already there were early morning swimmers navigating up and down the pool, no doubt Germans ready to place their towels on the best spots before breakfast. His Swiss contacts were due to arrive for dinner that evening so James decided the terrace was the place to rest after such an arduous journey and spend a few hours lazing around in the sun. Importantly, his bike was already parked ripe for the unauthorised interference, his Swiss contacts to confirm at some stage the doctored phials had disappeared.

After a continental breakfast James made for the terrace dressed in a tee-shirt and shorts; book in hand. It was warm, even though the hotel struck a deep shadow across the rocky terrace mounted on a small rocky outlet jutting out to sea. Step ladders were located at various conveniently placed points allowing swimmers to clamber out of the crystal-clear azure blue waters teeming with shoals of brightly coloured fish visible in the depths. So early was it that James sat there alone, engrossed in his book written by a business management guru, he was a stranger in paradise. Later he heard the odd voices in various languages. He couldn't help noticing increasing activity by the noise of sun lounges being continually moved around scraping along the rocky floor. Otherwise, he remained completely oblivious of their presence relaxing in the enveloping warm climate.

After an hour the temperature suddenly rose as the sun gradually broke over the top of the cliff face and James could feel the rays beginning to burn his forehead and arms. He placed his book by the side of his sun lounger and was suddenly shocked to discover, he was the only one, amongst around thirty people, wearing any clothes or bathing suits, the others were bronzed and stark naked!

Oh buggerama!

What to do?

Move to the pool, but they don't allow sun-loungers there.

All these thoughts raced through James's mind. Realising in an instant he was the one who should be embarrassed; unless he wanted to spend the day lying on a towel covering hard concrete there was no alternative but to join them. He replaced his book strategically on his lap, first took off his tee-shirt and then after removing his shoes removed his shorts. Whilst naked as God decreed, the book serving the purpose of maintaining his decorum, he started applying the sun cream. Unfortunately, his clever ruse wasn't going to work. A young blond lady, lying next to her boyfriend close by, saw James struggling to rub the cream onto his back.

"Can I help you," she asked in perfect English probably thinking only the English could be so prudish or perhaps she had read the title of the book?

James couldn't exactly refuse, He would only be drawing even more attention to himself, he graciously accepted.

The next few minutes would be absolute torture for James. Not through severe pain, but heavenly pleasure as the soft gentle hands caressed so adoringly his back. Maintaining physical control was an excruciating torment.

Despite this early encounter, James was soon able to relax and realise what an idiot he was to feel so embarrassed. The novel experience began gradually to feel quite normal; the hot sun beckoned for a cool dip in the crystal waters. As the maxim says,

'If at first you can't beat them, join them,' he was soon frolicking in the water with the rest, just like innocent children.

The day sped by and it became necessary to reluctantly interrupt the sheer pleasure of joining such a nice bunch of people and return to his room to wash-up and get ready for dinner at 7.30pm. His Swiss friends were to meet him in the foyer and hopefully could confirm the mission had been accomplished. They were to check the phials had gone. This was the very critical part of the trip.

Down by reception at 07.15pm he sat in the first available armchair and picked up a US international newspaper and scanned the articles. Just ten minutes later a group of middle-aged men arrived, the one in the lead immediately shouting across the reception floor,

"Hello James, are you ready to go with us to a nearby restaurant for dinner?"

James just smiled in recognition, put down his paper and walked over to shake hands with everyone and for the formal introductions to be made.

A table had been reserved at a restaurant, literally just 300 metres away. The patron knew the group well as they had dined there every evening after the day's session of the several lectures at an international conference for the pharmaceutical companies taking place in their hotel. His Swiss host told James the place was 'safe' and well away from prying eyes so he could relax. A few aperitifs were ordered and very soon the group engaged as though on a lad's night out helped by the fact all could speak English well. The host made it known they would hold-off the main course until another member of the group arrived, delayed by some 'administrative' work. James held back his growing anxiety and concentrated on the menu and a chance to enjoy some company at last after a few days travelling alone. As he was about to finish the first course, he distinctly heard the sound of cuckoo clock calling out the time of 8.00pm.

"Where's the clock," asked James?

"There isn't one," replied his host. "It's our friend doing his famous party trick."

"Which one," asked James?

"He is just outside on his way," replied the host.

"If you noticed and was counting, there were nine calls," said his host.

"Not really, I thought you Swiss were more meticulous with timekeeping," said James half-jokingly?

"But we are! Eight was for the time and the ninth that your phials have gone from your bike", said his host.

"The Ruskies have taken the bait, the plant pots! You can now fully relax my friend; your mission is now over."

"If he had made a mistake and there were ten, what would that have meant," asked James mischievously?

"Simple, it would have meant no switch, just your bike stolen," said his host.

Just as the exchange was finishing the extra guest arrived beaming from ear to ear. He whispered something in Swiss man's ear.

"Is there an issue," asked James.

"No problem, the mission has gone better than we could have expected. You now have some other cargo," said Swiss man.

"What do you mean," said James inquisitively?

"They have switched phials and replaced them with their own looking exactly the same, the cunning bastards. They may look the same but just contain probably their version anticipating we would believe they haven't taken the bait. But we recognised there has been a switch immediately from the small red dot missing at the bottom of the tubes, the plonkers," said Swiss man.

"Does this mean a change of plan," asked James.

"No," said Swiss Man. We continue as normal, make out we haven't noticed anything and we will eventually report back that the trigger samples after testing didn't work. The Ruskie's will believe we have not bothered producing it on an industrial scale and in effect they will believe they have disabled ours and weaponised theirs."

"I suppose we should be pleased," responded James.

"Pleased, we are ecstatic," said Swiss man.

"We need more wine for the meal."

The next morning, James waited by his bike and whilst making sure there was no one else around unlocked the seat, lifted it on its hinge and pulled out the Velcro secured bandolier of metal encased glass phials. His cuckoo friend was standing by as the switched phials were quickly stashed into Swiss man's briefcase before James returned to reception and took the local bus to the medieval port for an organised leisure trip around the islands offshore.

James hadn't realised how much adrenalin was stored in his system as the internal tension drained away, knowing he could now fully take in the magnitude of what had been achieved relax and enjoy the delights of the medieval town of Dubrovnik.

Organised tours were laid on at the old fortress town and a boat trip to a nearby deserted island containing unspoilt fauna and flora. There are probably no other sites in Europe to match the history and beauty of his new discovery. The old town of Dubrovnik still bore the wear marks embedded in the stone from the centuries of footsteps. Being a communist country there were no obvious signs of commercial trade, the shops well hidden in the recesses of the walls. If you looked down the street following the ramparts of the fortress walls you could easily imagine you had been time-warped to centuries before except for the few people walking around in modern dress. Departures to the nearby islands were from the centre of the medieval port in small wooden boats. Bunches of tourists would disembark onto these islands and allowed to roam at will amongst this naturalist paradise. Within minutes people would disappear in different directions to return a couple of hours later to meet the boat for the return trip.

James spent some of this time planning the outline of his return home. He had learnt the true measure of the distances and times involved in travelling through this terrain, he resolved to split the return journey through Croatia over two days and stop at the halfway point looking to cross the mountain border at around six in the evening of the second day and then rest-up at the next available hotel in Austria, probably again Klagenfurt.

James couldn't help but feel smug with himself that his mission had gone so smoothly and much better than anticipated; apparently at little personal risk. Tony is bound to be delighted with the outcome; it couldn't have gone any better. The trouble James had failed to recognise, in his exuberance, is that in all the best laid plans there is invariably a sting in the tail.

The trip back on the coastal road was a reverse of the experience before. It was daylight, in bright sunshine and the sea shimmered as though covered by a veil of diamonds right to the horizon. Apart from the odd car and lorry he was virtually alone, but not having that feeling of total isolation he had had before. All went well including the first overnight stop at a B&B and then onwards for the return trip over that border between Croatia and Austria and safety.

The traffic had built up as before, but still seemed to be at least moving at running pace. Nothing, apart from the odd van came the other way so plucking up courage he took up the same manoeuvre, hugging the line of the snail like traffic and headed for the mountain top. This time the reception was somewhat different. More soldiers and more vehicles were being selected as they progressed through passport control for a thorough searching and detailed document check. Nothing too unusual as an exercise in more intensive border controls, but there were observations that put him on edge. First there were no customs officers as before, they were all military. The selection of vehicles was not entirely random, they were all for British registered cars. Selected cars were being emptied and all the drivers and passengers were being asked to disembark, frisked and commanded to stand around as all their belongings were stripped out of the car and put on trestle tables for a secondary look.

Just as these thoughts raced through his head, he was directed by one of the officers to line up behind three other waiting British cars out of the line of the main traffic flow. James obeyed but instantly knew there must have been a tip-off that there were some nefarious activities going on in their territory by an Englishmen but they hadn't yet narrowed it down to a motorcyclist. If they found the switched phials, it would lead to instant arrest and no doubt some more planted incriminating evidence found. It was now or never, the downside risks made it imperative to take the initiative.

He nonchalantly rested his bike on its side stand but still stood astride his machine. He thought this wasn't the time for the electric start to fail. Luckily, one of the soldiers searching the car at the head of the line dropped a pot jar, no doubt a souvenir of the family's visit, momentarily attracting all their attention. There was a lot of agitation from the driver and apologies from the soldier as another went into his hut for a broom. James pulled the bike upright and as he kicked up the side-stand, pulled-in the clutch lever, he pushed the ignition switch and with the bike already in first gear lurched forward burning rubber on his rear tyre and went for the half barriers of the frontier. He knew his bike could go from 0 to 60 mph in less than four seconds. He had calculated that in that time, anyone who realised what he was doing, he could be at least halfway through the barriers. Someone would have to be a crack shot to have any chance of hitting him before he was in Austria.

That was the theory, but one 'Squaddie' decided he wouldn't bother taking aim and just swung round firing his rifle from the hip in one movement. His shot may have been a good one; James would never know. Unfortunately for the 'Squaddie, he failed to recognise his superior officer stood in the firing line and he took a bullet in the shoulder. It would hit him like a sledgehammer spinning him around and knocking him to the ground. The resulting mayhem prevented any follow-up action, including a second pot-shot. He was through and free. The Ruskie's would be convinced that they had the real McCoy validated by the Swiss reporting back to London that the phials were defective and now the courier evading capture by the Croats. Such information would be transmitted through Peter Voss. James was surprised he had taken the whole episode in his stride and thought one day, someday, someone in Hollywood would make a film of it! Perhaps called the 'Great Escape'.

8

Legging It in Prague

The journey back was somewhat of an anti-climax. From the awe and majesty of the Alps the roads flattened out and straightened into the far distance. Boring, mind-numbing concrete pathways broken only by the odd rest interval at a motorway service station to lift the monotony. It did, however, give James the time, in the seclusion of his crash helmet, to reflect on events; a great success tinged with moments of adrenalin pumping extreme danger. He had the sense of increasing fatigue as the adrenalin pulsating through his arteries began to calm. Holland beckoned, the clouds grew darker, followed by an enveloping mist of drizzle. Inside the all-weather wax cotton suit, James was bone dry and warm, but he could taste the raindrops passing over his lips in the driving rain. The stuffed dog was looking a bit the worse for wear, gradually slumping backwards in the damp atmosphere. The plastic bag over its head wasn't quite keeping all the weather outfit. The two tiny cut-outs for its eyes were a bit of a childish attempt at authenticity allowing droplets of water to enter. The weather was slowly penetrating even though 'Barnie' the bear was snuggly fitted behind the broad Perspex windscreen.

The target destination this time was not Zeebrugge, but Calais for the short ferry ride to Dover. Abord the ferry, he roped up the bike in the cavernous under deck then went to the cafeteria for a hot bite and a piping hot drink of tea. Just as he had finished his refreshments, he was being called down again to the bowels of the ship to prepare for embarkation along with all the cars. The rain had stopped but it seemed much colder. The oncoming winding roads and the need to navigate through the outskirts of London heading for the newly opened M1 was in a sense a bit of a relief from the sheer boredom of riding on the North European plateau. It helped passed the time away. Soon the welcoming signs for Leicester appeared, a first indicator that in another 45 minutes he would be home.

It came as a thunderbolt. Suddenly he felt a deep emotional reaction. He supposed from a combination of the magnitude of what had just achieved and at last to see his Mum and Dad in a warm safe home. It took the remaining few miles to 'gather himself' and become composed and self-assured. As he turned into his home street, he saw his Dad locking up the Mini just as his Mum was walking down the path to the front door with bags of shopping. Perfect timing, his Mum dropped her shopping and ran up the street to greet him. He couldn't supress his emotions anymore as tears welled in his eyes fortunately out of sight under his enveloping helmet and balaclava. No sooner had he entered the back door, his Mum had started making up some cheese and onion sandwiches, his favourite, and Dad was boiling the kettle for tea.

The next hour was filled with his adventures, except for the confidential bits, and a promise to get to Boots quickly to get the rolls of film printed. It was then his Mum reminded him he should nip round to visit his new girlfriend and put her mind at rest. She had been around every day since he had left asking how he was getting on, not that they knew that much apart from the odd short telephone message via 'Jiver'.

James was having a bit of a lie-in when there was a knock at the door. 'Jiver' stood there with a piece of note paper he thrust into his father's hand. This was the nod to get up and taste one of his Dad's delicious bacon sandwiches. Apparently 'Jiver' had said to his Dad,

"I am thinking of putting a red Post Office sign outside my house to denote I had a side line in telephone and telegrams."

Dad had apologised that he had been troubled so much of late but 'Jiver' just said he was joking, as a nosey parker he found it interesting what James was up to, or so he thought!

Before James could get a first bite into his sandwich his Dad put the note under his nose on the table. It simply said,

"Mountain coming to Mohammed, be at the Devonshire Hotel at Baslow today at 4.00pm for afternoon tea, TONY."

"I didn't know you had some Muslim friends," his Dad remarked sarcastically.

"It's just an office joke, I think he is making the point that I am always the one going to London and no one knows what lies North of Watford," said James trying to deflect a conversation he didn't want to pursue.

That hit a raw nerve as his father said,

"Bloody right, those southerners don't know the real world."

For perhaps for the first time James thought his father this time was the person in the wrong. Tony and his ilk knew a lot more about the 'real world' and the threats to everyone. Little did ordinary people know the extraordinary risks people like Tony were taking to keep everyone safe. James was being gradually drawn into this dark deep state no one talked about. Whilst James's Mum drifted through life from day to day just content with her family around her, Dad was more perceptive. He always seemed to go on edge every time James was 'away'. He wasn't stupid, he may not know what was actually going on, but these business trips were no ordinary run of the mill business affairs. James sensed on each return his father would be thinking to himself, thank God he's back home again, safe and sound.

James contemplated taking the motorbike to Baslow, but thought better of it. It's a posh hotel, the Duchess of Devonshire could turn up at any time, and perhaps the sight of him chewing up the gravel wouldn't go down too well. Off he went in the Rover 90 with his father saying as he left,

"Take care of the car, no scratches or dents if you don't mind."

Dad had become very attached to the new Rover 90, but James instinctively knew it was more directed at James not to take on any undue risks when meeting Tony.

Tony had arrived early, evidenced by the already half empty bottle of Chateau du Pape stood on the table. No time to allow it to breathe for Tony. Tony was more effusive than usual,

"Come here my little hero I have already ordered your favourite Bombay Sapphire gin, tonic and a tinge of lime for your impending arrival."

In a hushed tone that even James could hardly hear the words,

"You realise that our last mission ranks with the enigma machine. Unfortunately, as I am due to retire soon, it's a Peerage for me, and obscurity for you my friend."

Then resuming to his normal booming voice, he said,

"Let's have a slap-up meal, the bill is on the company."

As it turned out the meal was quite an experience. The food extraordinarily excellent, the ambiance highly convivial and Tony a joy as host. Soon the whole restaurant, diners and service staff were drawn into the exuberant atmosphere. This was no casual venue, most of the regulars knew Tony well, but they didn't have a clue what he did. Probably they thought he was some eccentric scientist, which he probably was, but with an unknown secret facet never revealed to anyone outside the circle. You felt he wanted to proclaim from the roof tops what exalted company they were in, but obviously couldn't, that's a key premise of the job, keep your mouth firmly shut.

For James it was an unexpected pleasure to share this moment of informality with his boss. But then as James was about to take the first mouthful of the cheesecake dessert the bombshell was dropped to kill the mood.

"You realise there is still a remaining task? We will have to make our friends feel we are genuinely concerned over our recent supposed delivery and why the switched samples didn't work. They will expect us to take some steps to find out what happened," remarked Tony momentarily putting on his serious face amongst the banter and frivolity.

"How do you mean," asked James as his heart sank to his boots?

"I am going to put it around the department you are going to conduct an in-depth review, making sure our friend Peter Voss is made aware," said Tony as he plunged his dessert spoon deep into the sherry trifle.

"I suppose it means meeting our Swiss friends again," enquired James?

"You are already ahead of me, except to make it interesting for you I would like you to meet them in Prague, again on neutral ground," responded Tony.

"Don't worry this is just a mild deception as a follow through, picking up loose ends," said Tony reassuringly but not totally convincing James.

"Just a quick meeting and then leg it back on the next plane," James said seeking some assurance the risks were minimal?

"Not quite, I want you to go by plane but use the one you now part-own with that building contractor friend of yours. We have to make it just a bit harder for our friends to easily track where you are. You will pose as just a normal businessman on a leisure trip with your mate."

James was feeling edgy, not just the fact that the other side had monitored his recent joint venture, but knew his boss wouldn't ask if it wasn't really necessary and that he was the best person to do it.

James would have been tempted to stay on for liqueurs but the bombshell news propelled him to finish straight after the coffee and head for home for it all to sink in. He had this premonition, not felt before, that this would be no routine trip, it didn't feel good.

Of course, on his return, his Mum and Dad were eager to know what happened at dinner in Baslow.

"The dinner was fine. I have been given a few days off and have planned a trip away for a break, this time with Andy to Prague in our plane. We have nurtured this crazy idea of tracking the Dam Buster raids and then go onto Salzburg and do the sites. It's a bit short notice but you know what Andy is like, once he has an idea in his head it has to be executed immediately. I was looking forward to a settled time around here for a bit longer," said James trying to make out he was reluctant to go, to which there was a grain truth.

"You are just missing your girlfriend", said his Mum teasing him for a response and an indication of how strong the relationship was and where it was heading.

"Possibly so, but all this travelling can be quite wearing," responded James.

"Well try working in a factory with a hundred hooligans for company and then come home with your hands cut to ribbons on all the sharp metal parts you are drilling, said his Mum in a mild rebuke. Little did they know he would rather take his chances with the hooligans than chance it with state sponsored lethal vicious thugs.

The following day, Tony called him into a spartan office in Nottingham comprising a table, two chairs and nothing else. Just blank white walls and ceiling lights. James guessed the previous tenants had just moved out judging from all the electric plugs pulled-out of their sockets in the wide-open work space outside. The new occupiers must be soon on their way given the main lights were operable.

"OK James, I know this is a bit of a bore but we have still the final act to play out. Here are your travel instructions; meet our Swiss friends and make out you are trying to find why the batch didn't work; fly back in your plane via Dresden and then refuel at Luxembourg so we know you are OK. Sometimes we have to do this stuff just to confuse our enemies, with no logical purpose in mind. It's all part of the game of deception."

James thought Tony seems to know everything even his mood. Nevertheless, he memorised the travel instructions and documents. Just to keep positive he said,

"OK chief, understood."

It was early December; James and Andy left Gamston Airport travelling light, except for a case packed with a smart executive suit and draped over by an Abercrombie and Fitch overcoat brought for both its casual business style and warmth. Miserably it coincided with James's 30th birthday.

It was quite a leg to get to Salzburg first and spend a couple of days there sightseeing the Castle and taking the tourist trips to Mozart's birthplace and the main sites.

The great attribute of flying your own plane is that you have to concentrate hard, helping to lockout those dark foreboding thoughts encroaching on

James's mind. Despite the dark mood, all went well and to plan. Helpful air traffic controllers making it easy for these newly qualified and inexperienced pilots. Fortunately, Andy and James had been trained at the East Midlands Flying School to exacting standards not just of the CAA but Bill the proprietor. Not for them the club airports, but a busy regional commercial airport to learn to fly. That's how Andy and James had met, James exercising a hidden passion for flying beyond motorbikes.

Flying to Prague was the most demanding of all the overseas trips they had attempted. Normally aerodromes are configured with runways running parallel and sometimes another running at a 30° offset to cater for differing wind directions. Prague is totally different, it is just like the sides of a square and on this particular day all the runways were being used requiring careful sequencing by the air traffic controllers and of course relying on pilots, including amateurs, doing what was expected. James was relieved Andy was his co-pilot because although the landing went straightforward, the taxing instructions took nearly a page of shorthand notes to know how to navigate across active runways and backtracks.

Finally drawing up to their allotted parking bay and stopping to do their shut-down procedures they were suddenly surrounded by three vans containing armed police and customs officers. James at first thought his premonition had proved right, until just two parking bays away, he spotted what was an unmistakable black and gold jet liner in the livery of the United States of America still displaying the star and stripes from the cockpit window. Ah, they just making sure we are kosha he thought. They climbed out of the plane, presented their documents and pulled out their limited luggage from the 'boot' in the back. All was fine when one customs officer asked,

"Are there any additional services you require?"

"Well, you could fill us up with AVGAS before we leave while we enjoy ourselves," he said naively.

"No gentlemen, services of a gentler and pleasing kind if you know what I mean," he added tapping his nose.

"No thanks, perhaps another time, we just want to see your fair city and meet some friends expecting us for dinner, but thanks for the kind offer," said James understanding fully the proposition and trying not to draw undue attention to themselves.

It still had to be explained to a naive Andy in the taxi to the hotel what additional services actually meant. Slavic ladies all seem to bear those exquisite forms of seductive females. High cheek bones and tall lithesome figures. They seem to come out of every doorway to tempt any passing lustful male. At least it appeared the Czechs seemed they were not on alert for 'interesting' recent arrivals. The plan was to have dinner at the hotel, get up early for breakfast and for James to meet his business associates over morning coffee while Andy went shopping for presents for the family as mementoes of their adventurous first long-leg trip on the Continent.

James's rendezvous was arranged in the main square in a café located almost directly opposite the famous astronomical clock tower containing the rotating sculptures and depiction of the sun and moon. In one sense it would be a place any tourist would head for but also an easy point to meet for a casual meeting. Arriving just on the hour of 11.00am coincided with the renowned display of this very old clock dating back to the 1400's. Momentarily, it distracted James from trying to identify once again his Swiss friends. He needn't have worried about locating them, he recognised a voice calling out his name; the swiss clock imitator.

"James, over here, a coffee and cake has been ordered for you."

Having done the formal greeting of shaking hands the coffee and gateaux duly arrived and everyone sat down in the cold sunshine, James grateful for his newly purchased overcoat. James opened the conversation heavily disguised as to the true objective of the meeting and kept to the remit that this was an internal review.

"Gentlemen you know why I am here. I know I am supposed to be doing an administrative task but just for myself have we identified the culprit who interfered with my luggage?"

"Not quite but we do know someone tipped off the Croatians that a foreign operator was exiting the frontier to Austria," said his cuckoo clock friend.

"The tip-off wasn't from home turf was it," asked James?

"Afraid so. You are going to have to do some navel gazing on this one," said cuckoo man.

"Oh, and by the way, the manifest contained their stuff in the hope I suppose it was a close match to ours apart from the additional extra.

"You have been more than helpful; thank you my friends our administrative objective has been achieved and you have confirmed I need to watch my back at home," said James with a knowing smirk.

"Let' have that coffee and perhaps a gargantuan piece of that delicious cream-filled gateau," interrupted cuckoo man bringing the meeting to an informal conclusion.

Just as the bill arrived James noticed someone sat on his own at another café just next to them. Perhaps to most people not unusual, but for James attuned to the Irish Troubles, someone sat on their own, dressed differently, out of the usual pattern in the surroundings, was something to note. Whereas everyone else were either couples or groups, mainly tourists in casual gear, this individual stood out like a painted clown in a busy railway station. Especially noticeable was the clear attempt to avoid accidental eye contact, especially as it would be difficult not to cast a glance in the direction of James's friends sitting at the precise angle, the very edge of the café seating area and facing away from the famous clock tower towards them. He concluded he was definitely being followed, but more sinisterly, two others in sharp suits joined the crowded throng of people sat at another café further away. You don't need three at a time in one place for effective surveillance, this was going to be a bit tricky.

James whispered to his friends,

"We have uninvited company; you pay the bill why I pretend to go to the loo and scarper by the rear door."

"Go ahead, if we can delay them somehow, we will," said cuckoo man.

James asked in German, in a slightly raised voice, for directions to the toilets as their waiter breezed by whilst also taking the bill for the others to pay. At the back of the restaurant he darted through the kitchen before anyone could notice left by the rear emergency door running like hell down a back street before it again joined the main tourist track where James slowed to a brisk walk.

He learnt later the delay tactics of his friends were to pretend they were fumbling around for the local currency to make up the full amount, one of them picking up James's overcoat as though they were expecting him back anytime son. His observers twigged though that either it was a decoy or James had a sudden attack of diarrhoea.

His pursuers must have been wearing leather metal tipped shoes because James, despite the distance, could clearly hear their collective clicks heading his way as they hit the stone pavement running at speed. The throngs of people were slowing James down, so he turned down a side street, stepped up the pace for some 200 metres and then dived out of sight first flat on his chest onto the pavement floor and then niftily rolled through a narrow gap in the wall falling gently onto a pile of coke stored in a cellar. He must have run or walked at least two thousand metres. It took some time for his pursuers to catch him up having split up at one point.

James sat motionless for at least twenty minutes trying hard not to disturb the nuggets of coke and to suppress his heavy breathing. He observed the shadows of the legs of his pursuers pass over the cellar glass aperture, watching them return in a slow walk but clearly unable to work out where their prey had gone to ground. James blessed that he had kept himself fit from his days as an article clerk; training with Notts AC. He recalled a film he had seen based on a true story of the pursuit of a spy in the same city during the days of the Nazis taking refuge as he had done, except then the prey was flushed out by flooding all the cellars. In all the mayhem he realised he had left behind his overcoat at the café as part of the subterfuge. Fortunate in the circumstances as it could have slowed him down.

He was wearing a dark grey suit so the coke marks weren't too obvious. Back at the hotel he arrived by the trade entrance, made his way to his room and cleaned up the best he could waiting for Andy. It was three in the afternoon when Andy strolled back with a couple of shopping paper bags that were quite bulky but didn't weigh much. He went to James's room with his beloved overcoat over his arm saying his friends had dropped it off in his room and left a note in a sealed envelope.

"Change of plan Andy, we fly to Luxembourg in two hours, I will explain later," said James.

"This morning before I went out, I prepared our planned route to Luxembourg so all we need is the latest weather and ATM's then we can go."

"There's no problem is there," asked Andy?

"No worries, it's just my boss has left a message that we must be in Luxembourg to pick up a parcel before we return to the UK. Sorry to be a pain, but hope you enjoyed a wander around as I did with my business colleagues," responded James.

Back at Prague airport the diplomatic cortège had already left and it was with some relief Andy was taking-off along one of the long runways heading for Luxembourg while James operated the radio and managed the navigation. There was no parcel at the Information Desk at Luxembourg Airport just a plain white envelope with James's name written on it. The message inside simply read,

"See you in London at your earliest convenience, Tony."

It may have been couched that way but James knew it really meant get your backside down to base by the quickest available means. As it transpired that meant continuing their flight as planned but for James to change travel plans and catch a train from Nottingham Midland Station to London St. Pancras as soon as they arrived back at East Midlands Airport. His pal Andy remarked whether his bosses ever allowed him any free time calling him down to the office at such short notice but then he did understand, he ran his own business and was not merely an employee like James.

As soon as James walked through the door Tony had an expression of concern and asked James to sit down, have a cup of tea and to give him a full report of what had happened in Prague.

"We are going to have to lie-low for a while, you and I, we are becoming too 'hot', said Tony mulling over the consequences.

"How do you mean," enquired James?

"I think they have identified you as a person of interest, and through you, me. Whilst they might be happy to have acquired the 'doctored nerve agent' they will be very interested in who formulated it. Ideally, they would like to interrogate me, or if not me, you."

James grasped immediately the significance of the conversation; he was a secondary target and Tony was their primary one. They were both high risk targets and needed to take care for their personnel safety even when in the UK; nowhere was now 100% safe.

"When you say lie-low what had you in mind," asked James trying hard not to show the 'jitters'?

"We have to disappear for a while, possibly for some years until the heat dies down," answered Tony.

"What does that mean?"

"Well for me they are talking about sending me to Washington as a scientific liaison officer seconded to the CIA. For you, something you might really enjoy, a stint back in South Africa where our secret service friends can keep you under their wing. They have an excellent intelligence service second only to Mossad so you would be very safe there. You might even contemplate marrying your sweetheart and start a family and live a normal life once more," Tony responded.

"When should we disappear," asked James.

"Not immediately but it will have to be soon, say two to three weeks," answered Tony.

James was struggling to take in the enormity of what Tony was saying. Not only a disappearance act but early entry into married family life, settling down and doing a normal job for years to come with no clear idea of what the long-term future might hold.

"Tony, I have the utmost faith in you and your desire to act in mine and your own best interests. I have experienced so much working with you, way beyond my wildest dreams. I will never forget the trust and confidence you placed in me. If I now need to disappear having done my national duty, then so be it. I had already started to think of my future with my fiancé and now you have given the kick up the backside I needed to take the plunge. I suppose I better start the wedding plans and take it from there."

Tony gave a forced smile realising that to a certain extent events had placed him and James in difficult situations. To a degree he was embarrassed that it had come to this dramatic turn of events. He then added,

"I have been in touch with your friend Bryan in South Africa and they have confirmed they would be delighted to have you back."

"Well I did enjoy working with them and it would be great to continue but this time on a more permanent basis," said James already reconciled to a new future path he hadn't altogether planned for.

At that point they both shook hands, gave each other a hug and looked forward to the day when they could again work together but perhaps more desk bound than active in the field missions.

Now it was back to Nottingham and work out how to break the news to his fiancé and then of course to the rest of his family. Fortunately, his future in-laws took the news in their stride and organised the wedding and even a reception within three weeks. James and his fiancé were married at their local church. Their marriage triggered the marriage of James's brother and sister eager for all to marry as a family before James went off to distant lands. James's parents were to be left to themselves in the house they had all lived together in a sort of organised chaos to be left as all their brood left in the quietness of a monastery with many happy memories. Jiver would no longer have to act as postal clerk.

9

The Falklands

James felt somehow, he had crossed over a kind of Rubicon. He returned to a conventional career; this time an accountant travelling abroad to a new appointment without an underlying agenda. All the exotic stuff left behind; a distant memory. It was as though it had all been a wild dream. He was married, suitcase in one hand and his wife held tightly with the other. Arriving at Jan Smuts Airport once more to meet Bryan and to introduce his new wife. He was sad to leave his family behind and break the link with Tony.

Since his last visit there were new personnel, but Fred and Duncan were still insitu. The head office had moved to Vereeniging, a town not that well known outside South Africa. Its main claim to fame was the site of the signing of the treaty for the ending of the Boar War; commemorated by a rather plain small brick building with a red corrugated iron roof, a feature on many houses in this mining area.

Forty miles to the north is Johannesburg surrounded by the many goldmines. James was use to those ugly coal slag heaps around the Nottinghamshire collieries but here the slag heaps were somewhat more attractive resembling sandy flat-topped sandcastles, enormous sand heaps glinting in the bright sunshine. On one there was even a drive-in open-air cinema.

The first month was spent in a hotel, then a move to a rented apartment in a district just a couple of miles from the centre of the town; Three Rivers. Every newly married couple faced the same traumatic changes; wrenched from their parent's home, finding a new place to live, putting in the basic furnishings and settling into a total new partnership. For James it was almost a joy to establish his independence and have the company of a wife in these different surroundings. Slightly to his surprise Sue settled like a duck to water. She had been brought up well, intelligent, social and not at all fazed by the minor challenges. The South Africans just adored her positive attitude and as a couple they were soon absorbed into a wide social circle.

James had a new boss too, Robin, who introduced him to the other accountants almost half of whom were South Africans and the others, like him, immigrants from the UK and Holland. Quite a mixed bag of humanity! They spent a few months in the Head Office before James was seconded to the Tube Making Division referred to as TOSA. The enormous factory situated halfway between the head office and James's rented apartment; perfect logistically.

TOSA was a vital supplier to the mining and farming communities for all their irrigation and pump equipment. The products ranged from those windmill pumps seen in many western films to six-foot gate valves controlling water and oil flows. They even assembled Honda diesel engines acting as emergency or mainline generators.

The re-introduction into accounting systems meant going back to basics; financial and cost accounting integrated into one coding system supported by sophisticated computerised systems. Reams of paper tabulations were spewing out massive chunks of data needing checking and processing. For the accountants their ultimate action were the reams of journal entries. The controls were extremely strict and highly disciplined. It was a full-time job just managing this veracious beast but then other challenges were thrown in. For example, a major reorganisation of all the manufacturing sites located onto one site and the cleared sites converted to distribution depots close to the end user customer.

It was not all work and no play. The South Africans love their sports especially rugby, cricket and football. James was determined to keep fit but running on the dusty verges of the roads was too risky. The company sponsored the local professional side so he asked if he could join the players in their training session. To his delight they were quite happy for him to join in. It coincided with the preparations for the start of the season so the training was geared to fitness and stamina building rather than honing their football skills.

James introduced himself to their coach dressed in his Notts AC green and gold tracksuit and was told to just follow the instructions and the others. There was a warm-up and then a series of sprint exercises involving progressively extended sprints at full belt and changes of direction. Sprinting was not James's forté but he did manage to hold his own. The session was closed by a jog of five times round the football pitch, the last one at full speed and the first one as a warm up. James just loped along with the rest but when it came to the full sprint, he left them all standing in his wake. At the end of the session the coach came over and said,

"Can you play football?"

"Well not as good as you guys, but I did play a season for my college team and in one game scored three hat tricks playing on the left wing."

"OK", said the coach, "Next time bring some football boots and we can assess what you can do."

James could never match the skills of the professionals, especially a certain Geoff Hurst he played against during a cup-tie. The coach did though suggest a different strategy than trying to match skills of opponents. He was instructed to run the opponents right back ragged for twenty minutes until he was shattered from the effort and then just push the ball passed him into any open space, run with it down the wing and try as best he could to put in a decent cross. He was to practice everyday crosses and running with the ball until he had some level of competence.

At matches Sue would tag along and prepare the cut oranges and hot tea for half-time; even with two very young children in tow. The football was highly competitive amongst the men but the women used the occasion for a good social get-together and chit chat. James just loved his new family life, his social and work friends and of course the country. To him it was just perfect. There was even talk of him filling in his education gaps, take a degree and then onto an MBA whilst still receiving a full salary. What more could he have wished for in fulfilling the ambitions of a modest working-class lad? But there was a fly in the ointment. Fatherhood does change your perspective on life and your responsibilities as a father. You can no longer just think of yourself; you also have to think of the well-being of others, and above all your family.

The apartheid system was for James something he found hard getting his head around. He had been aware of it before, as he was with other political and social system's he had no particular liking for. He didn't believe either his monarchist democracy was exactly a total paradigm of virtue. Why had his social class found it so, so difficult to make only the modest of ambitions work for them. Reasonable aspirations such as absence of severe poverty, a decent education, a nice place to live and some acceptable security shouldn't be beyond the reach of any citizen living in a highly-developed country.

Apartheid in foreign lands is portrayed in shorthand as racism of the worst kind. But on the ground, it was difficult to reconcile this with the absence of hatred between the many races. Some 'academic' Afrikaners post-rationalised the system with their version of man's development. This made the bizarre assertion that Africans were uncivilised because of the size of their brains, a notion shared by other Europeans!

'Black Africans' were disenfranchised from a democratic parliament, were subject to pass laws restricting where they could work and even disallowed from having a relationship across the various race barriers. You would think this would create a deeply held hatred but it wasn't evident in any mass sense. 'Black Africans' received free medical cover whereas whites paid privately, unemployment was almost non-existent, housing and electricity (where available) was free, children had free education and starvation was unheard of. Many of the women became nannies to Afrikaner children and were treated as surrogate grandmothers. They were trusted to ensure their children never came to harm. Some children were more attached to their black nannies than their natural white mothers. None of this made any sense to James. It wasn't until he recognised that whilst in the west it seemed highly racially driven, in fact it was tribal and that the Afrikaners as well as the African tribes were all determined to separate themselves culturally not just from Black ethnic Africans but also from other White English.

Whatever the resolution of the baffling conundrums to eventually emerge, it wasn't a lifestyle James felt he could allow to bear down on his family for too long. The decision had to be faced, either emigrate to Australia or North America. The pull of their families made it preferable they, however, returned to the UK. He hoped the several years of absence would have gone a long way to achieve the low-profile Tony had planned for James. Personal effects were all loaded into a large metal trunk, their excess household effects sold or given away and now James new family was prepared to return to the UK with the addition of one large suitcase.

James and Sue watched as the ship departed from Cape Town, Table Mountain disappearing to the horizon on the SS Oranje, but with their two additions, a toddler of three and a babe-in-arms of six months. They would spend the next

12 days heading north to Southampton adjusting to a different climate and a way of life that would now be foreign to them.

James never made contact with his previous lords and masters, under his own initiative, he set up temporary home with his in-laws and secured a job with an international conglomerate based in London. He started a new career much as before, concentrating on some minor head office roles, but then was asked to undertake more and more control rescue missions amongst the many subsidiaries losing management and financial grip on their businesses. To his surprise the UK systems were somewhat lax and lacked the sophistication he had become use to. No matter, his skills learnt in South Africa were being applied to good effect and with it a growing recognition amongst his peers he had special gifts for dealing with any troubled company.

After two years the importance of the work increased until one morning, he was called into the Deputy Chairman's office to be told he was being sent to Brazil. A man-made fibre plant was being offered for sale by an Italian Group and the board required a full investment appraisal. The project was complex. There were three languages to overcome, English, Italian and Portuguese. The Italians were notorious for keeping three sets of books; their internal version; the statutory version and those for the tax authorities. To make matters worse the accounts in Brazil were subject to inflation accounting. All this had to be converted to a UK version so a board could understand the history and the projections if the ownership was to change.

In a sense James was flattered his new company had expressed so much confidence in him to undertake such a major and important exercise. He had to remind himself that it wasn't that long ago he was doing sole trader accounts in a professional practice. In closing the discussion, the Deputy Chairmen did make a very surprising statement,

"Ronnie, you have done well with us and worked hard while you have been with us. It's time we gave you a bit of a rest. We think you deserve a couple of weeks sabbatical once your next project is completed. We have organised a guide to take you, before you return to the UK, on a four-wheel drive in a Land Rover down the west coast of South America all expenses paid. Your guide will be a man called 'Tony', who we are led to believe you already know."

Ronnie had so concentrated on the briefing making sure he had fully understood what was required that this reference to Tony threw him completely. Struggling what to say he admitted he knew a Tony, thanked his boss for thinking of him in such a way but admitted he was taken aback about an adventure he didn't know whether he was equipped to take. The Deputy Chairman went on to say,

"Don't worry, your friend Tony has asked if you could just pop over to his office where you have met before this afternoon and he will spend a couple of hours explaining the adventurous trip of a lifetime before you go home."

Tony's office was literally just down the road from his office in Hanover Square so James happily consented trying hard not to reveal a call from Tony was no idle adventure to gain a little R & R and a tan!

Nothing had changed, including the view of Marble Arch. Betty was her normal effusive self, hadn't changed a jot in her appearance and importantly still remembered the Jacob orange chocolate biscuits. Only Tony was missing, on his way in a taxi through the heavy evening commuting traffic from his ministerial office. In he bound, smiling bravely and saying,

"Hello young man, long time no see."

They gave both a hug, not a handshake, after all Tony was no longer the boss and James his subordinate.

"Have I got an adventure for you," said Tony.

There then followed a brief on the reason for the surprise meeting. Apparently, trouble was brewing in the South Atlantic. The Defence Secretary had decided, against military advice, to remove the only naval vessel based in the Falklands, giving an unintended notice of the UK's desire not to protect its far-flung dependencies. The military top brass took the view this would send an encouraging signal to the Junta in Argentina to mount an invasion and occupy and claim sovereignty over the islands. Worse still, intelligence was coming in that the French were in the course of shipping 20 Exocets missiles to Buenos Aries. These missiles made naval ships very vulnerable until counter-measures were developed. Tony had been working in his Department of State on such technology and had been trying to gain from the French how they worked to no avail.

James listened intently but then asked,

"So why are you telling me all this?"

"You are going to Brazil and if we are being tracked, we need to create a diversionary tactic that you and I are working in Brazil and then spending a short holiday together as old working pals. After dealing with the business in Brazil, which has government's full support by the way, you and I will journey down the west coast of South America to the most southern point of Chile, a stone's throw from the Argentinian border."

"And then what happens," asked James?

"You sight-see around Punta Arenas while I and a few SAS pals drop into the warehouse where these Exocets were delivered and stored in Santa Cruz. The security is very lax and we can be in and out in a few hours unnoticed," Tony now at full beam with his smile.

"Are you going to take them out", asked James.

"No, here's the cunning plan James".

"More cunning than the professor of cunning at Cambridge University?"

"Definitely, you will just love this one. We did ask the French how their guidance system worked and was told the guidance system was driven by a radar scanner sweeping in front of it until it identified a chunk of metal. It would have been useful if we knew for sure which direction the system swept the horizon, right to left or left to right. They told us right to left. I knew it was the opposite as they drive on the right and why would you drive off the road to hit an oncoming vehicle. We will soon know if I am right because with my SAS specialists in engineering, we are going to re-programme all the missiles to do the opposite. Unfortunately, those already on the ships we can't get at, but they will soon run out of 'ammo' should they do what we fear."

James was on the one hand relieved he wasn't being put at undue risk, he was just a passenger in this escapade but for Tony, given his lack of fitness and despite what he said, was literary walking into the lion's den.

"Couldn't the SAS do it themselves, they have the engineers and you can relegate yourself to a briefing role," asked James in his concern for his close mate.

"Possibly, but if they encounter a surprise, we need to deal with any issues on the ground there and then, it's too important to leave to chance", answered Tony.

"Now I am a married man I would probably have refused to entertain such an idea, but given it's you and I doubt I could live with my conscious if the worse prevails, I will do it," said James with somewhat of a heavy heart.

"Good man, I wouldn't have bothered you if I didn't feel it was important.

Within a week both were on a flight to Rio de Janeiro in a sombre mood. James had set to work at his Italian company for a week processing all the financial stuff while Tony did the sight-seeing tourist nonsense now dressed in shorts and a Bermuda shirt. To James's surprise the business side went well. Clearly the people in charge of the fibre-plant were highly competent but clearly concerned about their futures with a potential new foreign owner. The business was sound but James doubted it would make a good strategic fit. Yes, they were in the same business but with a completely different raw material source, a separate market and very little merger benefits, if at all. In a sense this made the work far simpler and straightforward to report back to his board. It had to be a resounding, No.

James had been worried that his normal forensic concentration had been disturbed knowing of the task remaining in hand. Leaving the factory with some trepidation he caught the flight from Rio de Janeiro to Santiago. They weren't going to travel the full length of Chile; nearly 2,000 miles was far enough. They booked into a hotel where all their new kit had already been placed in their room including medical kits, small arms, grenades and some camping stuff. This was going to be no walk in the park. The green Land Rover arrived the next day at 9.00am driven by a member of the embassy staff loaded with even more equipment. The Land Rover was equipped with satellite phones and locators so they could be tracked by GCHQ. Stuff had moved on since those Zambia days of old.

After breakfast James made a call home from the hotel bedroom just before he left, settled the bill and waited for Tony in the hotel reception area surrounded by potted palms and fans slowly whirling around above his head. He thought he could have started loading all the luggage onto their 4 x 4 but Tony had kept the keys and was still at breakfast taking in huge quantities of food as though it was the last decent meal for a week, which it turned out it was!

Initially the journey was on normal roads staying in the equivalent of two or three-star hotels enroute. Halfway the tarmac ran out and now they were travelling on minor roads and at times had to camp out under the stars. In a strange way this help to take the edge of the tension James was feeling deep down. No longer the gung-ho approach but a more measured appraisal of the risks. He recognised he was now a middle-aged family man. It was over the camp fire of the second night in the open night air that Tony opened up more on the mission.

"I can tell you now James that my military friends think the Government has made an enormous mistake in their foreign policy. Should General Gualtieri, in a fit of madness invade, the effort required to regain British territory would be at high cost and high risk. Success in their mission was an absolute imperative, turn the battle in their favour and could save hundreds of lives."

"Aren't we getting a bit too old for all this stuff even though I am just here as your cover," remarked James.

Tony didn't respond.

Chile is a beautiful country with a range of high snow-capped mountains running down its spine. For a few days James and Tony could put to one-side the challenge facing Tony at the end of the journey and used the time to enjoy the ride, the casual meals along the roadside, meeting the locals and a few cold beers in the evening to wash away the dust of the day. But at the end of the day time marches relentlessly on. Early on a Thursday afternoon they arrived in Plaza Munoz Gamero and made for the main hotel at the corner of the square. Parking outside they grabbed their personal belongings and extras to take to their room; the Land Rover parked in a nearby secure underground car park.

It was great to at last get under hot shower, change their clothes, unpack and stroll down to the bar. No phone calls home that could be traced, just two tourists experiencing an adventure. Tony ordered them a few beers and nibbles and both sloped to a corner booth to talk in coded fashion of the plan ahead.

"Well Tony, when do you expect your friends to arrive," asked James?

"Tomorrow and we depart for a couple of days the next day and leave you to take in the main sites."

Sipping their beers, they conversed for a couple of hours before moving into the hotel restaurant. Tony was no longer the jovial chappie; he knew how serious was the task in hand. It was agreed James would have a lie-in while the new group arrived at 08.00am making sure they never made close contact. The following day James couldn't avoid peering out of his hotel bedroom window watching Tony depart surrounded by six slim and not very tall young men leaving in two shiny black limousines. Locals must have assumed they were part of the criminal fraternity drawing undue attention which James thought they could well have done without. They were almost advertising their presence. He would still have his wits about him just in case foreign agents were operating in their field of activity.

The waiting around trying to work out what to do was excruciating for James. He almost wished he had gone with them, but that might have compromised their cover and now there was his family to think of.

Just when he thought he could relax and do the tourist thing strolling around viewing the old buildings and idly sitting in cafés he saw as he passed by a headline on one of the street vendors pile of newspapers, it read, 'Islas Malvinas Invadio'. General Gualtieri has had a mental storm. 'Buggerama', I hope Tony and his mates will be OK he thought to himself. The security may have been lax before but it is bound to be beefed up now.

James had never felt so anxious and nervous before. One afternoon he was so fraught he decided to sit in a seedy bar drinking several tumblers of the equivalent of gin and tonic gradually becoming inebriated to dull the pain and anxiety. He was beginning to gain attraction from some Latin ladies looking for rich pickings from a vulnerable tourist. It forced him to leave before their 'minders' turned up and made a fight almost impossible to avoid if he was to keep his wallet and possibly his life. He made for a Tapas Bar and enjoyed a selection of dishes that not only were they delicious but despite the gathering crowds the service was impeccable.

Still no sign of Tony so in the evening, rather than sit alone in his hotel bedroom, he frequented the bar. He post-rationalised that doing so would add to his alibi rather detract from it. What would ordinary tourists do alone in a foreign country, sit in their room and play a card game of solitaire? He did meet an American business man and engaged in idle conversation about their own countries making the occasion appear perfectly normal. Again, there were attempts to gain attention from some of the ladies of the night but he made out they were talking business and were not to be interrupted.

It was 10.00pm, just an hour after his casual acquaintance had departed for dinner in the town when Tony breezed through the door as though he had no cares in the world.

"Ah, Tony you are back. I was just about to turn in."

"No, my friend, not now, let's celebrate a great deal done," responded Tony eager to go out on the Town and have a slap-up meal but not quite the one at the Devonshire Hotel in Baslow variety.

"You must have heard the news," asked James?

"What news."

"The Argentinians have invaded the Falklands," answered James genuinely surprised he was totally ignorant of developments.

"We were just in time then," said Tony.

"The meeting went all to plan then."

"Sweet as a nut, the rations though were a bit to be desired though," said Tony.

Tony continued, "The proof of how well we have done will be seen in the next week."

A task force of a cobbled together naval convoy had been dispatched from Portsmouth and was heading for the South Atlantic. All-out war was imminent.

The battleship 'Belgrano' was dispatched from Buenos Aries to greet them but didn't get far. A nuclear sub laid in wait and sunk it before it could get within striking range. The Royal Navy was to taste the same medicine with hits to HMS

Sheffield and Coventry by Exocets. This was not going well. As in all wars there is a stage when the paperwork is filed away and the bloody engagements begin. Had Tony and his team succeeded? The first week it didn't appear so.

Back in London, James had nipped round from his office in Hanover Square invited my Tony to read a message sent by Admiral Sir Terence Lewin. They sat at the coffee table with a telex message simply saying 'Top Secret', No more problems by sea, their rockets have all gone squew whiff! Tony was almost in a state of high emotion with tears welling in his eyes.

"What does it mean," asked James?

"It means Bozzo, our plan worked, the guidance system was reversed, they shooting at themselves now. Who's a clever boy then?"

"You mean you didn't just make them miss but reprogrammed them to fire back at their own ships,' responded James.

"Precisely, that is what I call real cunning don't you think. Just like the professor of cunning but this time from Oxford University!"

James was delighted British lives had been saved but couldn't bring himself to rejoice in the deaths of others in a cold unforgiving sea, even though they were the enemy. It was a lot to take in. The paras and marines were able to gain a strong foothold on the islands and kettle the conscript army of the Argentinians into Fort Stanley where ultimately and thankfully they surrendered before any more lives were lost.

Tony promised that would be the last of their projects together and for the sake of themselves and their families he resolved there and then to resume a normal life, be left alone and let others take up the baton. They did promise one another to meet up somewhere in retirement, have a meal and a few drinks and be allowed to reminisce in their own company.

James said his goodbyes to Betty, gave her a hug, and then went home to continue working as a financial accountant in London.

10

From Russia with Love

Had James entered what is euphemistically termed 'a middle-age crisis? Life had become so normal and so predictable. Up at 05.30am, breakfast, the daily ritual of the motorbike ride into Central London. He began to know intimately the route, predicting where the traffic jams wound be and how to position yourself on two wheels to weave your way through uninterrupted. The same journey back, in reverse order, to try and see his children before they went to bed after dinner. The sheer mundane monotony only broken by the need to stay on at your desk until his ultimate boss, the Deputy Chairman, decided when he should go home and you were relieved of your duties for the day. Yes, the work was at a high level, pressured and highly disciplined, but the brain became numb and engaged the automatic mode to make it through the day.

It's true there were days of excitement, like the Lancaster House Independence negotiations on Rhodesia. Park Lane had been completely shut down, waiting for the diplomatic motorcades to pass by, James was invited to ride down the pavement for the entire length of Park Lane by a thoughtful police officer as long as he was careful. Then there was the installation of the first scanning machines at Waitrose supermarket. The regular weekly Saturday morning food shop made much more efficient once the bugs had been taken out of the system. The weekends were always the best. You get to play and have fun with the children and at last be able to have a normal, non-work conversations with your friendly neighbours.

Mike and Pat their next-door neighbour in the village of Copthorne were gems. The relationship with their new neighbours, however, didn't get off at first to a good start. Before James moved in with his family, he went on his motorbike 'solo' to turn on the electricity and gas and allow the house to warm-up for a few days while the furniture was delivered before finally moving in. On the day of their arrival all the family were sat in their lounge getting ready to do that first food shopping trip. Suddenly they saw a man walking up and down on the front lawn. Peering through the front door they saw Mike mowing their grass.

"I thought I would give you head start because you will be too busy settling in," said Mike switching off the electric mower and looking across to formally introduce himself.

Then came his wife, Pat, with a tray of sandwiches and cakes followed by several mugs of tea. James thought southerners are not supposed to be friendly as people in the north would make you believe. Until much later were they made aware that Mike and Pat were so relieved that a Chapter of the Hell's Angels wasn't moving in as they had feared, but a normal young family.

Mike was a do-it-yourself fanatic with access in his job to all sorts of specialist tools not found in the general hardware stores. James serviced his own bike so tools to take out circlips, delicate files for the intricate fitting of replacement parts or an instrument to balance the twin Ventura carburettors; Mike had access to them all. Any maintenance jobs required around the house; Mike would be a fountain of advice. He did come unstuck once when he fitted a cat flap to his back door. For his cat, the measurements were precise and perfect and worked well. What he hadn't allowed for is that his pet corgi dog would try and replicate the cat's entry. One day Pat came around in a terrible panic with the dog wearing the remains of the cat flap around its neck. It wasn't helped by James and his wife bursting into fits of uncontrollable laughter at the comic sight.

Their neighbour the other side was completely different version. Paul and Sue were outward going people, especially Paul. He was a county class golfer and managed the affairs of a Middle East Airline with direct access to the Emir. Their new found relationship was soon firmed up after a day to the country fair in the village. All the normal crazy stunts were there, including welly throwing and tossing bales of hay over a high wire. Paul soon spotted the beer tent housing 20 different varieties of craft beers. While the ladies sauntered around the various displays and exhibitions, admiring the various farm animals, Paul and James decided they would try a sample of each beer from the 20 barrels on display; a half pint at a time. By late afternoon it was time for James to go home for dinner and take the children back. His wife was still waiting for the judging of the cattle and sheep, so James left Paul in the beer tent, went to search for his wife and then made for home. Early the next morning there was a frantic knock on the door, it was Sue from next door.

"Do you know where Paul is, he never came home last night?"

"Didn't he come home with you yesterday?"

"No, I couldn't find him and thought he was still with you so I came home alone."

James was just having a quick breakfast before going off to work but put on his motorcycle jacket and went back to the country fair site where Paul was last spotted. Everything had been cleared away so James walked around the massive open field and soon found Paul propped up behind a large oak tree fast asleep!

And so, for a year, life was particularly normal and James was gradually being sucked into the middle-class life he was so enjoying. The work might have been mind-numbing but the social lifestyle was fantastic. Sociable neighbours, easy access to London and the South Coast, and for the annual holidays to the continent, easier and rapid access to all the ferry ports. The children were settled into the schools and making new friends. James had resigned himself to a quiet and contented life. Just earn enough to get by and that would be enough.

Eighteen months went by following the same pattern; until that is, the arrival of a certain Lucy Poliskia. She was a new recruit to the accounting department adding highly-skilled resources to a rapidly growing conglomerate. She came with first class credentials. A PhD in economics, chartered accountant, mastery of three languages and above all looking as though she had stepped off the pages of Vogue magazine. She was good to have around, nice on the eye and excellent when trying to grasp complex financial issues. She knew best how to analyse masses of data for the main board to understand. James was able to strike up a good working relationship because for him she filled the wide educational gaps he had missed out on. But for her that wasn't enough. James sensed she was subtly coming onto him. Why he couldn't fathom. He was happily married with a wife and children he adored. He wasn't exactly a Cary Grant, full of charm with looks to match. He wasn't exactly ugly either but he didn't feel he warranted the growing close attention.

Whenever he was alone in his office, she would make a point of suddenly appearing. James thought at the Christmas Party she was about to make her move when one of the main board directors, just in time, breezed in and decided to stay for a while munching a selection of the warm sausage rolls, drinking a few beers and warming his backside on the hot plate that had just been turned off. Lucy was not dressed exactly casually; she was wearing an almost see-through evening dress that had all his male colleagues in a bit of a lather.

Around the corner from Hanover Square is Oxford Street. As Christmas was closing in, James decided to make a call into the Selfridges departmental store and see if he could spot a nice present for his wife. Talking to one of the assistants at the perfume counter a voice came from behind,

"Don't turnaround now, it's Tony. Meet me at McDonalds, near Marble Arch in 30 minutes, it's vital I talk to you."

James continued the conversation with the sales assistant as though nothing had happened and purchased a small bottle of Chanel No. 5 for her to wrap as a present. He put it into a small green Selfridges bag, walked around the ground floor a little longer trying to ensure there was no other person watching him. Then he made for McDonalds, ordered a Big Mac, and sat on one of the window ledge seats leaving his overcoat next to him to reserve a spot for Tony.

In a few minutes Tony turned up clutching a Double Big Mac, fries and a large coke.

"Keep looking out of the window and don't make out you know me, we maybe being followed," said Tony raising the level of intrigue to heights that made James very uncomfortable.

"Your friend Peter Voss is about to engineer you losing your job. A member of the KGB is trying to compromise you, entice you into a hotel in Mayfair and for you to dispense a sample of our Dubrovnik product into one of their rogue agents gone native. Two teaspoons full, disguised as sugar into his tea. It is planned you will be left there with the body, your pockets contaminated with the stuff, as it were 'holding the baby' while waiting for the emergency services to arrive," said Tony.

"The person you have in mind doesn't happen to be called Lucy by any chance," James beginning to put the dots together?

"Precisely the one; you are progressing in your old age," commented Tony.

"Remember, what she doesn't know, but you do, is that our product isn't as active as she thinks, so it is going to get complicated," remarked Tony.

"Our subterfuge is about to be blown apart and as a result we are going to have to keep you away from the authorities, change jobs and disappear from London. I am not sure the Ruskie's have yet worked out how you are implicated with me, but it won't take long," Tony continued whilst James contemplated his new found cosy life was about to implode.

"What do you want me to do, shall we tell Special Branch to stop it before it happens," asked James?

"No, I want you to play along and see if you can confirm the target and that he is who we think he is, there is at this stage no innocent British life at risk."

"And what do I do about my job?"

"Next week I have got you an interview with a man, all you need to know is called Tom at the RAF Club on Piccadilly."

"So, Lucy is a licensed killer?"

"Just as you are, but were never required to exercise yours."

"Order a drink, I will leave and get in touch later."

The conversational exchange must have lasted all but ten minutes but James's world had just collapsed in tatters at his feet. The questions he had no time to asked were now flooding his brain. The Ruskie's are going to be as sore as hell and start looking around to practice their vengeance. How does he explain this to his family? What's the new job interview about? Will he have to resign before he can move? This was turning into one big awful mess. He felt as though he was turning into a fugitive from the clutches of the Mafia thirsting for his blood.

Then a further thought put a shiver down his spine. Lucy crossing his path was no coincidence. Peter Voss was planning a bad end for him. Not only had he to disappear but he needed to ensure, through Tony, he was well off the radar screen to avoid Peter Voss tracking him down again. Where he was to go, only Tony should know, and then only in case it was necessary for Tony to provide protection in the future and access to state resources. The bike ride home was not the usual routine. Fortunately, the demands to be alert in the commuter traffic at least helped him not to dwell too much on his plight.

He decided not to broach a pending change of plan to his wife until matters had crystallised a little more. First had to be the meeting with Tom, what was the interview for, when and could it be held secret? The weekend beckoned allowing James to be surrounded by some normality while he had time to absorb the magnitude of the events unfurling. All the family social activities took on a sharper edge. Each minute, each second, James measured as precious and tried very hard not to reveal to those close to him the dark thoughts circulating in his head.

The Monday morning routine came around as usual and it was off on the morning commute. It didn't take long before the object of the conversation with Tony appeared in his office. It was approaching Wednesday lunchtime on a bright sunny day but still James was hunched over his desk checking the final draft for the monthly financial board report to be out by Thursday so the directors could read it over the weekend. Lucy's head popped round the door to say,

"How about a walk into Grosvenor Square to eat our sandwiches and have a coffee. I made a thermos of coffee up in the kitchen we could take with us. I could do with some fresh air being stuck in this building all day."

James recognise this was possibly the queue that Tony had predicted and that James, who may have previously made an excuse that he needed more time on the board report and stay in, had to play along.

"Good idea, it's a bit stuffy in here at the moment the heating system and climate control doesn't seem to be working that well," it never did but it wasn't likely that such a spurious inaccuracy would be challenged. James wondered how could, what seemed to be a totally innocent invitation by a work colleague, lead into what Tony feared. But as instructed James just went along with it.

The short walk in the bright winter sunshine to Grosvenor Square proved quite an enjoyable stroll. There were people exiting their offices and no doubt heading for Oxford and Bond Street to do some Christmas shopping. The old black cabs were busy plying their trade amongst the busy traffic, only the odd one now and again denoting they were available for hire. It was cold and crisp and as long as you had a hat and a pair of warm gloves the weather wasn't too challenging. James and Lucy chatted away as they strolled along making way for the odd pedestrian trying to rush through the crowded pavement. The talk was mainly of office gossip and James having the chance to ask whether Lucy felt she had now settled in being the latest recruit. There was even a chance to make fun of their bosses.

Surprisingly there was a park bench available in the gardens across from the American Embassy. The sun was so bright that, out of any chilling wind, the need to wear gloves while eating your sandwiches proved unnecessary. The flask had two stainless steel screw top lids doubling up as cups. As their coffee steamed into the air and sat away from the main traffic noise James felt quite good that he had decided to have a walk outside. All seemed perfectly normal until Lucy said,

"Sorry to be a pain but I must go to the toilet I forgot to go when we left. I will ask if I can use their toilets in the Mayfair Hotel over there. Could you keep an eye on the flask?"

"No problem, take as long as you like, I will stay here in the sunshine," responded James.

Lucy clutched her handbag and walked off to the Mayfair hotel dressed in her black fur trimmed coat. James rapidly deposited the paper debris, emptied the dregs from the cups and took the flask as he waited for Lucy to enter the hotel. He followed her to the entrance and saw her walking straight into the main reception but instead of turning for the toilets turned in the opposite direction to a lounge area making for a man sat at the small table with tea and the remnants of some cakes still on a side plate. An Aspidistra plant was a useful camouflage for James to keep out of sight and for him to observe what happened next.

The suited man with blond hair and thin gold rimmed spectacles greeted Lucy and immediately took out of his inside pocket a thick brown envelope, passed it to Lucy who then quickly dropped it into her cavernous handbag. The man made some remark, left his belongings on the seat and started walking in James's direction only to walk just 10 metres away past him arriving at the gent's toilets. Once he was inside James glanced back at the table to see Lucy take-out a thin glass phial having first put on some plastic gloves, empty a few drops onto the sugar cubes, place the glass phial in a nearby bin along with the plastic gloves. She picked up her coat, waited momentarily for the man to return. They chatted briefly and in the course of the conversation he picked up three of the sugar cubes in a teaspoon and gently lowered them into the china cup. Stirring slowly as the conversation continued and then the moment came, he took a couple of gulps.

For Lucy these seconds seemed an eternity. She had planned to be on her way by now hoping James would still be sat at the bench and would not see her depart the same way she had arrived. She had deliberately positioned James facing away from the hotel at the selected park bench. James would eventually realise there was an unplanned delay and come looking for her. Timed correctly he would walk in just as the results of the evil deed took effect.

This was all taking too long, not a flicker of a reaction from her friend apart from a minor grimace as though the tea was unexpectantly too hot. She panicked and left, bid farewell and departed. James quickly back-tracked to the park bench and made out he was about to come over as Lucy stepped outside the hotel. As Lucy exited, he gave a wave and Lucy noticing him in the distance turned into his direction.

As James wandered over to the pedestrian crossing on the way back to the office, Lucy opened up first,

"Nothing worse than the need for a natural break and wondering where you could go, even in London," said Lucy cool as a cucumber.

"I agree, I tidied up and was about to come over anyway as I need to get back for that pending board report hoping I hadn't missed you," said James.

"We must do this again sometime," said Lucy as calm as anything, believing no doubt she had just killed a man, even if delayed, as anticipated.

"Yes, it was quite nice for a change not stuck at our desks," responded James wondering what is going to happen next.

That evening, after seeing the children of to bed and kissing them goodnight he turned the television on for the London News and nothing! It seems no one had mysteriously died that night at a Central London Hotel. All that possibly could have happened is the mystery hotel guest required a second visit to the gent's toilet for a grumpy stomach and nothing more. The following day was the meeting after work at the RAF club to meet Tom. James told the doorman who he was and instantly the doorman said,

"Tom is expecting you; I will show you into the bar."

There were only two people at the bar Tony and another man James guessed was Tom. Playing the game, he approached both and asked if either of them was Tom making it clear he wasn't going to make it obvious he knew Tony already.

"I am," came the answer from Tom the stranger.

"Could we all just adjoin to that table over there for a quiet drink; James, I would like to introduce you to Tony who is looking for a bright young man to work in a brewery as their finance director," said Tom.

Tony kept up the pretence and made no mention of James. Tony went through the job role, specification and importantly the main terms of employment. The vacancy was immediate due to the internal promotion of the present incumbent. James made it known he was under a month's notice but often this was waived for senior personnel moving out and would try his best to keep the notice period as short as possible.

The whole process was surreal and unlike any normal interview. An already printed and completed job offer and contract of employment were produced requiring only James's signature.

Within two weeks James find himself in a northern brewery starting his six-week induction programme. The sale of their house went just as quick and a new house purchased only 12 miles away from the brewery so that the children's schooling would not be unduly disrupted apart from the trauma of a major move and making new school friends. His wife's in-laws filled the space between the moves. James had gone to ground, moved away from the City and hopefully removed himself from the limelight.

It took a year to properly settle in again but James and his family managed to resume a normal life despite desperately missing his neighbours who were quite shocked he was moving so soon. He wasn't to know this time this would be their last house move before James finally retired.

In a strange way the fact that James was working in a brewery and not a standard manufacturing company or retail group allowed them to settle-in better. Everything was new and different. The social side of the business, given its nature, made life fun again. James could put behind situations where literary lives were at risk. The need to enter restaurants with your back to the rear wall, checking on each new entrant. Casting an eye over a crowd picking out the 'mis-fits' and avoiding advertising yourself or where you might be going. None of this appeared any longer necessary. Just going into a pub or for a meal with friends was a joy he had forgotten.

The lingering question was how long before the Ruskie's after a failed assassination checked their nerve agent's stocks and started making assumptions closer to home. At first, they would question the efficacy of the delivery by their young agent. They would try again but with some other lethal cocktail. Of course, there would be the usual disinformation by MI6. They would feed the line police forensics had detected high concentrations of minute particles of an unknown agent at the hotel requiring its temporary closure. The concentrations were too small for them to verify exactly what the substance was that made a number of diners fall ill and to inform the authorities. All the time trying to point to a delivery problem and the concentrations administered. They would confirm it was not food poisoning but some visitor contaminating the hotel with a virus which had now been thoroughly cleaned and posed no further problem. At some stage though if someone would decide if it was a stock problem, rather than a delivery one, that's when the fun could start.

Nothing appeared in the national press just the London Evening Standard. Just two months' later, however, the balloon went up. A Russian dissident took ill in the very same hotel and died within a couple of weeks. This time it was from a radioactive isotope traceable all the way back to Moscow. This was the clue that they had determined their nerve agent was useless and no doubt now were looking for blood. Tony being the prime target. James was probably seen as a side-kick and perhaps an innocent carrier but just might be used as a route to Tony. Life was about to get nervous and twitchy.

James never checked back to either Tony or whether Lucy was still around. That could cause more problems than it would resolve. No, just keep your head down and hope for the best. The Department would decide to make contact if this proved necessary. But everyone is human. Complacency can set-in, the guard allowed to be lowered, the standard precautions abandoned. Then just what happens in a heavyweight boxing contest, out of nowhere a killer blow and the lights go out. You awaken dazed and confused trying again to make sense of your surroundings.

11

Betrayed in Warsaw

The public perception of accountants is that they lead predictable and boring lives. In truth, those in senior positions hold a great deal of power and influence over the organisations they work for. This is probably also true in government; what Prime Minister would countermand his Chancellor of the Exchequer? Such an event would inexorably lead to losing their positions. So, it is in public companies. The tentacles of the finance men run wide and deep. The power of the manager stems from his ability to influence decisions carrying a financial impact. A finance director can neutralise a management decision by just withdrawing the economic power they wield. Therefore, such men have to act highly responsibly and be aware and alert to all the issues that could impact on the decision-making process.

James couldn't argue his new role was boring. Yes, operating the accounting systems and ensuring no 'sticky fingers' attached themselves to the monies belonging to shareholders could be mind-numbing but at the executive level the tasks to be overcome could be very challenging. To do the job properly and communicate effectively required the CFO at time to act as though he is a schizophrenic. What one person believes is entirely rational a CFO may view as utterly delusional. He may at times have very strong, tough, uncompromising and cruel antipathy to his subordinates. Show no emotional response, just a cold hard stare would normally suffice. Then on other occasions he'd gently educate a person on their weakness, instil great motivation delivered in a humorous almost playful demeanour. The really good ones can take such posturing to such extremes that no one can fathom the man behind the two masks. James's past life helped him to take such matters as a normality to both extremes.

No one year was the same as any other, there would be some major initiative and set of demands to meet. They came in a variety of forms. First there was a marketing promotion on his arrival that could have sunk the total business or at least damaged it over several years before it could recover. Developments of brands and new more efficient filling lines using plastic PET bottles to meet the insatiable needs of the major supermarkets. A major acquisition, the first the brewery had achieved against the national competition in over 50 years. A thriving export business to of all places Russia; and the USA. On a purely financial basis there was the tax avoidance schemes saving literally millions of pounds to the company's coffers. If that wasn't enough external impacts such as a coal miner's strike disrupting both the economic and social fabric of their trading region. James took it all in his stride even the promotion to CEO despite knowing he always felt better acting as a number two and particularly as he didn't wish to raise his public profile. This presented a challenge of reformulating the whole of the main board and creation of new strategies under the direction of the key shareholders. All this in just two short years.

At the weekends and at home, James kept himself busy living a comfortable middle-class lifestyle. A nice four-bedroom home with double garage and paved driveway, education of his three children in a local private school before they shot off to the various universities of their choice and a developing band of social friends. Every summer all the neighbours would hold a barbeque on the open stretch of land opposite their houses bordered by a picturesque babbling brook. As a communal initiative they had a rota of the tasks needed to create an open manicured lawn including the collection of the leaves dropped by the several birch trees. In the winter and just before Christmas there would be a rotation of couples visiting each other's houses to drink mulled wine, taste the mince pies and have a good gossip.

For most chartered accountants this would all have been more than enough. A decade or two of this would see them drift into quiet retirement and working in their allotments, building model planes or scenic train sets mixed in with a few doses of reading and walking in the countryside to balance everything up.

James still retained 'an itch' for the old excitement. The national challenges and life-threatening risks should a mission go awry. He had to discipline himself that those 'games' were now over. Leave it to the younger men and those much brighter Oxbridge graduates he thought in order to rationalise his inner frustration. He would have to content himself riding in long-distance charity rides for the military over gigantic hills and in the foulest of weathers, adventurous motorcycle trips. Or, such activities as swimming amongst the sharks or repairing a 'combi' in an African Game park while a white rhino grazed just 50 metres away and what else might be lurking in the long grass. In the African bush the wild animals considered those in 4 x 4's as meals on wheels!

He had kept a casual eye on the outside world noting the Russian Empire was crumbling. Satellite communist states were showing signs of rebellion and were no longer tolerating direct control from Moscow. A wall in Berlin had been built as a gesture of securing the outer frontier but resistance was becoming ever more futile. To James the whole edifice was about to sheer off just as a chunk of ice breaking from a glacier in Antarctica, whole countries moving slowly to freedom and democracy. He had a desire to see events in the Eastern Bloc first-hand and what was happening, but reconciled himself he should act responsibly and not entertain such thoughts.

Fiddling with his gold propelling pencil around his fingers like a poker player at one of those Las Vegas Casinos the group's buying director was running through the various initiatives he was considering triggering to lower the group's input prices and thereby enhance the already excellent profitability.

James had to admit to himself he was only half engaged when suddenly his mind was switched to full alert by a suggestion that 50% of the breweries glass supplies should be changed from local UK suppliers to the new factories springing up in Poland. It was the next statement that really got him going. It was necessary to undertake a feasibility study and visits these factories before a major change could be enacted.

James interrupted the flow and said,

"This could be quite a risk for us if the proposed new suppliers don't measure up."

This broke the meetings flow and was a somewhat surprise response to the group's buying director. He was only asking for a 50% change which could easily be reversable if the gradual implementation was showing signs of going wrong after a rigorous due diligence series of checks. But he didn't realise that James had hidden motive revealed by the next statement.

"I could do with a foreign trip for a change, I would like to come with you and test the opportunity first hand," said James.

The buying director was going to have to get any change endorsed by James anyway so no better way of doing that by involving him right from the start and then the board approval would be a 'slam dunk' with James behind it so much was his influence.

"It's been awhile since I have driven on the continent. I could drive through Germany over a few days and meet you in Warsaw and then go together to the plants. You could go fly direct from Heathrow," suggested James.

James wasn't going to travel the whole distance by car. He thought he would make his way to Hanover by plane, hire a car at the airport and then drive to

Warsaw at the hotel they would stayover for a night before the business trip really started.

James was tingling with excitement as he left three days in advance with the tantalising prospect of a visit beyond the iron curtain and a crossing at Checkpoint Charlie no less in Berlin. He readily had his visas arranged for him in the UK and with £500 of traveller's cheques and a UK Passport off he set. The autobahn from Hanover to the border crossing into East Germany at Helmstedt was straight forward enough. His documents were inspected, duly stamped without fuss in the office while two frontier guards checked over his vehicle for any contraband. The offer of a bottle of Scotch whiskey no doubt eased the administrative process.

Entering East Germany was quite a cultural shock. The towns seemed to be simply made up of drab concrete apartment blocks, the few cars were mainly Trabants throwing out a long trail of blue exhaust smoke mixed in with horse and carts for carrying the heavy stuff. It was quite a feat to discover where the shops or hotels were, given the absence of any signing just small plaques at the side of doorways. Petrol stations were constructed from merely corrugated roofs on simple steel girder frameworks and two or three petrol pumps selling either diesel or petrol. The people all seemed old and shuffled around the streets in the drabbest of clothes. The only relief from the lack of colour were the red stars endorsed on all the military stuff parked in large tarmac areas visible from the road. They included helicopter, lorries, tanks and field artillery guns.

James pressed on and thanked he had had the foresight to fill his tank with diesel before crossing the border having seen the long queues at the pumps. His first stopping point would be Magdeburg and then access to West Berlin to crossover to East Berlin via Checkpoint Charlie. The scenery may have been drab but in a strange way he felt excited to be in an area so recently indelibly marked in modern history.

Despite its connotations as the frontier of East and West, Checkpoint Charlie was nothing more than two control points. One manned by some GI's at one end and Russian guards at the other. No whisky this time, he was just ushered through with a beckoning hand and he was on his way through the rest of East Germany and then to the Polish border. In all the excitement he had forgotten to eat or even have a coffee so decided to pull in at the next petrol station and see if he could find some food. The queue at the pumps was just four cars in length, and in the wait, he asked for directions to a restaurant or café for somewhere to eat in the best German he could muster. The driver in the car waiting behind spoke perfect English having instantly recognised the accent and pointed to a non-descript shop at the corner of a street.

Entering the shop, the door triggered a bell above the door, a reminder of his childhood visiting the corner shop of his grandparents either for some sweets or as a special treat delicious home-made ice-cream. The owner was delighted to meet him and the chance to meet a westerner and no doubt access to some valuable marks or dollars, worth far more to him than the official exchange rate. Instead of a ten-minute stop it turned into nearly an hour but was more than compensated by the owner making up some fresh cheese sandwiches, biscuits and a large cup of steaming black coffee. Despite the simplicity of the meal James enjoyed both the encounter and a few moments to have a tasty snack despite the sparsity of the food available.

The strangeness of the environment began to fade and he convinced himself that he should take-in every moment as this was an experience, he was unlikely to repeat. The road to Warsaw was flat as a pancake and the roads began to deteriorate. The main road was metalled over with several potholes but all the by-roads were just dusty tracks probably leading to a small hamlet or farmhouse. Rapid progress couldn't be made since every few miles there would be a horse-drawn cart. It isn't the oncoming traffic that delayed his passage but the need to navigate around the carts who took up two thirds of the road and you needed to avoid steering into a drainage ditch at the side of a field.

Most people in the UK had never experienced being out in open country completely on your own with just your wits to ensure you were on track. James had remembered travelling along the roads of South Africa watching the sun descend to the horizon on the one side and the shadow of his car stretching gradually to the horizon in the other direction. The feeling of being alone was profound. Poland was much the same interrupted by several sightings of peasant farmers in the fields or as nightfall began to fall, the twinkling of lights in far-off dwellings giving some comfort he wasn't completely alone and at the mercy of the elements.

As luck would have it, the need to drive purely on his headlights subsided as he entered the outskirts of Warsaw. The next challenge was to find his hotel. He knew he had to head for the Vistula River along the Aleja Solidarnosci. The hotel would be somewhere off to the right. A couple of times he stopped for directions and at the second stop was given directions in perfect English. This time the entrance to the hotel was rather grander with a Romanesque frontage that wouldn't have seemed out of place in Rome. The concierge at the front asked him for his car keys, emptied the car of luggage and beckoned him to make his way to the reception while the car was securely parked elsewhere.

From the spartan surroundings of East Germany this was somewhat better. He decided to park himself at the hotel bar for the next hour waiting for the arrival of his colleague due anytime from his flight from London. A message was left at reception to let his associate know where he could be found for a drink before dinner. The hotel was full of foreigners and clearly had been designated a tourist hotel, the locals confined to the grubbier establishments. A sip of gin and tonic accompanied by the obligatory salted peanuts just made life seem so much more civilised. He missed his colleague's arrival but after 45 minutes there was a tap on the shoulder and the easily recognised voice of his colleague Frank said,

"Ayupp siree, you made it then".

This was Frank using his Nottingham slang to bring a sense of normality to this strange new environment they had both been plunged into. A couple of aperitifs and they were both ready for meal.

Over the meal Frank slipped James a list of the organised visits, the addresses, key personnel and contact details. Each factory had organised picking them up, ferrying them to the factories no more than 60 miles away and to return them to the hotel the same day. Once out of Warsaw you were soon out in open country on endless roads through enormous forests. Sat in the back of the car James couldn't help but ponder on those poor souls sent to this barren land to the so-called 'work camps' to ultimately die in this desolate landscape. In winter it must have been a living hell. These melancholy moments were dispelled by Frank briefing James on the visit and rehearsing what the deal he was looking to secure.

Suddenly out of nowhere would appear several enormous factory sheds obviously built recently housing hundreds of workers. No housing could be seen so they must have all been shipped in by bus given the absence of any cars other than the managers. Each visit began to blur from one to the next and it became difficult recalling the characteristics of each without reference to notes and some minor point of differential observation. Even the canteen meals were the same; pork with loads of cabbage and potatoes.

Frank had done his homework and at the end of each day was able to agree a scale of shipments, the prices and delivery dates. The only material conditionality was that the level of shipment breakages would not exceed 1% of the total shipments for the dispatches to be accepted on arrival and the international bill of lading authorised for payment in US$. Little did James know the arrival bit he was never going to be able to accomplish. There is always a sting in the tail.

After a full five days the business side of the trip was complete and Frank and James decided to visit the Old Town of Warsaw and sample an authentic Polish meal in one of their best restaurants. Along with local wines they both had an enjoyable meal, possibly too much to drink and some conversations with the local natives eager to know more about the western world. The next day Frank was to catch the 11;30 return flight to London while James organised the return of his car duly filled with diesel for the return to Hanover. It was already late November; the nights were closing in and the weather decidedly chillier even by normal Polish standards.

After a hearty breakfast, as best continental breakfasts can deliver, his car keys were handed to him on the forecourt after his luggage had already been deposited in the boot. The difficult bit of navigating had been overcome and all that was required was to take the same route back but perhaps this time take it a little faster if he could. The first couple of hours went well and he was soon nearing the crossing at the Polish border. Some sprinkling of snowflakes hit his windscreen but rapidly thawed and were cleared by his windscreen wipers of his Mercedes. Out into the barren countryside with the traffic materially thinning the snow began to come down in earnest. For about an hour he didn't meet any traffic until he saw through the white blizzard made more pronounced by his headlights a horse and cart coming the other way.

A little late unfortunately, forcing him to manoeuvre, the nearside of the car went onto what he thought was a minor grassy bank. Passing the horse and cart the nearside wheels suddenly dropped down and there was an almighty bang as the car caught what turned out to be a large rock hitting the underside of the car. He managed to turn in the wheels to return the car under its own momentum back onto the road and stopped. Keeping an ear open for any traffic he put on his overcoat, placed a car mat from the rear passenger seat onto the ground and had a look underneath. He could clearly see the scrape marks but no obvious damage except for a steady drip of engine oil form the engine sump. The force of the strike must have opened a gasket seal allowing for oil to escape. He calculated that at the rate of loss he probably only had 150 miles before the sump would run dry and as a result the engine seize up.

There was nothing for it but to try and get help from a nearby farmer and telephone for assistance, that is if he had a telephone. To make matters worse it was proving more difficult to define where the road actually was. There were now no snow tracks from other vehicles not even telegraph poles to give some indication of the lie of the road. Just as he was about to get back into the car, he heard a tractor coming from behind with its distinctive chugging diesel sound. He ran up the road in order to wave him down and to prevent the back of his car being ran into.

What good fortune, the farmer immediately assumed James had broken down, he too looked under the car and then beckoned James to follow him for the next few miles before he turned off the road, which by now was covered in three inches of snow. How the farmer knew when to turn off was a mystery but travelling along the side road, over a small rise they descended to a group of small buildings. One was obviously a cottage and the others farm outbuildings, one a huge barn with aircraft hangar like sliding doors. James was told to drive the car in to see three other tractors, a Trabant and of all things a lorry parked inside. In the middle was an inspection pit, James was guided over it before coming to a final stop. James's luck seemed to be getting better and better. Strewn along the walls were all manner of tools along with fan belts, gaskets and even several sizes of earthing wires and spare batteries.

James was led into the farmhouse to the sight of a roaring coal fire, the farmer's wife cooking the evening meal and two small children highly inquisitive by the arrival of a foreign visitor. Sat at the kitchen table he learnt the farmer's wife, understood English well and had studied mechanical engineering at Warsaw University, where she had met her husband to be. It turned out she would diagnose any problems with people's cars and lorries and leave her husband to do the actual rectification work.

Having her husband report on the damage she suggested the most practical solution was to weld the sump underneath as a temporary repair as the alternative meant raising the engine from its mountings, decoupling the engine from the clutch housing and also finding a Mercedes replacement gasket. That would take a week in all and James needed to get back for his flight from Hanover. She strongly counselled her husband to go steady with the welding touch as any accidental contact with the fuel lines would mean it wouldn't be just dinner that would be burnt to a crisp.

Dinner would be an hour away giving her husband enough time to do the remedial work. The worsening weather forced James delaying his departure and staying overnight until the morning. After the dawn her husband would guide him back onto the main road and then pick up the snow tracks hopefully cleared by the snow ploughs or marked out by the heavy lorries. It had been a long day for James and after a delicious and simple meal he was led to a deep feathered bed in a guest room and fell fast asleep.

Six in the morning he awoke naturally to hear noises of people walking around downstairs. He had a quick wash and shave in the basin available on a dressing table, got dressed and by the glow of the coal fire made out the farmer and his wife drinking coffee and preparing breakfast. He bid them a good morning and said he must pay them something for all the hospitality and car repair. The cheerful couple wouldn't hear of it and said it was just an act of kindness anyone would offer in the same circumstances. Despite forceful remonstrations no payment would be accepted. James anticipating the problem had already tucked a US$100 bill under his pillow to be discovered later.

The breakfast started with hot porridge; tasting delicious from the full cream fresh farm milk. Just as he was finishing the last mouthful there was the distinctive sound of several lorries coming down the farm road. At first James though it may have been more of the farmer's clients coming for maintenance or to pick up the lorry in the hangar. Pulling back the window curtain the farmer's wife gave out a gasp of sheer fright. The farmer and James joined her at the window to see Russian troops descending down from the first two lorries rifles in hand. Their officer didn't bother knocking on the door waiting for an invitation to come in he just burst through the door and ordered everyone to put up their hands including the children still dressed in their bedclothes.

The men were searched and then asked for their papers. The farmer went to a kitchen drawer but James said he needed to return to his bedroom for his passport. Having gone through the farmer's family documents it came to James's turn.

"Ah, an Englishmen."

"Yes, I......," James tried to finish his sentence but was ordered in perfect English to keep quiet until spoken too.

The passport was past to a subordinate who went outside presumably to radio headquarters.

"Are you a spy," the officer said?

"Are these people harbouring you."

James realised this could be serious and was no idle threat. His non- arrival at the hotel on the way back had tripped an alert. More than that he began to feel he had made a terrible blunder. Hadn't he realised that any unforeseen mishap in enemy territory would put him at grave risk and more than that of innocent people. At least he should try and explain the reason for his unplanned stay and to keep his hosts out of the fracas. Before he did the farmer explained fully the circumstances of the unplanned visit and offered to take the officer to the hangar show him evidence of the temporary repair. All seemed well when the pair of them were intercepted on their return by the junior soldier calling from the lorry with radio handset clutched to his side. The farmer continued walking towards the cottage as the officer went over, grabbed the phone and listened intently.

James just stood transfixed with the farmers family as all this went on and at least a dozen Russian soldiers stood around waiting for orders. The officer returned, ordered one of his men to handcuff James behind his back as the officer lectured the family, presumably for taking a foreigner into their home without question. As this went on James was manhandled to the second waiting lorry and told to climb into the back. He tried to protest but didn't see the butt of a rifle plunged into his kidneys, the acute pain took his breath away and momentarily made him unsteady standing up. Lifting his leg onto the back ladder was almost impossible but helped by a pair of helping hands pulling him upwards and into the back of the canvas covered lorry. There were just four soldiers inside looking expressionless.

Every jolt along the uneven road caused even more acute pain but not to the point there was a danger of him passing out. James had to fix firmly on his account in his head and not to allow his physical distress allow his mind to wander and give unintentionally slightly different accounts of his 'unauthorised overstay.' This was no need for an alibi this time just a true account that could easily be verified and he could then be released and sent on his way.

It took an hour to reach an army base just off from the main road. Grabbed out the back of the truck, two soldiers pulled him with either arm and frogged marched him to a nearby hut furnished with just two chairs and a table. The two of them pushed him by the shoulder onto one of the chairs and stood away against the wall at ninety degrees to the entrance door. A good half hour passed by until the door sprang open, the officer strode in, sat opposite to James whilst throwing a blue file on the desk. James sat motionless as the officer slowly turned the pages of a thick file pausing now and again at various photographs having read the report narrative.

All this took place in stony silence until the officer took a deep breath and said,

"Youngman, you seem to have been causing us some mischief over the years. Where's Tony?"

The alarm bells were really ringing now. James knew he was in deep, deep trouble. This was no routine security check. They had linked him to Tony and were making it very clear he was swimming in deep waters now, no doubt infested with veracious sharks.

"We know who you are so make it simple for us and just answer the question."

"Tony who," responded James?

"I know lots of Tony's."

"Again, I will make it very simple for you, Tony in MI6," came the answer.

"Oh, that Tony, why didn't you say," said James in a slightly mocking manner.

"I haven't seen him in years, why the interest, responded James?

"Since you stopped working for him, he seems to have gone to ground just like you. We didn't want such a relationship to wither on the vine so in the kindness of our hearts thought it a great idea if the pair of you renewed your acquaintance."

James half expected Tony to walk through the door at any moment. The questions stopped and both sat in their chairs impassively peering at each other. A glass of water was brought-in and with just one sip James passed out. Perhaps it was from the sheer exhaustion of the day. The next thing he knew he was being propped up and prevented from tipping over in his chair by the two sentries either side. Pushed in front of him was a picture of the brewery where he worked. In the few seconds he was allowed to look at it several thoughts went through his head. The picture was clearly from an old album. It was a classic view of the side of the brewery building subject to planning controls whilst around the side was the main entrance. That would have been the normal view if you were to convince someone they knew more about you. Whilst he had been 'roughed-up' it wasn't intensive. He rationalised it was just a preliminary. They weren't that serious to extract information otherwise he would be suffering from several deep bruises, bleeds and possibly some broken teeth. No, they had something else in mind and they didn't at this stage want to go too far and take unnecessary risks.

He speculated the Ruskie's had been tipped off and the breakdown was just a minor diversion from the search as they tracked him across East Germany and Poland before returning. It was worth a try to take the initiative knowing they were fully aware of a relationship with Tony, probably their main target, and perhaps in a subtle way interrogate them.

"If you couldn't find Tony, why didn't you tap on Peter's door," asked James?

"We know where he is so don't worry about him," said the Russian Officer.

James thought what a plonker, the Russian arrogance enabled him to confirm the connection and compromise a double agent, but maybe they didn't care. James was well on the path to being 'dispatched' as soon as his worth to them had been exhausted. He remembered from his limited training on interrogation that when it looked hopeless, expect the worse, prepare your mind and your last prayers.

Then the interview was ended. The Russian officer turned to his subordinate and said,

"Tell General Serov our friend is on his way, could he book a room for a few nights," smirking as he said it?

James knew this reference was not to a two-a-penny chocolate soldier in the army, he was a very high- ranking officer in the KGB. He took some comfort that he wasn't being dealt with by the standard thugs and sadists, this man was the real McCoy. A time for last prayers and a hope the end would be quick and painless.

12

The Gulag

Still sore from the rifle butt in the back the transport by car seemed almost luxurious than a bumpy, canvassed-covered army truck. No one said where he was going, but he guessed it must be Moscow. Apart from the odd stops for fuel and toilet breaks it took 24 hours to make the continuous journey. No food just the odd black coffee, but at least they put some sugar in it. On entering the Meschanky District of Moscow, rumbling over the cobbles of Lubyanka Square dominated by the surprisingly beautiful building housing the headquarters of the KGB, James was pulled out by the rear door and ushered across the pavement as some pedestrians strolled by. A person in handcuffs entering such a building was taken as a normal occurrence. They took absolutely no notice.

The inside betrayed the grandeur of the outside façade. The brick un-plastered walls were painted in a two tone, a light brown lower level and then a cream colour covering the top half of the walls and ceiling. The corridors were long. Dotted on the ceilings were regular clear light bulbs and off-white plain shades. Interspersed during the long promenade over the concrete floor were several steel doors opened as soon as they approached. Not by some sophisticated mechanism but manually from the sound of the bolts being unfastened and keys turned in massive deadlocks. Eventually after a couple of 90° turns they reached the bottom of a railed set of stone steps rising quite high above two floor levels to again access to another steel door. This time though the door opened to what appeared to be the inside of a palace, bedecked with marble, gold fittings and oil paintings.

James had already reconciled himself that he was likely to die, but at least it wouldn't be yet in such grand surroundings. In a peculiar way he took some solace that someone from his background was at the epi-centre of the Russian Empire to whom at least, despite his humble beginnings, he had at least irritated them a little. Not many could boast that nor were they, however, likely to find out. The three of them went up the marble staircase, James held firmly under each arm, still handcuffed before they were removed at the entrance in front of a very large double door. Once removed after a tap on the door, they marched in, James directed to sit in the one chair facing his next interrogator, the infamous General Ivan Serov no less. Not dressed as he had expected in a military uniform but a dark grey herring-boned suit and tie endorsed with the emblem of the Russian State.

Ivan didn't move except for fiddling with his red fountain pen around his chubby fingers peering at the single piece of paper on his desk. Suddenly there was the flourish of his signature and then he turned his round black eyes housed below bushy eyebrows towards James and gave him a hard stare.

"Do you smoke," he asked

"Only if I overdo the sunbathing," answered James.

Not a flicker from Ivan, he flicked open his packet of Marlborough cigarettes, took out a cigarette and lit it with a gold cigarette lighter. Drawing a few puffs, he said,

"You seem young man having difficulty answering our simple questions?"

James just stared back thinking you so and so's don't intimidate me, do your worst and let's get this farce over with.

"If you co-operate, I can assure you that you could be on the next day's flight out to London. You are not that important to us. All we require from you is some minor information and to help us tie-up some administrative loose ends," continued Ivan.

"Look, you kidnap me from a farmer's house when my rental car broke down; I was on a verifiable business trip with a colleague; you come out with random names like Peter, you dream up associations, yet you still haven't told me what law I have broken to warrant such treatment. I demand to see my British Consulate representative before I answer any of your ludicrous questions," said James as a pure act of defiance.

James did see a flicker of anger that an idiot had unconsciously confirmed a double agent in reciting the name Peter. James pretence of sweet innocence may be just sowing some seeds of doubt in their minds they had in their enthusiasm picked up an innocent bystander in a greater conspiracy. James felt he was scoring some points of his own, it was not just one-way traffic underlined by the next comment.

"Our concerns are matters for us. You may be just an innocent bystander or a bag carrier to others who have ill intent towards our Federation. All we need are the answers to a few very simple questions. If it is true what you say, what have you to worry about," said Ivan?

"Next you will be asking if I believe in Santa Clause, do you really think I am that naïve," said James showing his feint irritation.

"Under our system we can keep people of interest for as long as we want, innocent or not. All we have to decide is where to keep you while you reflect rather more deeply on your responses before you tell us what we need to know," said Ivan.

At that point he pressed a button on his desk and two other escorts came into the room, handcuffed him again outside the door and took him down to the basement to a bare cell with a bowl of porridge and a coffee. James had to admit he felt a little smug. The 'Ruskie's' were up to something but at this stage it was too early to speculate. So far, the roughing up had been tolerable but could about to become more intensive. He resigned himself this could happen but practiced in his mind over and over what he had already said and the stance taken. No alibi was needed as he was non-operational and he had a perfect reason for being in Poland. He mustn't, however, allow his mind to wander onto other issues or mention names even if severely provoked mentally or physically, that could incriminate him. In the time he had available he must indoctrinate himself, rehearse all the key phrases repeatedly, then hopefully pass-out if it got too tough.

He didn't have to wait long for the next move. After an hour the cell door opened letting in the poor electric light and in came a Russian in a business suit. They both walked down the corridor, no handcuffs, to a waiting car. In just 30 minutes he was standing in a railway goods yard surrounded by at least a dozen soldiers and shown to a specific carriage on a long steam train. He remembered well casting a glance at the locomotive, shiny black and throwing off the spare steam and the two tankers behind brim-full of lumps of anthracite. The carriage contained a platoon of other soldiers just armed with side-arms sat in each of the compartments. James was directed to the middle compartment completely empty but marked out with the grill up against the window and the bulb removed from the ceiling light. This was to be the longest train journey of his life and probably the longest for most other people. For five days he ate, slept and gazed out at the scenery, the only break from the repetitive monotony were the toilet breaks to the end of the carriage. Clearly his carriage was sealed from the rest.

In all other respect the journey was like any other. The first stop was five minutes away, Yaroslavsky Station, which if James had known was the gateway railway to Siberia. Not far out of Moscow the snow had just settled amongst the vast fields and sparse woodlands. There were other small towns on the way and stops to let-off and let-on a dozen passengers at a time. Three days in, the snow deepened until by the fourth day it was four to five-foot deep and the few roads the railway crossed were deserted apart from the odd horse-drawn sledge. The compartment was heated, but only to the point of avoiding freezing. James was offered a few pullovers but no overcoat or woollen blankets. At the last station all the passengers disembarked along with the conductors. James was told to sit down and keep still. This is it James thought, transport to a drab concrete building, dragged into a centre square to be shot against a wooden post by his guards. No religious rites, no blindfold, just a couple of short ropes to secure him against the post while sat on a small wooden stool. James mentally said goodbye to family and close friends, made his confession to his maker thinking he had always tried his best. He had made mistakes but never wished ill of anyone. Peter Voss had denied him retribution, time had run out. A piece of bad luck as he saw it; divine intervention preventing him from inflicting a savage and vicious vengeance not naturally in his character, unless provoked.

To his surprise no premature passing away. The same routine, a bare room, an investigating officer interspersed with slaps on the face but no fists or rifle butts. May be this was the debut of a punishment schedule leading to his ultimate demise. It went on for several hours until the sleep deprivation forced him to intervals of a deep coma. The interrogation stopped and he was virtually carried to his cell and dumped in a pitch-black cell, a straw-strewn floor and a few blankets. He managed to come around and feel on the ground, wrapped in what he could gather around him to keep warm. There must have been some heating since the coldness was not as severe as you would expect given the weather outside. He fell into a deep sleep.

He awoke in the pitch-black darkness except for the very small rooflight where the stars in the night sky could be clearly seen. He had no idea of the time but guessed it wasn't far-off dawn given the sky wasn't as ink black as you would expect. There was complete silence, not even the call of a dawn chorus. Then he had the strange feeling he wasn't alone. He couldn't be sure but was there someone with him shallow breathing in the stillness? He shuffled round the cell on his right hip still wrapped in a few blankets and then he came up against another body who gave out a jolt as they touched. A hand reached out, took the finger of his hand and placed it against his lips after the other hand felt over his face. James took this to mean don't make a sound. The strange figure then took James's finger and moved it over the cold ground to spell something out. He didn't get it at first but at the second attempt he was sure it said,

"I'm Tony don't react."

Then his finger was directed at the 'Tony's mouth' making a sign he had zipped his lips. James took this as a confirmation he hadn't talked. It was James turn to answer and repeated the exercise but this time guiding 'Tony's' finger over the ground spelling out the statement twice over to be sure,

"OK, I understand. My name is James, should I know you?"

There was at first a momentary pause and in Morse code James finger was tapped on the floor, dash dot dash dash; dot; dot dot dot; (Yes). They both huddled up together James happier he had a companion, Tony not only a trusted colleague but the one person with great bulk, a great advantage in the circumstances. James sussed the motive for placing them together. He had been bought in to try and prise open Tony's mouth. James tapped on Tony's arm again in Morse code, 'Hold out my friend, we will eventually get out of this stew.'

James guessed an hour went by as the light through the skylight began to increase but he still couldn't make out Tony, just a very dark outline of a shadow huddled in blankets on the straw floor. Suddenly the door flew open casting a shaft of poor light from the single light bulb in the corridor and in marched two soldiers, one holding a bowl of porridge and a lump of black bread while the other went to pull-up Tony. It was then James first properly saw Tony but only just recognised him. His head was blue and his eyes almost closed from the intense swelling on his face. His lower jaw was ajar revealing a bottom tooth pointing at right angles to his chin. Either it had been broken or worked lose from all the treatment. There were signs of blood patches on his shirt as the blanket fell to the ground. He was yanked up, once the second soldier had dispensed with the breakfasts, such as it was.

Tony had held out and was still refusing to answer their questions. Perhaps they believed the sight of James would finally break him and make it totally clear he was in a hopeless situation and no help at hand. Even his bag carrier could be kidnapped to make the point. There was also the opportunity to plant in Tony's head that his colleague would betray him as had Peter Voss, who no doubt helped to succeed in his capture. This went on for the next three days confirming to James Tony was having none of it and despite the rough treatment wasn't to be compromised. James sought to lift his spirits when he returned by sharing some humour, always conscious there could be microphones or hidden cameras to capture any indiscretions.

"I think they are trying to impress us with their five-star hospitality," said James.

He could feel Tony's body slightly shake chuckling to the inane humour. Before they both fell back to sleep James would recount English memories, be they recollections of fish and chips, steak and kidney pies and foaming ale. He rattled on recalling his favourite comedians and retelling the few jokes he could remember. Tony would still resort to writing on the floor so his responses couldn't be detected but never anything that would connect them to the work they had done. At the end James spelt out his own statement,

"If I ever get out of here Peter will meet his maker, be in no doubt my friend."

"I can't take much more of this but if you do, make it slow and excruciatingly painful," spelt out Tony.

"I vow I will do my best my friend," responded James writing on the floor with Tony's forefinger.

The same routine continued for the next few days. James stuck in a gloomy cell and Tony dragged out each day to return in a poorer state than before. Again, they would huddle together in the evening and converse in a rudimentary way the best they could. But suddenly Tony gave out. He momentarily clutched James's hand with what strength he had left and then gently released it and went into a terminal coma. James thought of calling the guards but knew that wouldn't save his life; he was already dead. He decided to talk through the night, always putting up the pretence they hadn't known each other before, reminiscing over England and what a great nation it was and that their families would be protected. He also said at the end that he always kept his promises. Perhaps their plight would be a reminder of the nature of the enemy they, and the nation, were dealing with.

It must have been around 03.00am when James too gave in and went into a deep sleep through sheer exhaustion. He was still sound asleep when the guards came in with the obligatory bowl of porridge and lump of black bread. His slumber interrupted by the sound of shouting as more guards entered the cell followed soon by a doctor. James just sat slumped against the wall watching the panic unfolding before him. This wasn't something they had expected. Clearly internees before were in a better state of health. Tony was a big man with a family history of congenital heart problems leading to premature death even in normal circumstances. Would this mean he was next?

James sat impassively until then he was dragged out to an interrogation room like the others before and perhaps the same one as Tony's. What came next, he didn't expect.

"Did you kill him," the officer banging his cane on the table?

"In my country we do not kill our fellow countrymen," answered James.

"You can stop the pretence now; you are both working together. There is no need for any false thought of protecting one another," continued the officer changing tact.

"Your trouble is you couldn't see the truth unless it smacked you in the eye," said James trying to take the initiative once more and hoping he was sowing the seeds of more doubt into his interrogator's head.

Then another surprise, the interview stopped and in Russian the command was given to remove him from sight. Back in his cell, another surprise, a three-course dinner, dessert and mug of hot coffee. Now this was really confusing especially as the meals became frequent again and he was seen by the doctor every day and fussed over. Now he knows what turkeys felt like around Christmas time. Fattened up, cossetted under warm heat lamps, dry straw to lie-in and then wallop, you are first stunned and then have your throat cut before they cut you open and remove your inwards. What will it be for him, no matter, whatever it is, it will be, he reconciled to himself? Enjoy the food while you can and wait for the inevitable hoping a quick, clean and painless termination.

Just over a week had gone by since saying his last farewell to Tony when there was another change of routine. No longer the cold-water bowl to wash and shave but he was led to a shower block with nice warm showers and great bars of carbolic soap and hair shampoo. On the bench seat was a change of ironed clothes including a nice woollen red jumper. Trust them to choose red, they never cease to make a point. At this point he was not returned to his gloomy cell but a one round cell with a window masked by steel bars, a clear view of the forest beyond and a nice warm bunk bed. He comically speculated himself that he must have been moved to a five-star hotel.

Another week and he began to feel his normal self. Then another surprise he was summoned by the governor of this 'reception centre' and just told,

"We are sending you home."

James had great difficulty accepting this news. Is it just a trick to confuse him? The rough stuff hadn't worked on Tony, so let's try the gentle approach with this one and reduce his defences before he gets to know what is coming. James wasn't going to fall for it and followed the line he always had done,

"At last you seen through your mistake and you have at last accepted you have the wrong man. I am just an ordinary businessman that by bad luck crossed your path at the wrong time," said James almost to the point he began to almost believe it himself.

While he was in custody, he wouldn't allow his mind to stray any further to avoid giving rise to other suspicions. See if you get free first, then work out what is actually happening. It seemed they were right. Next, he heard a car door, not a lorry turn-up, which whisked him to the railway station that he had arrived in those weeks before. No isolated compartment this time, a normal

223

compartment accompanied by two burly men in dark suits, woollen overcoats and black fur hats mingling with the other passengers.

This time James was able to take in the vastness of Siberia. Hour after hour they would speed through the countryside of birch trees, pines and thick snow. It was as flat as a pancake and no sign of life right to the horizon once you went over a small incline clear of the tree tops. Even if you managed to escape, had all the food and water you could carry, you would certainly perish in a savage and hostile country as this.

Arriving back in Moscow he was taken straight to the airport, checked over by a medical team, given a hearty meal and hot drinks before one last quick interrogation the last sentence of which James would remember to the last of his days,

"Remember young man and remember it well, there are no frontiers for us in pursuing the enemies of the Federation."

With that chilling remark he was on the BOAC flight to London but accompanied by two British civil servants, Graham and Ricky. They made it plain they were to accompany James to Britain but were not allowed to talk beyond why they were there. All the other passengers disembarked before James was allowed to descend the aircraft steps to a waiting black Jaguar saloon and whisked well away from the terminal buildings to another part of the airport driving into an open hangar whose doors were open just enough to allow a car through before the doors were immediately closed behind them. There was an executive jet parked inside but nothing else except what appeared to be a row of offices at the other end.

Walking into one empty office and sat at a desk strewn with flight plans and aeronautical maps, a mug of tea was brought with three digestive biscuits parked precariously in the saucer, the door closed and he was left alone. It seemed an eternity but was probably only ten minutes. The door then opened to reveal Malcolm beaming away holding a brief case.

"Doctor Livingstone I presume," was Malcolm's first words and then they just hugged each other.

"Are you feeling OK after your elongated holiday," asked Malcolm.

"I am fine now but never thought I would see Blighty ever again," remarked James.

"I know there is a lot for you to take in but let me try in the bit of time we have to brief you on what's been going on and how you are to conduct yourself in the outside world," said Malcolm.

Malcolm, his personal lawyer over many years, then explained that to the outside world and to his wife, James had gone missing in bad weather in the farmlands of Poland and there was a search on for his whereabouts. It had been put out that the Russians eventually found him lost in Western Russia, disorientated, out of petrol and suffering from hypothermia. A kindly farmer had taken James in until he felt better and he could be driven to the nearest town some 80 miles away. Nothing had been said of Tony's absence, only the 'Department' knows there is a problem. At all costs they do not wish to compromise Tony.

'You know Tony is dead," said James?

'No, I didn't know, nor do I believe does anyone else," remarked Malcolm.

James, despite the whirlwind enveloping him, tried to rationalise what was actually going on. He concluded that Tony was a vital part of military intelligence and to a degree the Department would be relieved he never compromised his position. Importantly, the role of Peter Voss as a double agent was blown and the 'Department' could no longer exploit their intelligence. But had the Ruskie's yet 'twigged' the tampering of the nerve agent? Of course, the next question was what did Malcolm know and to what extent.

"How is it you are here and not my family," asked James?

"You don' think I was going to swallow their cock and bull story; you know me better than that. I don't wish to know what on earth you were up to, I just wanted to get you returned pronto when it seemed those with power of influence seemed to have given up," remarked Malcom.

"Who is Lucy Polaskai by the way, you haven't been fooling around have you," asked Malcolm?

"She worked with me in my previous job, why do you ask," enquired James avoiding the inference.

"Because in my research on you she is another who has gone missing without explanation."

It was all beginning to make a sort of sense to James. The nerve gas poisoning failed and the Ruskie's were keen to check Lucy's explanation of failure against any account supplied by Tony. When this drew a blank, James was extracted to hopefully get all three together to spill the beans but Tony's premature departure upset the master plan. The penny finally dropped when James learnt that the Russians had sent some agents over and contaminated a target's house in England. That had nearly worked had it not been for the NHS, but it was probably a fresh batch in order not to raise suspicions of access to a chemical warfare stockpile. Tony had held out to the bitter end, what a hero!

"I have not seen Lucy since I left and I assure you she was just a work colleague," James continued to say.

"You probably saved my life but I can't explain to you why I say that," said James.

"I understand, Mum's the word, I am just overjoyed to have my mate back."

They were just about to finish went two men wearing a dark pin-striped suits and jet-black shiny shoes marched in shook him vigorously by the hand and said,

"Let's get you home, your adventure is over young man and you can get back to a normal family life once more. Your wife is waiting downstairs with a chauffeur to take you back to the Midlands.

13

Newark Northgate

James was so relieved to see his wife. He gave her a great kiss and hug, struggling to hold back the rising emotions, held in check for so many weeks in a lonely cell.

"I am not going to ask awkward questions; Malcolm told me not to, let's just get back home and let your friends know you had gone AWOL and were taken into custody until you were vouched for," said his wife in her usual phlegmatic manner she always displayed despite acute pressure. James wondered many times perhaps she was better at his role than he was. At first it all seemed a long drawn out adventure but he was beginning to realise the enormous risks he was taking. Family life had changed him, potential exciting adventures or challenges ceased to raise the adrenalin they use to. He began to worry whether he would ever get back a normal life enjoyed by others facing closing down their careers before retirement.

At these fleeting thoughts and reflections, they both clambered into the back seat of a black Humber Snipe still holding hands not wishing to let go for a second from one another.

James set in his mind a determination to leave all that 'exotic' stuff behind. He should plough the furrow of his own destiny just as had been planned from the outset. That was before he was drawn through high ambition and lack of opportunities that his working-class background had bestowed on him. He had allowed others to dictate the terms for his advancement. He didn't want in the end to change the prison of his social class to exchange it for just another, not even one housed within a five-star accommodation.

James just kept staring sideways at his wife as she in turn stared silently out of the window as the rain droplets began to smear across the window pane. He thought to himself, what agonies she must have gone through without complaint, not knowing at any time where he was, what suffering he may be enduring and what he was doing. He resolved it was time he acted more responsibly as a husband and provide her greater certainty and contentment. Both of them sat in the car in monastic silence for the next two hours just squeezing each other's hand as though they were new found lovers embarking on a future romance.

The next few weeks were a bit of a blur. Lots of gathering of friends and meals out. The Department said they would retire him early and pay him an interim pension until he could find a settled job; not to worry if it took some time. They would give him an exemplary reference as a valued civil servant in the Department of Trade and Industry.

The settled job never arrived, he couldn't countenance a fixed routine with a predetermined job specification and those vacuous job interviews with so-called superiors who were still wet behind their ears. Through a series of networking initiatives, he alighted on setting-off independently, a challenging mix of building his own small businesses with various investment partners, and in between, helping out on sizeable corporate acquisitions.

The odd big lucrative corporate deal bonuses came in helpful as he bridged the leap from one enterprise to another. Should the deals succeed, which most did, great dollops of cash would fall into his account. His private businesses were not far from home base at Southwold but the corporate stuff meant regular train journeys to London from Newark Northgate to King's Cross and onwards to the City. He always felt a return of that old buzz walking around the 'City' once more, meeting the crème de la crème of financiers, lawyers and accountants. He doubted there was any other place in the world that could match these people. Whilst the stakes and rewards were high, he had enormous respect for city people, their attitude to hard work, deployment of skills and above all their unquestioned integrity. The cherry on the cake were some nice non-executive positions thrown in for good measure to give James a nice little mixture of 'earners' that kept his mind fully occupied and his modest finances robust.

Life at home became normal at last. For the first time James got to know his immediate neighbours, took up private flying again and at the weekends a social life properly separated from the Monday to Friday routine. His children were progressing well at school and very settled. His wife had done a great job keeping the house and home together, dealing with all the domestic dramas everyone experiences with little fuss. They even managed to go on enjoyable holidays either camping with the children or later staying at nice villas out in the continental countryside. They managed to visit the USA several times revealing a side of his wife he hadn't known before, a love of the casinos and gambling on a modest basis. She was pretty good at it and James revelled in the regular winnings; not for the jackpots but the sheer thrill of his wife hitting the jackpots. She at least deserved some reward for a hard family life. At last he had got his life back and would have been contented to roll along, eventually retire and then disappear forgotten into the sunset.

Real life is not like that. His past was about to catch up on him, suddenly and bizarrely.

Advances in medical science had opened a greater understanding of Post-Traumatic Stress Disorder - PTSD. To the general public it became well-known during the First World War but its victims would be treated with little sympathy. Experiencing severe and tragic events most people are able to cope with it as long as they are not too overwhelming or frequent. For the most part the scars remain hidden even to the victim and life goes on. But to some the constant flashbacks and emotional triggers prevent people from conducting a normal life or simply a capacity to have a restful sleep. James would probably admit he was a minor sufferer but was able to cope with the odd emotional outrage when for example known terrorists were glorified or their actions given nonsense post rationalisation. He knew them as men committing unwarranted cruelty and distress to whole communities living under their terror campaign and to bequeath decades of suffering and deprivation for a 'cause' that could have been pursued and resolved by democratic and peaceful means.

There still remained though the issue of Peter Voss. That could have been an ongoing problem but having witnessed his internment he believed he could bury any latent problems along with his corpse at Berry Hill. He did from time to time visit the cemetery on the pretence of just wanting to pay respects to his old buddy Malcolm, but always managed to wander over, peer at the headstone and feel a great inner satisfaction. Not a particularly Christian feeling, but one James felt he could easily justify.

After the funeral the meeting with Mr. Brand and his father slightly disturbed him. They had known he had been to Berry Hill to pay respects to his old friend Malcolm and passed on their condolences, but Mr. Brand made a passing comment that didn't fit.

"Sometimes when someone passes away it is taken as some form of finality and their internment the last act of a life. I am not so sure, that past has a nasty habit of returning when you least expect it."

The years rolled by and James was able to play out his years heading towards retirement in relative obscurity. He may have had a mix of work, and sometimes great challenges, but behind it all was finally a routine of sorts and lack of extreme situations. There was the ability to work at home with the advent of the internet and any travelling normally only involved a train journey to the City. Most destinations were within the square mile except the Docklands being redeveloped and offices springing up around Canary Wharf.

James through frequency, would soon navigate the underground without reference to a map, leaving the last part for a taxi drive avoiding time-consuming research of the best navigation to his precise destination. James tried to make the best of the time and would arrange at least two meetings in a day. The dead time was normally confined to a light lunch spent on his own either in a café and sometimes in one of the Royal Parks sat on a bench enjoying a sandwich in the warm sunshine.

Such trips were the routine he desired. It was good practice to get an early start getting to the nearest railway station at Newark Northgate for the 7.07 or 7.40. This meant he could be in Kings Cross at or before 9.00am and make for the first meeting by 10.00am. On a good day there would be three meetings with a return on the 5.30pm or 6.05pm return train ride. They may have been just meetings, nevertheless James always felt completely spent by the end of the day such were their intensity. If at least one succeeded in its objective that would be considered a good day. You couldn't always tell at the time.

Sometimes you get an infusive response only for the enthusiasm to leave once you left the building. Other occasions the greeting would be introduced with an opening remark such as, 'This doesn't get our juices going,' only for the process to accelerate when James was able to convince his hosts the opportunity was something they just couldn't pass over. Not that James was a snake oil salesman, he presented a balanced and truthful account but wouldn't waste people's time on just a nice idea but problematic investment, it had to have the capability of earning a load of dosh for everyone. Over the years he earned a good reputation and people would readily arrange a meeting knowing it would be worthwhile listening. You could always learn something even if it wasn't up your alleyway.

Then came that momentous day he would never forget. James should have prophesised something out of the ordinary was about to happen. His training and experience should have foretold that once a routine pattern is broken other factors begin to bear on an outcome.

The day started innocuously enough. This particular day the meeting was set for a change later at midday giving time for all the professionals and advisers to have the documentation properly prepared and very importantly the money standing online for the final completion and transfer of funds to the appropriate accounts. People would have worked overnight to make sure all will be in order for the final signing of the completion contracts. No other meetings as a result had been arranged.

James wasn't one to leave anything to chance. He would still depart at his usual time to ensure he would make the meeting even if there were transport difficulties or more likely a last-minute technical hitch arose and needed to be ironed out. If all went well the completion would be done within an hour and then straight into a celebratory lunch. If there was a delay there would be no time for a quick snack so rather than having at breakfast a couple of buttered slices of toast with jam, James determined to have a bacon and fried tomato door-stop sandwich to keep the sugar levels up, just as his Dad would have made. He hoped whatever happened, the deal would be completed and he would be home by 8pm if not before.

Newark Northgate was just 20 minutes away by car. They had recently expanded the car park so no sweat on parking and it was a quick walk to the ticket office to buy a first-class rail and tube ticket and pay for the car parking for the day. Just a couple of people were already at the ticket window all buying the same ticket, so within a few minutes James was pocketing the bank cards, sorting the various tickets for the journey and making sure the others were properly stored away in his briefcase for ready retrieval later, whilst holding the car keys between his teeth.

Postman Pat, the lookalike ticket collector, was there as usual. He was all of six foot six inches. Not a word spoken just a clip of the ticket after a brief inspection and then onto the next passenger. James went to the kiosk on the platform for a newspaper, held up for a few minutes as others were served their morning coffee and sometimes a bun substituting for the breakfast they had missed.

The slight delay meant James witnessed the direct Edinburgh – London Express as it hurtled passed at full speed almost forcing you to spill any coffee. The air wake blew you back and then immediately sucked you forward such was the train's speed. James wasn't carrying a cup of coffee as first-class passengers would be supplied with one shortly after boarding and an offer of a free daily newspaper. James preferred reading the Financial Times rather than a Daily Mail but would read the complimentary copy on the way back as a way of winding down.

As usual James headed towards the end of platform where there was the first-class passengers waiting room. James reflected on those 'Whites' and 'Non-Whites' of the days in South Africa and wondered whether there was much of a difference in cultural outlook. James preferred standing outside if it wasn't raining, given it was the only opportunity to take in fresh air once he boarded and disembarked again in London.

Just as he rehearsed in the past his alibi's, James ran through the key aspects of the deal to be sealed to ensure he had any responses ready that might be required, so to a degree he was lost in his thoughts. Looking down the track in the direction of travel he had noticed the two amber lights were still illuminated and before he could start to worry there could be a delay, they turned to green so his train had clearance to move off after boarding. Looking the other way, he could make out far into the distance the twin headlights of his train. The line was so straight it must have been all of three miles away.

He stood there motionless looking across to Postman Pat dealing with the late arrivals and trying to make sure everyone could leg it over the bridge in time for the train's arrival. The first- class passengers still huddled in their comfy hut timing their arrival on the platform to perfection having gone through the routine many times before. The announcement would be made and then they would depart from their cosy den clutching their brief cases to saunter towards the end of the platform and position themselves three carriages down from the locomotive for embarkation.

The next sighting, he encountered froze James to the spot. Such was the shock he couldn't move; he was totally transfixed. Had he seen a ghost or more logically a 'doppelganger?' In the next split-second to regain his faculties, he got an answer, this was no ghost or 'doppelganger' it was the real thing. The image that greeted him gave him a momentary glance under the black trilby and immediately ran in the opposite direction towards the end of the platform. The other passengers didn't notice someone seemingly going the wrong way or what happened next as their eyes were peeled on the third door down to get on the train as soon as possible, throw off their overcoats and open their papers whilst waiting for the morning paper to be thrust onto their table.

His eyes had not deceived him, it was Peter Voss in rude health running away and making for the opposite end of the platform before making a rapid turn to cross the tracks before the train came to a final stop. Unfortunately for him he never saw the express train hurtling towards him from the other direction, nor did it seem anyone else. Their train obscured the view. The driver must have seen him cross but then disappear into thin air. He had reported it to the guard that he saw a man cross the track but no one saw him reappear. That is until the train had arrived at Retford to the North by which time James 's train had already departed.

The incident was reported in some detail in the London Evening Standard when James sat reading the paper on his return home. Apparently, the mystery was solved when a woman standing at a level crossing just before Retford Station saw a severed head roll down the track with its eyes still blinking. She fainted on the spot and a few men who went to help to find out if she was alright, vomited at the grotesque sight.

Peter Voss's complete head, detached from his body stood in the middle of the tracks as though he was looking rearwards down the track still looking for James. The rest of him was stuck over the front bumper, his left-arm extended. As the train had slowed the crumpled body mass gently slid down the bonnet of the train leaving a visible blood-stained smear over the blue livery.

The transport police weren't able to piece all the information together until the London train had already departed from Peterborough and the Metropolitan Police completed the tale when waiting at King's Cross, they interviewed the driver as a potential witness. All the passengers were totally oblivious to the event and carried on their normal business, until, like James, they had read it in their evening paper.

So, was Peter Voss's internment a complete sham? James wondered whether it had been a ploy by Peter to escape before the Department caught up with him or an ingenious plot conceived by the Department itself to cover up the activities of a traitor who's cover at some stage would be blown by the media and the neutralised chemical weapons scheme exposed. James never got to know. No one in the Department made contact, the whole matter was kept quiet and hushed up.

Having to focus on the completion meeting helped James cope with the shock of the unexpected encounter. It was only when he boarded the train for the return journey, did he feel the shakes coming on, calmed by a small bottle of wine. He closed the newspaper and spent the whole of the return journey thinking of his past and perhaps contemplating he could now really put to bed the reoccurring nightmares. He cast his mind back to poor old Tony hoping in the spiritual world he too could now lay at rest at last realising the final deed had been done.

He made a snap judgment. That's it, I have had enough. We are going to live abroad, in France, enjoy a different culture, divorce himself away from all the historical reminders even those of his schooldays. No, now was the time for a brand new and fresh start. He did manage to return home for just gone 5,30pm and on entering the house shouted to his wife in the kitchen he was home as she was about to start preparing the evening meal.

"Don't bother cooking a meal tonight dear we are going out for a slap-up meal and a few drinks; I have something to tell you. I'll book a taxi; I feel like a few 'bevies' tonight to wind down."

This was unusual for James. Suzanne would normally question what lay behind the outburst of enthusiasm, but she knew James had had a heavy day and with her sixth sense knew deep down this was not going to be a normal dinner out between the two of them. Having changed, James reserved a table at the Café Bleu, his favourite restaurant in Newark. They spent the evening at a table for two surrounded by other diners enjoying the exquisite food. James then leaned forward, and in a hushed tone, said to his wife,

"It's about time you and I spent some quality time together in a better climate with no distractions."

"What on earth are you getting at," murmured Suzanne not letting on that she had a premonition something of major significance was afoot?

"I have been thinking a lot about our future. I don't need to work anymore. I have a good pension and the children are striking out on their own with their own families. I suppose I have been thinking about this for some time especially during my impromptu extended holiday. Let's go to live in Brittany. It has a better climate, plenty of fresh air and fantastic scenery and beaches, good restaurants and wonderful farming countryside. We are not too far away from any potential grandchildren and for the first time in our lives we can enjoy the fruits of our labours," rambled on James trying to be rational slurring his speech under the growing influence of the glasses of fine wine.

"This is all a bit sudden," said Suzanne.

"Not really," responded James.

"My old age is catching up with me. I no longer have the drive and ambition I had before."

"Well if you really feel that way. I suppose it is about time we took the demands of a career and family behind us," said Suzanne resigned that whatever she had said it wouldn't have changed James mind anyway.

Probably for the first time in their lives they mutually relaxed, spent the next hour finishing the remaining dregs of the 'pichet' of wine before tackling the desert and coffees. By the time the bill arrived, Suzanne had moved from resigned acceptance to eager anticipation.

14

AGM at Dinan

A visit to the boulangerie is always a delight. James volunteered to go every other day to take in that wonderful smell of fresh-baked croissants and assorted patisseries. James's French wasn't that good, so in the early days there was some confusion over the questions from the sales lady. It wasn't good enough to point to a round loaf or croissant and give a number; bread is too important to be relegated to just a simple food selection. How do you want it baked, a little or well done, sliced, white or wholemeal, cereal etc., etc? The simplest to order were the wonderful tarte aux frais (strawberry tarts) and beignet a la crème (cream doughnuts). It was tempting to throw in these delightful patisseries at will but James relegated that to Fridays only for the sake of his growing waistline.

Having arrived in France the most demanding challenges were to understand the French system of acquiring a property and organising the supply of public utilities. A bank account with all your account details on a 'RIB' document was a first essential. It served the purpose of validating who you were and where you lived. No cash transactions allowed, all had to be subject to Napoleon Bonaparte's system of bureaucratic documentation. Everyone is registered with the Social Security. An absolute necessity if you wish to have access to the medical services or in other cases an ability to take a job. Once through the pain of registration, the systems worked well and smoothed your life for later on.

Within six months James and Suzanne knew they had made the right move. Their lifestyle was healthier from the fresh foods, clean air and ability to take regular exercise. No longer the rigours of getting up early, time slots and working late; at time when the treadmill of life didn't allow for the processing of personal administrative stuff left unattended between all the business meetings. Now, James could properly relax, no longer having to continually worry where the next challenge may come from. Saying all that, it didn't mean a routine wasn't established. Days were fixed for shopping, market tours and visits around the ramparts of Saint Malo, rain or shine, to keep fit.

Suzanne always accompanied James except for one pre-determined annual excursion. They had once tried the boat trip down the River Rance from Saint Malo, through the barrage at the estuary and onwards upstream to Dinan. It was a good five-hour trip and in the summer sunshine, was a delight. James had determined that once a year he would make the walk on the last part of the route along the riverside from Taden to Dinan; a respectable 5 kms. It gave him a chance, once a year, to engage in what he called a mental annual recalibration.

He had lived his life very much on the edge and at very high stakes. A mental downgrading readjustment was necessary so he could enjoy his retirement and as a backdrop absorb the beauty of his new home. The walk was a little too far for Suzanne, and in any case, she recognised there were times when James would become very pensive, lost in his own thoughts. Not much company when he was in that sort of mood. Perhaps she also knew he was coming to terms with all his past experiences only a part of which she could guess. She readily accepted he needed a period of quiet solitude to help him come to terms with the magnitude of his past endeavours. Perhaps it was a kind of amateur psychotherapy to avoid mental health problems later in his advancing years.

The walk was timed to allow for a couple of hours strolling gently along and then in Dinan, lunch by the roman bridge traversing the river. The beautiful arched stone bridge straddled the narrowest point where the river became a series of rivers and canals leading once again out to the Atlantic Ocean. His chosen resting place before returning was overlooked by huge medieval fortress stone walls protecting the town from medieval intruders perched high on the overlooking hill.

There was always a good choice of food at one of the many restaurants dotted along the water's edge, but he had his favourite very close to the bridge and situated right alongside the river. From inside the restaurant he would be able to observe customers outside on the terrace, and beyond, passengers disembarking off the pleasure boat from Saint Malo, happy and smiling from a memorable trip. Old habits though die hard, he had to sit with his back against the kitchen wall facing the entrance opening. He never felt comfortable not being able to observe the comings and goings of others. Mental profiling them all at the shutter speed of a kodak camera. Click, click and in an instant, he knew them and their likely background.

Starting at Taden, there is a lock linked to the other side, but this time, by an adjoining narrow barrage on which many wild birds would perch. Opposite there were two café restaurants for those wishing to stay routed to the spot. One restaurant, on special days, has delicious fish and chips on the menu, a particular favourite of James and a reminder of his humble childhood. Locking the car and dressed in his blue shorts; casual gawdy shirt and trainers, off he would stroll along the riverbank. There were two important accessories; a hat to stop the fierce sun burning the top of his balding head and a good pair of anti-glare sunglasses. No longer the Glock as an essential accessory. Whilst useful in the bright sunlight the sunglasses were indispensable if you wished to observe against the fierce glare the shoals of large carp swimming just below the rivers surface.

The chosen day was memorable as much for the weather as the scenic views. The warm sun peering through a morning mist hovering over the very still waters, trapped between the limestone cliffs on either side. A whole variety of birds perched on the barrage. They were mainly black gulls but on the odd rock sticking out of the shallow waters cascading over the rim of the barrage would perch a few cormorants. A rotating road bridge stood just 50 metres further downstream so anyone could get a closer look by just crossing the bridge when the road was open, taking in the views upstream peering at the audience of birds and downstream observing several sailing and motorboats gentle navigating mid-stream, along the waters of the river.

James set-off making sure he hadn't forgot his wallet and placing the car keys safely into a zipped side pocket of his shorts. At first there would be a few people walking in either direction but once you had turned around the first bend most people disappeared not wishing to venture much further than a few hundred metres. Sometimes you would get mountain bikes flash by on the wide sandy bridle path or a sailing yacht meandering slowly in the gentle breeze; for the most part you would be left all alone in the silence of the river. The sides of the limestone cliffs were covered in small trees giving in some spots some welcome cool shade. On the far bank he saw a kingfisher with its vivid colouring as though several pots of paint had been splashed over its body by a clumsy artist. James could already feel the difference. No adrenalin pulsing through his veins or the necessity to rehearse an alibi, just absorbing the tranquillity. If you glanced downwards at the river's edge you could often observe those shoals of carp swimming lazily along as though they were keeping you company.

James never took a drink with him on the assumption he would not raise enough of a thirst for just a couple of hours exercise, but today he began to contemplate a nice cool glass of beer before tucking into lunch with a glass of white Bordeaux. The river twisted in both directions with no sign of houses or roads. One turn of a bend would reveal another enchanting view that Gainsborough could have been inspired to capture on canvas. Just a few kilometres on, the hills would start to recede until on the last bend the roman bridge would appear in the far distance, and before it, several stone buildings on either side following the direction of the river. To the left were a couple of hotels and to the right a string of shops and restaurants.

Already many people were milling around. Some on tiny for hire tourist motor launches, others viewing the various shops merchandise and artists productions whilst others sat outside the cafés taking in light morning refreshment.

In the few months James and Suzanne had been in France they had observed the town was a magnet for an open market, exhibitions or gatherings of all manner of social groups. Dinan was well-known regionally for its medieval fair; everyone encouraged to dress in middle-age costumes. The standard would be very high and it felt you were on the set of a Hollywood movie with knights and maidens milling around as though waiting for the next shoot sequence. To dress up was an imperative otherwise you were not allowed into many of the attractions including a full-blown jousting contest. James was relieved he was dressed casually as walking around in the costumes must have been most uncomfortable in the hot airless weather. That is especially if you were carrying a two-handed authentic sabre sword.

Before he became into easy reach, James decided to give himself a generous coating of suntan cream on face, arms and legs even though he would shelter under one of the enormous branded umbrellas. He avoided the tables for four or six people and selected a two-seater table inside according to his usual habit. Slumping in the bench seat, his back resting against the restaurant kitchen wall he took a well-earned breather. It was well before lunch time. He first ordered a nice cool lager and began to take in the panoramic view. He still couldn't shake off that habit picking up every new customer so they could be 'clocked,' observed and assessed. He couldn't kick the other habit either of profiling all the customers, as he had done before, but for a wholly different purpose. Now it was just for the fun of it, making-up mentally stories about each person or group. Perhaps one day he would try his talents and write a book about this idyllic life and the characters stories formed in his mind?

He removed his sun hat but retained the sunglasses so he could take in all the surroundings. All the usual stuff was going on. Tourists strolling along, some of the children licking an ice cream cone, all the time building the fortitude for the right-angle turn and the long steep climb up to the town at the top by a gently arched narrow-cobbled street. At frequent stops, to get the feeling back into their legs, they would take the opportunity to peer into the many artists galleries lined along their way, moving along ever upwards to the distant very top and relief from the agony in their legs, entering as a reward the centre of the town.

All was as it should be, but then he noticed a cortege of brightly coloured cars arriving; Italian Fiat 500's led by an old British Riley. The old nationalistic nostalgia returned for his beloved Rover 90; he had to go over and have a peek as they lined up neatly along the bank just 50 metres away.

Making his excuses to the waiter, saying if he could reserve his place and that he would return in half an hour. He casually sauntered over, hands in his short pockets making a shy approach. The Riley had its bonnet up to reveal to all admirers the pristine engine beautifully restored underneath. James was soon into his old routine charming his way in, asking the questions demanded by his curiosity.

"You are bit far from home," commented James?

"My wife and I live in Guernsey so we thought after spending two years on the old girl we give her a few days out," was the response.

"I hope you are referring to the car and not your attractive wife," joked James.

The joke went completely over Riley man's head and he continued,

"We are on our way to Brest, don't fancy testing the old gal on that steep hill."

"I am sure your wife could manage it," James persisted.

Then a smile emerged and the Riley owner realised he was reciting his prepared script rather than listening to the conversational repertoire. In a strange way it seemed to break the stiffness of the man but his wife was already enjoying the banter from this English stranger with a slight whacky sense of humour and who was not completely lost in car mechanics.

"Are these your friends, the Italians in their Noddy cars," asked James cheekily?

"We all belong to a European Veteran Car Club. They posted on their website a request for a guide to tour of Brittany, so we volunteered to be the lead."

"Do you mind if I have a wander over to meet them?"

"Not at all," said Riley man, "I will introduce you."

"What's your name by the way?"

"James."

Now it was Riley man's turn.

"So, when you drive your wife home she says, home James."

That did it, at last it proved they were on the same comic wave length and were soon conversing like old lost friends.

"Look, we are having lunch, is there anywhere you would recommend and perhaps you could join us," said Riley man?

"That is most charming of you, that would be great. I have just popped over form that restaurant over there by the bridge. The food is simple and the service excellent. They could soon put a few tables together for say 15 of us."

"Perfect," said Riley man.

The next twenty minutes was taken up discussing the intricacies of refurbishing a Riley starting with the bare chassis.

After a brief meeting with the Fiat car owners, James headed off in the direction of the restaurant, soon organised the tables in one long row for James to beckon with an arm movement for the others to follow. James placed himself in the middle to be followed almost immediately by Riley man and his wife sat next to him. She seemed relieved to at last get away from solely car gossip.

The rest of the table began to fill and then James swore he could hear a cuckoo clock chiming. It seemed totally incongruous to hear such a sound in a French restaurant in the middle of a roman and medieval town. The more he looked around the more bemused he became. And then again, the same call but this time apparently just behind him. He turned to receive the shock of his life. It was his Swiss contact, last seen in Prague. A cold shiver went through him, such was the surprise.

"I wondered what happened to you. The last time we met you were legging it in Prague. Hadn't you paid the bill," said Swiss man smiling away?

"Just practising my lap times", said James not wishing to highlight any details.

"I did hear you had an extended holiday in Asia and then no more word, so we were very worried about you."

"Don't let us dwell on that sorry chapter for the moment, let's have a chat later to avoid boring our fellow guests, I am dying to know how you got here and listen to your adventures with your friends," said James.

Swiss man suggested they had quarter an hour at the end of the meal to have a 'catch-up' while the others prepared their cars ready to go to their next overnight destination before arriving in Brest. He would explain to them James was an old friend and just wanted to exchange addresses and telephone numbers before they left.

In an open conversation he explained to his Fiat friends that James was no stranger to him and they had been business associates over two decades ago but had over the years lost touch. So, it wouldn't happen again they would have a private chat to exchange contact details and organise another reunion as soon as they could. The other participants were just delighted that their enjoyable adventure had enabled two old friends to meet again.

Swiss man recounted he had now retired from Roche and had settled in a tiny village on the border with Italy. Often, he would venture over the border on shopping trips to Milan buying the superb clothes and footwear so prevalent in the many shops. Sometimes they would stayover in Bellagio for a weekend stay, enjoy the view of Lake Como and the exquisite dinners at one of the fine hotels strewn alongside the lake shoreline. It was on a walk around Bellagio, after a sumptuous meal, hoping to burn-off the excess calories, that he came across the Fiat Enthusiast Group parked in one of the small piazzas. Although not a Fiat owner himself he was made an honorary member and then treasurer and ever since, every year he organises their annual sojourn across various parts of Europe. It was the turn for Brittany to receive them. Trust the Swiss man to end up handling timing and the dosh thought James to himself, even when socialising.

To keep it simple for a large group, and in order not to put undue time pressure for their departure, everyone opted for the many types of pizzas. What else would you expect from a bunch of Milanese? They stretched it to a dessert and coffees, so the meal was still two hours long influenced as much by the meal as the interludes skilfully orchestrated by the waiters to permit the natural flow of several individual and group conversations; they all happily chatted away.

For James this was an unexpected pleasure to what he had expected at the end of a pensive and melancholic promenade. Oddly, he found it all therapeutic, distancing him far away from recounting all those historic recollections. Despite his idyllic new lifestyle, he did miss being with his mates but not the dangers and the risks that went with them. At the end of the meal the Fiat Owners slowly left and said their goodbyes along with Riley man and his wife to pack their car and freshen up. Swiss man, the treasurer, was handed the total bill whilst at the same time pulling out the 50-euro notes, checking the items on the bill and calculating a fair tip.

Soon he and James were sat alone drinking the last remnants of the fifth large 'pichet' of wine.

"This was no casual accident was it," asked James?

"Well, you have proved to me you haven't lost your mental faculties," replied Swiss Man, his cuckoo chiming clock friend.

"You are checking-up on me."

"I wouldn't put it quite as crude as that. Before I talk about how I managed to be fortuitously here, I would like to pick up on what happened after your unfortunate experience in Asia and the loss of your boss and friend. That assignment we were on in the Balkans and our success we still believe prevails.

We did have a fright when Putin came on the scene with his thuggish henchmen. The old regime was in the habit of knocking off their individual opponents should the old USSR interests be crossed. But he decided to move on from the dagger and the bullet to a slightly more sophisticated way of dispatching opponents with a stab in the leg with a poisoned umbrella amongst others. Of course, this methodology was developed to induce terror into their opponents and more importantly those contemplating defection which had become a major problem to them. Our friend Vladimir decided this wasn't enough, not only did he believe he needed to remind us lest we forget he had access to lethal weapons, he was prepared to deploy with impunity and with no regard to accepted norms. As you Brits would say, not playing to the rules of cricket."

"Yes, I still read the papers I know all that," said James tersely.

"I am coming to the point. You no doubt read that they progressed to carrying nuclear isotypes around in their pockets knowing full well that the scent of the wolf could be traced, straight back to the Kremlin. Just Vladimir's modus operandi to make clear that if you cross him you are not safe anywhere, even when having tea in a central London hotel. We had a bit of a fright when he went a step further using a powdered nerve agent, we knew of it but had no samples. We thought we had been rumbled but were puzzled whether he had actually learnt to deactivate the neutraliser, a gift from us. One person did die from a brazen attempt at assassination, but it seems from a very heavy dose application from the thrown away receptacle designed as a cosmetic product. Others were very poorly but the agent wasn't as lethal as they may have believed," continued Swiss man.

"I see your concern. The last thing we need is for such weapons to be personalised," said James.

"Precisely. Fortunately, Porton were able to confirm this was not a development of the old stocks hidden away. Rather than reveal their presence by risking the route back to the stockpiles they decided to manufacture a very small batch for 'slotting their prey' and replicated the old stuff and then closed the temporary laboratory in Siberia. Given what happened they may have a concern they didn't quite get the manufacturing process right or the deployment was clumsy. Usefully, it reinforced their false belief they still had sufficient stocks for a mass deployment."

"Well thanks for that update and it is reassuring that the high risks we took were worthwhile and still operate, but doesn't explain why you are here," said James.

"Again, I am coming to that. As you will know any new Prime Minister or Leader of the Opposition is briefed on national security. When the new PM came in, we appraised him of our past mission and then he asked where you were. None of us really knew but believed you had retired to France. To be frank, we then got a bit of a roasting. He said that what he was being told was we had on the loose, unprotected and unsecured, an agent capable of blowing the whole scheme apart should Vladimir's thugs manage to identify him. We did say in our feeble defence that if we provided opaque protection that would raise the risk of revelation. The PM did discuss it with her Majesty who was visibly shocked that they had allowed someone to be so exposed and potentially provide a crack in the nation's defences. She insisted you were found and someway a plan put in place to keep you out of harm's way."

"The Queen was concerned for my well-being; I don't know whether to be proud of her concern or worry myself and my wife sick," said James.

"That s why I am here. I came up with this proposal and discussed it with the Queen after informing how we first met. After our talk she produced a present selected for you which I have in my car. I was told to tell you it was her majesty's personal choice and she formally presented it to me to do the same to you. I took the liberty, with her Majesty's blessing, to add a feature to it.

We agreed with her Majesty and the PM that I would meet you every year by simply I sending you a postcard of where the veteran car club was heading for their next annual outing and we would meet at the same time and on the same date as of today. I also took the precaution of checking, asked for a full security clearance, for all our present and future members of our Veteran's Car Club to be sure. Any 'foreign or suspicious activity' in your area we would be put on full alert for your security. So, if you don't mind, should you go anywhere outside a 50km of your home send me a postcard and we will assume you will be there in a month's time from the time we receive it. Doing it this way we have the perfect cover," said Swiss man in a serious tone.

"You Swiss guys love the precision and meticulous accuracy, don't you? I do understand. Don't be unduly worry I will let you know if ever I have any suspicions. I have every intention to die of natural causes well into my nineties."

"I am so relieved you have taken it well. Good luck my friend and let's look forward to our next meeting and having a great time. Next time bring your wife, I would love to meet someone who could put up with you for so long," said Swiss man now cracking a smile.

Returning to the car he brought out a box wrapped in gold paper and printed with an emblem of a portcullis. Tucked under the tied ribbon was a simple piece of white paper edged in gold. It just said,

'From a grateful Sovereign.'

He passed the parcel to James, gave a formal salute. Swiss man then explained his own modification. He told James the package contained a Swiss clock but with an important difference. It would only chime once a day at 8.00pm. If on any day it chimed nine times, he was to pack his case that evening and the next day with his wife meet him at the roman bridge the next morning. It would serve as a reminder of the success of our mission and as an early warning system if it was felt he were at risk.

After the exchange they both hugged each other and James stood around for the next half hour and waved them off. As he reflected on the thoughtfulness of his Sovereign and her concern for his well-being his eyes became moist and he felt a great surge of emotion. If he hadn't realised before, he did now, he became aware his nerves of steel had been shot and his retirement was well timed, a very good decision on reflection. Losing your cool in his job was not only bad for you, but just as important, for others as well.

He decided to have one last ice-cool lager, smiled at the waiters, picked up his sunhat and replaced his sun glasses. He then tucked the present under his arm and made the same journey back reflecting on a momentous conversation. The sun by the late afternoon had lost most of its fierce heat and in terms of effort the return journey was physically less demanding than his departure.

How was he going to concoct his alibi to his wife with the degree of credibility required? As usual he took the line of sticking to the truth as far as possible. He would say that he had enjoyed very much the walk especially as he met an old associate from decades before by chance from Italy and he had lunch with him and his friends. That would cover anyone who had spotted him in Dinan or indeed seen him dining with others and gossiping to one of the men's wife. It would explain away everything. It just then left how to explain away the clock and future annual excursions.

The simplest answer would be to say Swiss man was keen to meet her and suggested meeting up at the Veteran Car Club's next annual meeting. He wouldn't go as far as suggesting this was a fixed annual fixture but felt confident that once she had met everyone there would be no objection to another repeated annual invitation. A very neat way of avoiding deciding where to go next for a short weekend break; it would be decided for you with company you liked. This still left explaining the neatly wrapped parcel minus the handwritten note.

That settled in his head, off he sauntered and with all his thoughts neatly filed away in the recesses of his brain he continued to absorb the beauty of the surroundings. Just a little way from Dinan the river opens into a wide expanse and on the far side there are small jetties over which huge fishing nets were hung. What the actual fishing method employed was he didn't know. There were no fishermen around to demonstrate how they did it and what type of fish they were after. The mist over the water had lifted as the river narrowed once more. This time there were more hikers and cyclists to keep him company so the feeling of solitary confinement abated. Even a Labrador came bounding up and begged to be fussed with a friendly pat and stroke of his head. The rather attractive owner apologised for the exuberance, but James just brushed it aside and they walked together for awhile chatting away until they shortly arrived to her 4x4 parked at the river side around halfway to his destination.

It had been a good day and those darker thoughts had been lifted as though a shaft of sunlight and beamed into his dark recesses of his mind. He had lived a good life, tried to do the right thing and now realised his ambitious efforts had reached and been recognised at the highest level of his nation. No bad achievement for a working-class lad educated at Players Academy for backward boys and forward girls and some reward for his ambition t breakaway from his social confinement.

It didn't seem that long before he soon could see his car, the birds still gathering round the barrage by the lock and the nearby swing bridge road. Probably for the first time in his life he felt total contentment although he realised, he was no longer up to the mark for repeating past adventures. As he entered the front door there was a call from the kitchen,

"Fancy a cup of tea after your walk; did you enjoy it", said his wife?

"It was fantastic, by chance I met an old friend."

"Oh, that's nice, did you do anything else while you were there? Did you try the climb into the town?"

"No, not enough time for that but I did have a gaze into one of those shops on the waterfront. I bought a surprise present for you. Go on open it."

"What is it?"

"Well it wouldn't be a surprise if I told you, would it, said James?"

"It's a beautiful cuckoo clock," exclaimed Suzanne.

"A cuckoo clock, what on earth made you want to buy a cuckoo clock," said his wife?

"More than you would ever know my love!"

THE END

Printed in Poland
by Amazon Fulfillment
Poland Sp. z o.o., Wrocław

64308308R00145